IN THE TRENCHES

AN OPS PROTECTOR ROMANCE

GIULIA LAGOMARSINO

Copyright © 2022 by Giulia Lagomarsino

All rights reserved.

No part of this book may be reproduced in any form or by any electronic or mechanical means, including information storage and retrieval systems, without written permission from the author, except for the use of brief quotations in a book review.

Cover Design courtesy of T.E. Black Designs

www.teblackdesigns.com

Photography by Reggie Deanching @ RplusM Photography

https://www.rplusmphoto.com

Cover Model: Guy Higgins

https://www.facebook.com/profile.php?id=100077795575275

❦ Created with Vellum

For Brad.

Thank you so much for helping me with this amazing storyline, and being my sounding board when I couldn't figure things out!

Here's a shoutout to all our heroes for all they do to protect us on a daily basis!

Not all heroes wear capes... some wear kevlar.

CAST OF CHARACTERS

Cash Owens- Owner of Owens Protective Services, sniper, and overall badass.

Eva James- deadly mistress of throwing knives and Cash's…person

Team 1:

Jerrod Lockhart- Complete hardass, rule follower, and generally the guy considered to always have a stick up his ass.

Edward "Edu" Markinson- Hater of hospitals, slow drivers, and references to anything in the 80's.

Brock "Rock" Patton- Wannabe model, obsessed with his looks and constantly combing his hair…A ferocious fighter for a man so obsessed with his looks. Also, as a side note—he can't act for shit and hates the word 'loins'.

Scottie Dog Thacker- Tactical vomit expert, hater of flying planes, and always up for a good time. If you're with him, have a barf bag in hand. Has never had even a sip of alcohol in his life.

Team 2:

Marcus "IRIS" Slater- His name stands for *I Require Intense Supervision*. EOD expert that has taken up a new love…blowing up shit.

CAST OF CHARACTERS

Mick "Slider" Jeffries- Not Slider from *Top Gun*. Sorry, ladies, I know he was gorgeous, but it's not the same hottie.

Tate "Thumper" Parsons- No, not named for the adorable furry rabbit. Thumper got his nickname after losing a foot to an IED. Now using a robotic foot, he is probably the fastest person on the team.

Team 3: Now known as The Ditty Boppers

Eli Brant- Fierce team leader, but will put you in your place with a good practical joke when necessary.

Red Warren- Funny, meat-eating, California-hating, rifle owner. Proud to take out the bad guys in any way possible.

Bradford Kavanaugh- Son of a senator, terrified of mummies, scarabs, and basically anything from ancient Egypt. Loves practical jokes, except when they're about him.

IT Department:

Rae Dennon- Sarcastic, witty, badass woman. Terrified of nothing, will take down any man with little effort, and has an intense feud with Dash.

Dash- Awesome with computers and a skilled fighter. Constantly being compared to Rae, the sexier version of him. Still trying to convince Fox he's just as awesome.

Black Ops Team: Also known as The Three Js

Jack Cox- Team leader who loves aviator sunglasses as much as a good gun fight. Willing to take one for the team as long as the mission is long and hard…just like his johnson.

Johnny Wood- Dangerous cowboy, loyal to Rafe—a man that would kill his own mother if it finished the job. Respects a man willing to get the job done.

Jason Long- Number 3 of the baddies. Dangerous and dark, always full of threatening wisdom. Stay out of his way.

The Other Guys:

New Guy- Also known as FNG- Doesn't have a death wish, but firmly believes he can never be killed. Willing to take horrible risks to prove he's unstoppable. Medic and smart as a whip, but also one of the most ridiculous men you've ever met.

Jones- Spotter for Cash during their military days, with a bad attitude since losing the use of his leg. Like you really need one of those.

Rafe: Evildoer posing as the good guy. Or is it the other way around? Dangerous antihero with not a single redeeming quality who stays hidden in the shadows. Unknown relationship to Cash.

Fox: Works in training, has an undeniable fascination with throwing knives, and loves singing show tunes…sometimes a little too much!

IN THE TRENCHES MEANING

Origin:

Trench warfare is a form of land warfare using occupied fighting lines consisting largely of trenches, in which troops are significantly protected from the enemy's small arms fire and are substantially sheltered from artillery. The most prominent case of trench warfare is the Western Front in World War I. It has become a byword for stalemate, attrition, and futility in conflict.
https://military-history.fandom.com/wiki/Trench_warfare

OPS Definition:
In the fight.

1

CASH

Breathe.

Adjust two clicks.

Check the anemometer one last time.

The sand blowing in the distance was all we could use to gauge the wind speed. I needed to be accurate. If not, I'd give away my position and put the rest of my Marine Scout Sniper Team at risk.

With the wind blowing hard, the bullet could land damn near anywhere. If the wind either picked up or died down, my shot could completely miss the target and hit the brick wall one building over. Not to mention, the target was nearly a half-mile away, and only part of his head was visible. It was an impossible shot, one that many would not even take a chance on at this point. Our team could move out and try to sneak up on him, but the chance of him catching our movement was greater.

Even though we'd cleared the small village when we first arrived in town, we had to keep our guard up. In the desert, there were always hidden tunnels and passages where someone could easily slip in and out. We couldn't be sure that he didn't have reinforcements in the shadows, waiting for us to make a move. Either way, I had to take out that sniper if we had any chance of leaving here alive.

I took a deep breath, checked my target's position one last time, and placed my finger on the trigger. He knew we were over here somewhere. His rifle had shifted in our direction. It was now or never. Kill or be killed.

I took one final steadying breath, my heart slowing to an even beat as I prepared to pull the trigger. The only sound filling my ears was the thumping of my pulse as I blocked out everything else, including my team.

Deep breath. Exhale. Squeeze.

I watched through the scope as the target shifted slightly. His body appeared to slump away from his rifle, but it was nearly impossible to tell if it was a clean shot. I waited, staring through my scope for any sign of movement. Five minutes passed before I pulled my gaze from my scope.

"Jones?" I asked, waiting for confirmation.

"Target down," he confirmed.

But there was only one way to be sure. Handing my rifle off to my spotter, I pulled my pistol from my holster and slowly moved from my position. He gave a slight nod, resuming his position beside me, his rifle at the ready in case something went wrong.

After laying in the same spot for the better part of two days, my muscles were protesting the movement. But nothing would stop me from collecting that HOG's tooth. It was well-known among snipers that there was a round waiting out there with your name on it, meaning as a sniper, another sniper would eventually have his sights on you. It was a superstition that in collecting that bullet, you couldn't be killed by gunfire on the battlefield because you collected the bullet that was meant to kill you.

Sticking to the shadows on the crumbled rooftop, I left my team behind to collect that chambered round from my enemy's rifle. They didn't think twice about me leaving. They knew all too well that it was something I needed to do. I pulled out Betty, pressing my lips to my good luck charm just before I turned the corner.

I crept down the stairs, gun in hand and ready to fire. The rubble that had fallen on the stairs made it that much more difficult to make my way down without making any noise. The dust from the building clogged my throat, forcing me to stop and take a drink of water so I didn't give away my position by coughing. When I finally reached the entrance of the building, I scanned the area for any potential threats.

The sunlight reflected off metal from various pieces of rubble, making it difficult to spot enemy combatants. Now I had to rely on my team to keep an eye out for me.

"Ready to move," I said, placing a hand to my ear.

"All clear."

With one final scan of the area, I made my way across the open road to the buildings on the opposite side of the street. I should be on edge, wary of being so exposed, but I had my team at my back, and I trusted them with my life. I made it across the street and slipped between the buildings, hugging the walls as I ran down the alley.

Taking a moment to catch my breath, I searched the next street, the most dangerous part of this in my mind. My team couldn't see me anymore, which meant I was on my own. I continued weaving through the streets until I reached the building that housed my enemy.

With a final glance up and down the deserted street, I jogged over to the war-torn building. My enemy had chosen a good hiding spot. With all the rubble and destruction, he had much to hide behind and blend in with.

I climbed my way through the fallen pieces of concrete until I reached the roof where my enemy lay dead. Cautiously, I approached and knelt beside the man I'd taken out. His eyes were still open as he stared up at the clouded sky. Some men said words of prayer when they came upon a slain adversary. I had no words for this man. He wasn't just my enemy, but a man who fought for an unworthy cause. There was no justification for the cruelty his people inflicted on others.

I picked up his rifle and emptied the chamber, holding the round up in front of my face. A small grin split my lips as a weight was lifted from my shoulders. This was my calling in life. I'd known it from the moment I first entered Marine Sniper School. When that rifle was in my hands, I felt untouchable. I was unwavering in my duty, bound to the weapon that not only took lives, but saved mine many times over.

I was a Hunter of Gunmen.

2

BETH

"Have a good night," I said to my last patron, and by far my favorite person in the world right now.

Tom smiled at me, his wrinkled face reminding me of my grandfather. He was a kind man and had always made me feel safe in his presence. I tended to gravitate toward elderly people for that very reason. I figured they'd already been through the worst life could offer, so they didn't put up with any bullshit.

As usual, Tom left me a five dollar tip when his meal cost just a few dollars more than that. I caught him staring at me sometimes like he was trying to figure out my secrets, but I would never share them. That could get him killed, and he was too kind to me to risk his life, no matter how much I wanted to share the load with someone else.

I followed him out, locking the door behind him, then shut off the lights. As I stared out into the night, I looked for any sign that someone was watching me. No matter how far I ran, I always worried someone was still following me. I could never shake the feeling, but if someone was hiding out there in the shadows, why hadn't he made his move yet?

Tearing my gaze away from the dark sky, I went through the motions of closing up for the night. The cook was still in the kitchen cleaning up, leaving me to take care of putting the chairs upside down on the tables and sweeping the floor. When I finished, I grabbed the mop, taking pride in making sure everything was up to standard for the next shift.

"You almost done?" Art asked after shoving open the kitchen door.

"Yeah, I just have to handle the register."

He nodded at me and let the door fall shut. Art was a bigger guy, heavily muscled and tall, who wore a blue bandana around his head every night. Though we'd never really spoken much, I got the impression that he liked me, or at the very least, tolerated me.

Popping open the register, I went through the process of printing out the daily receipt and making sure the register was balanced. Sid, the owner of the diner, always took the cash to the bank in the morning. I just had to lock it in the safe for the night.

By the time I locked the safe, I was dead tired. My feet were killing me and my neck and shoulders ached from carrying the trays all evening. I grabbed my jacket out of the back and grabbed my purse from the back room. I never carried too much money on me because there had been thefts around here since I first started.

"Goodnight," I said to Art as I headed for the back door.

"Yeah, you're on tomorrow, right?"

I nodded and gave him a wave. "See you then."

He jerked his chin and started turning off the lights. On my way out, I grabbed the last trash bag and hauled it over my shoulder. Slipping out into the night, I glanced around first to make sure I was alone. When I didn't hear anything, I let the door close behind me and headed across the alley to the dumpster shoved up against the fence. I grimaced at the terrible smell when I lifted the lid and quickly tossed the bag inside.

Just as I spun around, something hard came down on my head, instantly making me sway on my feet. My hand shot out, grasping for anything to keep me from falling, but then my hair was yanked harshly and I cried out.

"Is this her?"

I tried to turn and see who it was, but between the black spots dancing in front of my eyes and the way the man was holding me, I couldn't see anything. I tried to bite back the panic and think, but fear flooded my veins, making it impossible to think straight.

"Yeah, that's her."

"Then let's go."

Panic overwhelmed me and despite my head spinning, one thing was clear—I needed to run. I swung my elbow back, making contact and hearing a grunt. I took off, only to feel a hand grasp my arm and yank hard. Blinding pain shot through my shoulder, making me scream as I fell back. I nearly passed out, but the urge to vomit kept me from escaping this reality. Bile rose in my throat and I turned just enough to avoid throwing up all over myself. The man released me, stepping away from me as I spewed the contents of my dinner all over the alley.

I collapsed to my knees, choking and sobbing as my arm throbbed painfully. I looked up to see two men staring at me with so much contempt that I prayed for a quick death. Whatever they had in store for me, I would find no mercy with them.

"Get up," one of them snapped.

Holding my arm against my chest, I struggled to my feet, my head growing dizzy as the pain overwhelmed me. I thought about trying to run, but I knew I would fail. And what would that get me? What had I ever gotten by running?

The back door swung open and Art stepped out, quickly assessing the situation. His eyes locked with mine for just a moment. "Run."

But my feet were like lead weights, refusing to let me move. The fear had overridden my adrenaline, blocking my mind from making any decisions, no matter how beneficial they might be. I was vaguely aware of Art swinging at the first guy. The second rushed over to me, grabbing me by my broken arm and dragging me away.

My feet dragged across the gravel as he pulled me away from Art, my only hope of salvation. A scream bubbled up in my throat as he yanked on me even harder. With the remaining strength I had left, I swung out, hoping to hit him or stall him in some way. I narrowly hit him in the balls, and he bent over, cupping himself as he kept a firm grip on me. I struggled to break free of him, but just as I thought I gained some leverage, his fist shot out and slammed into my cheek. I stumbled back as he let me go and collapsed in a puddle on the ground. My face slammed into the gravel and pain exploded in my head.

I watched Art fighting the other man, unable to get up and move. My body hurt everywhere, my vision blurred in and out until I finally closed my eyes, hoping I wouldn't wake up to see what they would do to me.

But I was yanked up roughly and shaken until I opened my eyes and looked at my attacker. "You're not getting off so easily, bitch. The boss wants you back at camp to deal with you himself."

I wheezed in pain as he hauled me up over his shoulder and took off down the alley. My ribs bounced painfully on his shoulder, but something hard hit him and I went flying from his grasp, falling once again to the ground. I wasn't sure what happened after that. I slowly blinked, watching a fight in front of me, but barely processing who was fighting.

Then I was lifted in the air, cradled against a large body as we walked down the alley. A door was opened and I was set inside a car, my head lolling back against the seat as the buckle was stretched across my body.

"Hang in there, Beth. I've got you."

Rolling my head to the side, I saw Art staring intently at me before shutting the door and walking around the car. I closed my eyes, just wanting to go to sleep until I heard him speak.

"I'm going to get you to the hospital."

"No," I said as urgently as I could. "Don't. No hospital," I croaked out.

"What? Beth, you need to see a doctor."

But I knew if I went to the hospital, I would never be safe. Art didn't know it, but he not only saved my life tonight, he saved me from something worse than death. Reaching across the seat with my uninjured arm, I used every ounce of strength left in me to plead with him.

"Art...take me home," I gasped.

"You're in no condition—"

"Please," I begged, staring at him through my rapidly swelling eye.

He watched me for a moment, and something in my voice must have gotten through to him.

He started the car and sighed. "Where am I taking you?"

"The…Fairfield Apartments," I wheezed.

His brows pinched for a second before he shook his head. They were basically slums. No one dared go there unless they absolutely had to. And I absolutely had to. It was the only place I could rent in cash.

We drove quickly through the streets, neither of us saying a word. I drifted in and out of consciousness, barely aware of anything going on around me. I squinted at the overhead light in the car and realized we stopped. Art came around to my side and helped me out, putting his arm around me as I struggled to reach my apartment complex.

"My purse," I mumbled, just now realizing that it didn't matter if he took me here or not. I couldn't get in.

"I've got it. Where are your keys?"

"Pocket," I answered, swaying on my feet as he released me just long enough to grab my keys. He quickly caught me and hauled me up against his body as he shoved the key in the lock, only for the door to creak open. I could practically feel the anger coming off him as he realized just how shitty this place was.

"Which apartment is yours?"

"1A," I answered, thankful that we didn't have that much further to go.

He nodded and got me down the hall, then opened the door and helped me inside to the couch. Sighing in relief, I allowed myself a minute to catalog just how bad my injuries were. I wouldn't make it far in my condition. One look down at the way my arm hung limply at my side, and I knew I had dislocated it.

Art sat down on the rickety coffee table across from me and leaned forward. "Let's check out the damage."

I closed my eyes as he shifted the hair from the side of my head and sucked in a breath. "You're bleeding pretty bad." His fingers prodded at my head. "How bad does your head hurt?"

"Pounding," I responded, unable to say more than that. My

stomach was still churning from all the pain, but I kept taking deep breaths to ward off the nausea.

He let out a deep sigh and started to unbutton my coat. "I'm going to check out your arm. Do you think you can help me with your coat?"

I nodded and allowed him to shift his arm behind me and help me sit upright. I pulled my right arm out of the sleeve, wincing when he slid the other sleeve off my limp arm. His face crinkled as he looked at my shoulder.

"You need to have that set."

"Can you do it?"

He shook his head. "Beth, I'm not a doctor. We need to take you to a hospital."

"No," I said firmly, pushing aside the pain long enough to remind myself what was at stake. "I can't."

"If you don't have insurance—"

"It's not about that," I said weakly. "I…" Against my will, tears leaked from the corners of my eyes and I quickly swiped them away.

"Are you in trouble?"

I couldn't even look at him. I wasn't ashamed, but I couldn't confirm what he said either. The more he knew, the more danger he would be in.

"Hey," he nudged gently. "If you need some place to lay low for a while, you can stay with me."

Looking up at him, I wanted to believe he was right, but if they found me at the diner, they could find me at his place, and he didn't need to risk his life for me. "I just need a bus ticket out of here."

He nodded in understanding. "I get it, but you're in no condition to travel." Sighing, he studied my arm again. "I have a friend that might be able to help. He's going to school, but…it's the best I can do."

"Do you trust him?"

"With my life," he said sincerely. "I'll pack what you need. Then we'll get you to my place."

"What if—" I said quickly, but stopped myself before I said too much. My gaze flicked to the window, and he caught on to what I was thinking.

"We'll be careful. Whoever was after you…if they knew you were here, they'd already be breaking down your door."

He had a good point. Now that they knew where I worked, it wouldn't be a stretch to think they could find my apartment. "What happened with those men?"

"They're dead."

I gasped, covering my mouth as I looked him in the eyes. "You killed them?"

"They were trying to kill you. Did you want me to leave them alive?"

"But…the police?"

He shrugged. "Nobody cares about dead people here."

"Maybe not, but that doesn't mean they won't investigate how they were killed."

"If it comes to that, I'll deal with it."

"Art, you have no idea what you've done."

His jaw clenched hard as he watched me. "What I did was protect you. They were going to kill you."

I knew that all too well. I still couldn't figure out how they found me, but I'd worry about that later. Right now, the pounding in my head was interfering with my ability to think clearly.

"I'll grab your things. Is there anything special you want to take with you?"

I nodded, sitting up a little more. "The corner," I said, pointing to the corner of the living room. "I have some money stashed under it."

Frowning, he moved to the corner and yanked back the carpet, staring down at my stash. It was everything I'd saved since I ran. He stalked into the bedroom and returned a moment later with a backpack. After packing the cash, he returned to the bedroom. I could hear him in the other room, packing my things. With my head pounding, I couldn't keep my eyes open. Everything inside me hurt, so I closed my eyes to rest until he was ready.

"Beth," his gruff voice pulled me out of the darkness. "I have everything I could pack. We need to leave."

I nodded, but I couldn't get up. Between the dizziness and the pain in my body, I had a better chance of flying to the moon. Seeing the pain etched on my face, he slid his hands under my legs and around my back, then lifted me effortlessly. With what little strength I had left, I draped my good arm around his neck and held on, resting my head against his shoulder. With every jolt of my body as he carried me down the stairs, I slipped further into oblivion until finally, I felt no pain.

"I'm not a doctor! I've only seen this done a few times."

"Please, I can't take her to the doctor. Do whatever you can to help her."

"I could get kicked out of school for practicing medicine when I'm not properly trained."

"Nobody's going to find out."

"Fine."

I heard footsteps come closer and struggled to open my eyes. Groaning, I saw Art hovering over me as another man approached, rolling up his sleeves. For a moment, I was worried who this man was, but if Art brought him over, he couldn't be dangerous.

"This is my friend. He's going to try and fix your shoulder."

I nodded, swallowing hard. I knew this would hurt, but it couldn't be worse than the pain I was already feeling. The man bent over me, taking my arm and pulling it away from my body. Then he lifted his foot, placing it in my armpit. Slowly, he started to rotate my arm. I squeezed my eyes shut, sucking in a breath at the pain. Art's hand found mine and I held tight, drawing from his strength until the pain became too intense. My head pounded with every torque of my arm until I finally passed out.

When I woke up, it was dark and the man was gone. Art was standing by the window, gazing out into the night. "Did he fix it?" I asked, drawing his attention.

He didn't answer the question. "Does your shoulder feel better?"

"It still hurts, but not as much."

He nodded and turned back to the window. "Beth, who are you running from?" he asked after a moment.

I rested back against the pillow and stared up at the ceiling. "I can't tell you."

"And I can't let you walk out of here with no one to help you. Beth, you're a fucking mess. Your eye is swelling shut, you have a gash on your head, not to mention the multiple bruises over your body and your dislocated shoulder."

I pushed myself up with my good arm, wincing when my shoulder pulled. "Art, I appreciate the help, but you can't get involved in this."

"And you expect me to just walk away?" he asked, turning to fully face me. The muscles in his arms were pulled tight as he clenched his fists and fought back the anger.

"Yes, I do."

"What if I want to help you?"

"Why would you do that?" I asked. I was nothing to him. We barely spoke.

He turned away, cursing to himself. "What do you expect me to do? I'm just supposed to send you to the bus station like this?" he spat. "You won't last a day."

"I've lasted this long," I retorted. "Look, this isn't your problem, and I'm not going to let you get involved. I just need a couple of days to heal and then I'll be out of your hair."

"Fine," he bit out, storming toward the door. "I have to get to work. There's food in the fridge."

"Thank you," I said sincerely. He gave a brief nod and then walked out of the room. Moments later, I heard the door shut. Tossing back the covers, I hobbled out of bed and into the living room. His apartment was sparse, but clean. I locked the door and then searched for some food. Now that he mentioned it, I was starving. The nausea I felt last night was gone, leaving me with stomach pains. I couldn't remember the last time I ate anything. So much of last night was fuzzy. But I could still remember that look of determination on Art's face when he walked out of the diner last night and saw me surrounded in the alley.

I grabbed some lunch meat and made a sandwich. He had some chips on the counter, so I grabbed those too, and went to sit in the living room. Paranoia swept through me as I thought of those men dead in the alley. I picked up the remote and turned on the TV, searching for the news. It was five minutes to ten, so the news cycle would be starting over in just a few minutes. I waited impatiently until, finally the news anchor came on. Story after story played, but there was nothing about any dead bodies behind the diner. If I had a phone, I would call the diner and see if everything was okay. But since I didn't hear anything from Art throughout the day, I assumed nobody found the bodies.

I needed to get away from here as soon as possible. I found an old laptop under a pile of papers on Art's coffee table. Pulling it onto my lap, I checked bus routes and tried to find my next stop. Part of me thought I should get as far away as possible, but the thought of staying close and flying under the radar was tempting. After this last attack, wouldn't they expect me to run far? If I stayed in California, I'd be hiding right under their noses. Decision made, I laid down on the couch and slept the rest of the afternoon.

"Are you sure you have everything?" Art asked as he took me to the bus station.

"Yes, I'm sure."

He nodded and pulled into the parking lot. I hesitated, looking around for anyone suspicious, but didn't see anything.

"Thank you for your help. I know I can never repay you."

"And you don't have to," he said, his eyes concerned as he looked around again. "What if…you could stay with me."

To hear someone offer that kind of help was an unnatural feeling. I had long ago shut down the idea that anyone would be able or willing to put themselves at risk for me. My mom and I didn't speak, not since I was a teenager. Her idea of taking care of her child was very different than mine, and as soon as I could, I left and never looked back. I had always been on my own, but the last two years had been more difficult than I expected.

At twenty-seven years old, this wasn't exactly where I thought I would be in my life. I assumed I would meet someone and be married by now. Maybe I'd even be thinking of starting a family. Instead, those thoughts were now banished. It was clear that was never going to happen.

"I have to leave," I said to Art. "I appreciate all you've done for me, but I can't stay with you."

"At least let me buy your ticket. That way you won't be seen by the cameras."

I nodded and got out of the car. My bag was slung over my right shoulder so I didn't further injure my left shoulder. I pulled the hoodie over my head, covering as much of my face as possible. I knew it wouldn't do much in the way of hiding my bruises, but if people weren't looking closely, they might not notice.

I hung back as Art went to the ticket booth and bought a one-way ticket. I kept searching the crowd, the hairs on the back of my neck rising as the minutes ticked by. But I couldn't see anyone suspicious, not until Art finally started walking back to me. My eyes went wide when I saw the two men scouring the platform, clearly looking for someone.

I couldn't be certain they were looking for me. It was just a suspicion, but their attire made it pretty damn clear that whoever they were here for, it wouldn't end well. Art's eyes connected with mine and I shook my head slowly, telling him not to come any closer. He slowed and walked over to a bench, sitting down as he looked back in the direction he came. I saw him tense when he saw the men.

I didn't know what to do. I needed to get away, but Art couldn't be seen with me. That would only put him in danger. He pulled up his own hoodie and turned away from the men. Then I watched as he tucked the ticket into a crack in the wooden bench. Casually, he got up and strolled away.

Licking my lips, I took my chance and walked to the bench, snatched the ticket and headed toward the buses. I didn't dare look over my shoulder, but I could already feel them following me. I started walking faster, hoping I could make it to the buses and get away from them.

"I'll distract them," I heard a voice beside me. "You run and get to your bus. I'll lead them in another direction."

I didn't have time to think before he shoved me toward the buses, making it clear that he was helping me. I took off, running as fast as I could, searching for my bus number among the numerous buses parked outside. I wove in and out of the crowd, hoping the men would lose me. Panting hard, I found my bus and ran for the door. I was just about to get on when I looked back. Art was shouting at a bus parked on the other side of the circle drive. The men looked over there and took off after him as he raced into the street like he was heading for me.

I got on the bus just as the driver was about to close the doors. "Find a seat," he snapped. I ran for a seat, staring out the window as Art rushed across the grass toward a parked bus filled with people. I pressed my face to the window, watching as he ran hard. He turned back to look at the men, and I gasped, seeing a car racing down the street.

"No!" I cried out, slamming my hand on the window. "Move!"

He turned back around, one foot on the pavement, when he saw the car. He tried to step back, but the car swerved in his direction, slamming into him. I watched in horror as Art's body went up over the hood, crashed into the windshield, and then catapulted over the car.

Slapping a hand over my mouth, I turned away from the window, squeezing my eyes shut as I heard the screams in the distance. Tears leaked from my eyes as I finally worked up the courage to look out the window again. People were racing toward his prone body. I waited for any sign of movement, but there was none. The bus jerked as the driver pulled away from the curb. I almost got up and told him to stop, that I wanted to get off, but something stopped me.

As much as I wanted to run to him and be with him, I knew Art wouldn't want that. He caused the distraction so I could get away. If I got off the bus now, then he died for nothing. Sinking back into the seat, I sniffed as everyone around me moved on the bus, staring out the window at the growing crowd across the lawn. I bit my lip to keep the tears from falling, but it was no use. I'd gotten someone killed today, a man that tried to protect me when I couldn't protect myself. I knew this would happen. I should have never let him come with me. If I had left on my own, he would still be alive.

I could never allow anyone to help me again, no matter how lonely my life got.

3

CASH

"Come in!" I barked at the loud rap on my door.

The door swung open and Eli Brant walked in, a smirk on his face. "Everyone's waiting in the conference room."

"And that's funny?"

He was quiet for a moment, the smile never leaving his face. "He's very…pretty."

I rolled my eyes. "Sinner?"

"I was just thinking, now that he's here, and the fact that he just looks so damn charming, we really don't need to rotate on close protection anymore."

"You want to shift that responsibility to him," I affirmed.

"Hey," he held up his hands, shaking his head. "I'm just saying, the ladies will love him, and we both know they're more likely to listen to that pretty face than the rest of us."

I laughed at that. "Yeah, you're all ugly." I jerked my chin at the door. "So, do you think he's ready?"

"You saw him. He adapted well to our team. He's a bit of a jokester, but I think he'll do just fine."

I nodded in agreement. "I talked with Cazzo, his previous team leader. He says Sinner's solid. No mistakes."

"I get the same impression."

"Good. Let's welcome him with his first mission as close protection agent."

I stood and walked around the desk, joining Eli as we made our way to the conference room. Sinner was lounging in his chair, but the way his eyes moved around the room, it was clear this was his way of checking things out discreetly.

"Alright, let's get this meeting started. As I'm sure you've all figured out by now, Mark is now joining your team. Eli is in charge when in the field. He's your commanding officer. Warren is your communications guy, and Bradford is your weapons guy. That leaves you," I nodded to Sinner with a smile. "You will be the close protection agent on most assignments."

"Perfect," he mumbled under his breath. It was clear he didn't like his new job, but he didn't complain any further.

"I thought you'd like that. Nobody likes to be the close protection agent, but it just so happens that you fit the bill perfectly for this next one."

I threw folders for each of them on the table. Sinner flipped his open, but then shut it, shaking his head immediately. "No, no way."

Great, just when I thought he would be a perfect fit for the team, he had to go stir shit up on the first job. "You got a problem with your assignment?"

"Yeah, I have a big fucking problem. Vanessa Adams? She was my last assignment at Reed Security. Let me guess, her dad just needs someone for a charity function or some bullshit."

Okay, that was not what I was expecting. "No, he wants us to find her and bring her back. What the hell happened on your last assignment?"

"Let's just say Victor Adams didn't give us all the intel and one of my team members ended up in the hospital, unable to feel his legs."

"Fuck," Warren grumbled.

"Details," I snapped, feeling extremely uneasy with this case now.

"We were her detail for a charity function. According to Victor, her last detail was incompetent. We were stepping in with the idea that we would take over permanently if everything went well.

Someone was at the function watching her, so we got out of there, but we came under fire when leaving. Reed tried talking to Victor about it and got the feeling there was more to the story he wasn't being told. Then he contacted us later, saying that Vanessa had run away. Reed's been digging into him, trying to get information, but the guy has a lot of connections. Whatever he's hiding, it's buried deep."

"Shit, well, doesn't that just complicate things," I said, leaning back in my seat.

"Why is he contacting us? He lives on the East Coast."

"He said that she has friends out here and would most likely come this way." I frowned, remembering my conversation with him. It had all been a fucking lie. If she was out here, either she ran away, or he stashed her out here and then she escaped. "Shit. Alright, Eli, start planning this out while I get Reed on the phone. The rest of you get your instructions from Eli."

I stormed out of the conference room, hating that this guy was trying to take me for a fool. Slamming the door behind me, I stalked over to my desk and picked up the phone, dialing Sebastian Reed.

It rang five times before he finally answered. "Sebastian Reed," he answered briskly.

"Cash Owens."

It was silent for a moment before he cleared his throat. "The employee thief."

"I didn't steal Sinner. He came to me for a job."

"Either way...What exactly can I do for you? Are you looking to raid more of my employees?"

"I'm calling about a former client of yours. Vanessa Adams."

"Fuck," he swore. "What's this about?"

"Her father called me to find her. Everything checked out, so I took the job. Except, your former employee says that Adams is responsible for putting one of your men in the hospital. And I take exception to anyone that purposely endangers the lives of my men."

"What do you need from me?"

"Information. Why is he looking for his daughter?"

"As far as I could tell, he was trying to use her for a business deal. I don't have any details. I was working on finding out who put my man in the hospital, nearly paralyzing him, when he shut us out."

"But she's an innocent," I presumed.

"All the information my men gathered from her points to her being a victim in all of this. I don't think I have to tell you how much she would suffer if she were captured by her father and used…for whatever his plans are."

"Understood," I answered. "If I recover her, I can't keep her here."

"I can hide her," he offered. "He wouldn't suspect us, at least not right away."

"Are you thinking of stashing her at a safe house? Do you have the resources for that?"

"I can handle it."

"What I meant was, do you have the men to spare for as long as this could take?"

"Don't worry about that. You get her out here and I'll take care of the rest."

"We'll need to keep this quiet. If he catches wind of my guys heading out to you, we're screwed."

"He'll definitely be keeping tabs on you." Sebastian sighed heavily on the other end. "Send her with Sinner."

"You're sure? I got the feeling the two of you didn't part on the best of terms."

"This is business and goes beyond any reasons I may have had for letting him go."

I was so damn curious I couldn't help myself. "He's been training with us for a few weeks. He's good. Really damn good. Why exactly did you let him go?"

When he didn't answer immediately, I didn't think he ever would, but then he surprised me. "You know he was Special Forces, and his skills speak to just how good he is. Trust that."

And then he hung up. Whatever happened between them, I might never know. But I did trust what I saw when Sinner was training, and that was all I needed to know. I headed back to the conference room where Eli was still planning with his team.

"Okay, we're going ahead with the mission as planned," I said as I walked back into the room. "The outcome has changed, though. It seems Victor has a few enemies who want to use Vanessa as a bargaining chip—Vanessa in exchange for a business deal. We don't have the specifics at this moment, so I don't know how accurate this information is. We're going to go ahead with locating Vanessa, but when we find her, Mark will deliver her back to Sebastian at Reed Security where he'll take over protection services. In case we're being watched, we'll have to have a female agent on standby to fill in for Vanessa so we can get her out of here safely. Any questions?"

"Will I be taking her by myself?"

"At this time, we think that's the best option. We need to keep it low-key. We may add one member to the detail, but we need to see what we're up against first. I'll have a packet put together for you by midday. Why don't you head home and pack a bag. If she's where we think, you won't have time to pack. I'll have an SUV loaded when you get back."

"Sounds good."

"Send Red and Kavanaugh over to the friend's apartment to keep an eye out. As soon as Mark's back, I'll send the two of you over to her place to pick her up. You make sure there's no interference and that they get out clean."

"Got it," Eli responded.

We walked quickly back to my office. This whole thing was making me uneasy. If we got Sinner away, we might just get out of this clusterfuck without any problems, but the sinking feeling in my gut said things weren't going to be as smooth as I hoped.

"Are we sure that Reed Security can handle her protection?" Eli asked.

"If Sinner didn't think they could, he would have said so."

I jerked my chin at Eli to close the door. Walking around my desk, I took my seat and started putting together the packet for Sinner.

"Still, why is he out here? You've seen his skills. Why would Reed let him go?"

"That I don't know, and frankly, it doesn't matter at this point."

"Unless there's something neither of them are telling us," he said suspiciously.

"I get the feeling that it's a personal issue. Reed said he was good. We've seen that Sinner can handle shit. Frankly, as long as he's not a traitor, I don't see any reason to dig into him leaving Reed Security."

"But hasn't it bothered you from the moment you interviewed him?"

I sighed heavily, rubbing at my face. "No, it hasn't. I told you I talked with his former team leader. Let it go. Right now we have a job to focus on. Go get the SUV loaded for him."

He nodded and turned for the door.

"Eli." He turned back to me. "You have to trust the people you work with. I know that's hard for you, but I wouldn't put someone on your team if I thought he couldn't be trusted."

With a swift nod, he opened the door and headed out. I stared down at the paperwork I was putting together and remembered when Eli first came to me. I was just starting up OPS and looking for recruits. He didn't exactly trust me, but that wasn't shocking, considering someone on his own team turned on the rest of them. It took forever for us to gain his trust, and I knew that while his head understood that Sinner was an asset, Eli wasn't sure of his instincts anymore.

After multiple calls, checking in with other teams, and finishing off some paperwork, I was just about to head down to see Sinner off. He should be back at the office soon. But then I got another call, this one from Red.

"Yeah?"

"She's at the friend's apartment, but it looks like someone's headed inside."

"Friendly?"

"I don't think so. Do you want us to intercept?"

"Follow and see what happens. If she's in danger, you step in and take him out."

"Got it."

I rushed out of the room, hanging up as I made my way to the garage. Eli was in there, finishing up the SUV. "Ready?"

"Good to go. What's going on?"

"Red just called. He's got a visitor."

"Who—"

My phone rang again and I quickly answered, "What have you got?"

"She climbed out the window. Kavanaugh has the suspect restrained, but there was a second guy who must have slipped inside. He followed her out the window. Her friend was working with Adams."

"Where is she now?"

"She took off on foot. I'm going after her now."

"Don't let her disappear. We need eyes on her."

"I'm on it."

I hung up and dialed Sinner. My heart pumped with adrenaline, but this was what I did. I lived for this shit, for an operation to go off without a hitch. But when it went off the rails and the energy ramped up, I was in my element.

"Cash, I'm on my way back—"

"She just ran out of the friend's apartment. Where are you?"

"About three minutes from that location."

"Get over there and pick her up. She's got company. Don't come back here. Head for Reed Security and call when you're clear. We'll set up to switch vehicles."

"On it."

I turned to Eli, who stood waiting for orders. "I need you to grab one of the guys and get this vehicle to a secure location. Sinner's picking up now. He'll have to ditch his truck. When he calls, we'll get his truck and bring it back here."

"What if they follow him?"

It was always a possibility, but if we were going to pull this off without letting Adams know that we weren't on his side, we had to put our faith in Sinner. "He's trained for this. We don't intervene unless he specifically asks for it."

"You're sure about that? He doesn't know his way around the city. Don't you think—"

"What I think is that we'll put Vanessa in more danger if we chase her down. Red has eyes on her. He'll make sure Sinner has this under control. In the meantime, let's make sure everything is set for him to get back to Pennsylvania. I'll work our contacts and have some vehicles arranged for him on the road back."

I knew he didn't like my plan, but this was what we had to do. It was a risk either way, but if Red and Kavanaugh intercepted to help, we'd risk the whole fucking operation. And right now, Adams needed to believe that we were on his side.

I headed back up to my office, but I didn't even get there before my phone rang again.

"Yeah?"

"Sinner just dropped off Vanessa at a motel with a man and another woman."

"Dropped off?" I asked as I shoved open my office door and settled behind my desk.

"I'm assuming he's ditching his vehicle. Do I follow Sinner?"

"No, stay with Vanessa, but keep your distance. He wouldn't have dropped off Vanessa with someone he didn't trust. If anything suspicious happens, move in."

"You got it, boss."

I tossed down my phone and pinched the bridge of my nose. I thrived in a situation like this, but the logistics of keeping Adams in the dark was a complication I was beginning to regret.

I was in my office with Red, Kavanaugh, and Eli, awaiting a phone call from Sebastian. The last anyone saw of Sinner was when he walked away from the motel with Vanessa and his two guests yesterday. But since then, a firestorm had erupted, possibly ruining the entire mission.

"I should have followed him," Red said again, sighing as he leaned back in the seat.

"Those weren't your orders," I reminded him.

"Yeah, but I could have left Brad at the motel and followed. We knew the situation was hot—"

"Red, it's not your fault," I repeated. "Let it go. He's fine now."

He shut his mouth, but glared at the floor. He took it seriously when shit went south. But this decision was all on me. Now, I had to hope that we hadn't completely blown this mission.

My phone rang and I picked it up. "Cash Owens."

"It's Sebastian. What's going on?"

"Sinner's headed toward you, but we have a problem."

"Fuck, why does there always have to be a problem?"

"Because that's just the way shit like this goes."

"Fine," he grumbled. "What's going on?"

"When Sinner picked up Vanessa yesterday, he was in his own truck. He had to ditch it after dropping Vanessa off at a motel. He had two other people with him, a man and a woman."

"Christ, I bet it was Sean and Cara."

"Who are they?" I asked curiously, looking at the others to see if the names rang a bell with them. They all shook their heads.

"Cara is his ex-girlfriend, and Sean is her brother."

"Any idea why they were out here?"

He was silent for a minute. "Cara has some issues," he said carefully. "I don't know the specifics of why they broke up, but I'm guessing she went out there for him."

"And she took her brother with?" I questioned.

"She has severe anxiety. She was kidnapped years ago by a serial killer. She got away, but not completely unscathed," he said, not really needing to tell us more. It was pretty clear by that short statement that she was pretty fucked up from what happened to her. But that didn't explain why Sinner left her and came out here. He didn't strike me as the type of man to leave a woman like that.

"Okay, well, that would explain what my guys saw as Sinner was making his way to pick up his truck. The woman, Cara, passed out and had to be carried the rest of the way. As far as Red could tell, she was fine. They took off and that's the last anyone saw them."

"I'm not seeing the problem," Sebastian said in frustration.

"When Sinner ditched the truck, whoever was after Vanessa found him. His truck was pushed into the river. Sinner almost didn't make it out alive. Apparently, an older gentleman jumped in to save him when he didn't come up. He dragged him out of the river, and after

Sinner walked away, a news crew showed up and interviewed the man."

"Shit," he said as he realized what this meant.

"As soon as he shows up, you need to stash her. Adams is going to come at you hard."

"Yeah, I got that."

"Let me know if you need anything."

"Trust me," he growled. "I'll be hitting you up for a favor in the future."

He hung up and I stared at Eli's team. "Well, that could have gone better."

Eli grunted from the corner of my office. "What do you wanna bet Sinner stays in Pennsylvania?"

Kavanaugh smirked. "There goes your idea to have only one close protection agent."

4

CASH

"Where the fuck is Sinner?" I grumbled as I stalked into the conference room, glancing at the clock again. "He was supposed to be in an hour ago." The man had been gone for a week and we needed to get back to work. When I called and told him to come in, that wasn't a request.

I sat down at the head of the table while Eli's team scattered along the whole fucking length of it. We had been digging into Adams, trying to find anything we could on the guy to take the heat off Reed Security. So far, we weren't coming up with much.

"Do you really think a meeting with Adams is smart?" Eli asked.

"We won't send in Sinner. As far as Adams knows, Sinner was still working for Reed Security when he took Vanessa."

Scottie Thacker from team one came strolling in holding up a phone. "Hey, anyone got any idea where Sinner is? I found his phone in the parking lot."

"He was supposed to be here a half hour ago," I grumbled, irritated he was fucking off.

"Maybe he's in the training room," Eli suggested.

"Nah, I've already looked around. I can't find him anywhere."

"Goddamnit," I muttered, shoving back from my chair. "If he's fucking with us, I'm gonna kick his ass," I said, storming out of the room. As much as I wanted to believe that he was screwing with me, my gut was churning, telling me that something was very wrong. I shoved open the front doors and stormed outside to the parking lot.

"Where was his phone?" I asked Scottie. I could tell everyone had followed me outside.

"Right over here," he pointed to behind a car. "Fuck, tell me he's just really clumsy."

"Dammit, if he gets himself killed, who's going to be the close protection agent?" Eli asked.

"Not it," Kavanaugh and Red said at the same time.

"I hate you fuckers."

I scanned the parking lot, seeing his rental at the back of the lot. "Everyone inside now. Lockdown procedures in place. No one goes anywhere until we find out what the fuck we're dealing with."

We all rushed back inside, and after everyone scattered, I slammed the alarm on the wall, letting everyone know we were under attack. Technically, we weren't at the moment, but that could change. The alarms blared and everyone gathered in the conference room, as was our procedure in a situation like this.

"What the fuck is going on?" Rock asked as he rushed into the room, his gun in hand.

Now that everyone was gathering in the conference room, I silenced the alarm, though the lights on the walls were still flashing. They didn't get turned off until we were sure the danger had passed.

"We believe Sinner has gone missing. When was the last time anyone heard from or saw him?"

"He was just here this morning," Eli reminded me.

"And I called him back in. Has anyone spoken to him since?"

Everyone shook their heads. Fuck, I could not lose a guy like this.

"Boss," Rae, my tech guru, said as she rushed into the room. She ran over to the clear screen on the wall and started tapping on it, bringing up camera footage. We all stood around her, watching as she brought up what appeared to be Sinner walking toward the office.

"When was this?"

"About thirty minutes ago."

We watched as Sinner walked toward the office, talking on the phone. Three men came up from behind, hitting him over the head and dragging his limp body over to a van.

"Why am I just finding out now?" I barked. This was a fucking disaster. We had sensors set up to detect threats outside the building.

"Because he never actually made it close enough to the door. I've found another camera angle from the street and pulled up the license plate. I'm running it through the other city cameras now to track their movements."

I spun around, facing Eli's team, which already looked like they were gearing up to move out. "Get everyone in here that's not scheduled for a job. I want everyone working this. Get the SUVs ready and get on the phone with local PD. Make sure they know we have a hostage situation and we're going in."

Eli nodded and practically ran out of the room, followed by the rest of his team. Rae worked through the footage, pulling up what the computer was already running in the background.

"It looks like they're heading out of town toward these abandoned buildings," she said, zooming in on an isolated location on the map. "But I can't be sure they didn't switch vehicles. There's a lapse of about three minutes, where they should be further along on the cameras, according to my software."

"Can you tell where the lapse occurred?"

"I'm working on tracking that now."

"What about the plates? Do you know who owns the vehicle?"

"Stolen vehicle. We're not getting anything from that," she answered succinctly.

"Fuck!" I shouted, slamming my fist into the wall. I took a deep breath as I thought through every move I needed to make to get my guy back. If they captured him outside our building, then the game was up. They knew he was connected to us, which was why we weren't getting anywhere with Adams.

"Do you have a location on Adams?"

"He's still in New York."

"What about his movements? Calls he's made?"

"I'll work on getting that information, but it's going to take a while."

"Get on it," I said urgently. "I need to know any contacts he has out here. Then we can start tracking down locations. And let me know if you find out if they switched vehicles."

I stormed out of the conference room and down to my office. I had to make a very uncomfortable call, but it was necessary to save lives.

5

RED

I ran along the edge of the building, stopping outside the window to peek inside. The thick dirt coating the window made it nearly impossible to see anything, and I hoped that worked in my favor as well, keeping everyone inside from seeing me.

"I can't see a fucking thing. Anyone else got eyes?"

"Negative," Eli said over comms. "I'm moving southwest."

"Copy that," I answered. "I'm shifting southeast."

With one final look inside, I took my chances that no one could see me and moved on. As I hugged the side of the building, I peered around the corner, watching for any guards. There was one man walking around the corner, and as soon as he disappeared, I hauled ass along the building until I came to a ramp leading down to a single garage door. I jumped down and ducked, waiting for a moment, listening for any sound. When I heard nothing, I peeked in the window of the garage door. Squinting, I could see something inside.

"I've got movement in the basement," I whispered. Taking a rag out of my pocket, I wiped the glass, hoping it would clear it enough for me to see inside.

"Guys, we've got movement out here," Kavanaugh said. "Five vehicles."

Peeking up over the concrete around me, I scanned for anyone else walking around. When I saw it was clear, I turned back to the garage window and looked inside again.

"Fuck," I muttered as I watched someone walk through a door with several other men. They were carrying shit from my nightmares, torture devices that would make any man talk. "I've got four men walking into a room down here. It's not looking too fucking good. We need to get in there now."

"We wait for Cash's orders," Eli commanded.

"Fuck, he doesn't have that long," I said urgently. "I'm on the southeast side of the building at the underground garage ramp. Get your asses here or I'm going in alone."

"Moving to you now. Just give us a fucking minute," Cash growled. "Reed, do you copy?"

"That's a go."

"You take the north side of the building. We're going in on the south side."

I glanced up through the window again just as I heard screams coming from inside. My heart beat a steady rhythm as I slipped into kill mode.

"Coming up on your six," Eli said. "Don't fucking shoot me."

I spun and raised my gun, watching as Eli, Kavanaugh, and Cash all came running down the ramp, armed and ready to go. Checking our surroundings one last time, I turned back to the door as we all spread out along the length of it. I grabbed my utility knife out of my pocket and slid the flathead screwdriver into the t-handle keyhole, breaking the lock. Turning the handle, I nodded to the others. Eli and Cash were on my right side, guns ready to fire when I opened the door. Kavanaugh was on my left.

"Don't let me get shot," I said right before I jerked the door up, flooding the basement with light. Gunshots fired around me as I pulled my weapon and prepared to fire. I moved to the left, taking up position behind Kavanaugh. We moved fast, firing off round after round at anyone who came in our path. Cash quickly ran to the door where the screams came from, standing next to it as he looked in through the window. He signaled that two men were in the room and one man was down.

Cash flung the door open just as a man stumbled over to Sinner, ready to shove the knife he carried into Sinner's chest. Firing twice, the man dropped to the ground, his body lying in a bloody heap. Cash rushed over to Sinner, who lay naked on the floor, curled up in a ball.

I quickly pulled my emergency blanket out of my pocket, something we carried at all times, and tore it open, laying it over Sinner. Tucking it around him, I shook my head. The guy wasn't even moving, and he stared up at Cash with the look of death in his eyes.

Cash tore his gaze from Sinner, the look on his face grave. "We need water and his clothes."

"Got it, boss."

Rushing past Kavanaugh and Eli, who stood sentry at the door, I searched two other rooms before finding them across the hall in an abandoned room. As I was heading back to Sinner, Scottie whistled to me from the bottom of the stairs, tossing a bottle of water at me.

"We don't have long," he warned. "Reed is holding them back, but we need to move."

"On it," I said, rushing back into the room.

"A few weeks on the job and you're already trying to get out of work?" Cash shouted at Sinner.

The gunfire picked up outside. We didn't have long to thwart another attack, not if we wanted to get Sinner out of here alive. He was already in bad shape. It was fucking freezing in the room and Sinner wasn't even shaking, which said a lot about the condition he was in.

"We need to move," I shouted at Cash. I fired at two men running in through the same door we came in. They must have had reinforcements show up. He tossed the clothes at Sinner after getting him to drink some water, but it was clear Sinner couldn't put on his own clothes. I ran over to him and helped him yank up his pants, keeping my eyes averted.

Sinner had burn marks all over his body, but a particularly nasty burn on his dick. I was surprised the man was even still alive at this point. I yanked up the zipper on his jeans and slid his shoes on, then helped him to his feet.

"No time for the rest," Cash shouted. "It's now or never." He shoved a gun at Sinner, but it fell right out of his grip, clattering to the ground. His hands were swollen and deep, red gashes circled his wrists. I picked up the gun and stuffed it in the back of my tactical pants.

"You good?" I asked him. He nodded, but I could see he was struggling to stay on his feet. But when the building rocked with an explosion, steely determination filled his eyes.

Cash gave me a grim look, his eyes flicking back to Sinner. "You got this."

I nodded, understanding what he was saying. We moved to the door, Cash taking the lead with Kavanaugh and Eli covering him. Climbing up the stairs, we slowed down so Sinner could keep up. Once we reached the ground level, there was no telling what we'd be walking in on. Scottie Dog, Rock, and Edu were positioned around the warehouse, laying down cover fire to keep these assholes back. Lockhart was at the door, shouting at us to get moving.

I glanced back at Sinner, watching as he struggled to hold himself upright with the wall. Still, I could see the determination shining in his eyes.

"Almost there, man. We make it across the parking lot and we're home free," I shouted over my shoulder.

The door opened ahead of us, sending blinding bright light inside the warehouse. I grabbed Sinner and hauled him forward as we approached the doors.

"Cash," I heard Sinner grumble from behind me. I turned just as he slumped against the wall, all the fight going out of him.

I was already headed back to him when Cash shouted, "Red, get Sinner before he falls the fuck over!"

"I gotcha, man." I bent over and hauled him up over my shoulder. I heard his sharp intake of breath as the wound in his side hit my body. I was trying to be gentle, but Cash was already waving me out the door, screaming at me to get my ass moving. I ran for the door, ignoring the way Sinner bounced on my shoulder. My team ran in formation around me, protecting both Sinner and me since I couldn't carry my weapon.

"Get him in the truck!" Cash shouted. I glanced over my shoulder just in time to see Cash kneel, laying down cover fire for us. Eli grabbed the door to the back of the SUV and flung it open. The ground shook with an explosion just as I was hauling Sinner into the backseat. He slumped over, staring sightlessly at the ceiling. I got in beside him, hauling him into an upright position.

Slapping him on the cheek, I shouted at him, trying to keep him from going into the light. "Mark! Stay awake, man. Don't go to sleep!"

If he closed his eyes, I feared he might never wake up again, and I had never lost a man. I wasn't about to now. Eli handed me his emergency blanket just as Cash and Kavanaugh got in the front seat. I tucked it around him, hoping I could warm him up just a little.

"Fuck off," Sinner said, his eyes slipping shut.

"Fuck, he's freezing," Eli muttered as he helped me rub his arms and try to warm him up.

Sinner's hand slid out from under the blanket, squeezing mine slightly. "Red…"

I squeezed it back, letting him know I was here. I swallowed hard as I watched him struggle to get any words out. He was losing the battle for his life, I could see it slowly draining from his eyes. I couldn't do anything to save him.

"Cara…tell…love her," he croaked out.

Determination swarmed within me. There was no fucking way I was losing him, or going to his woman and repeating those words. I couldn't.

I gripped his hand tighter and cupped the back of his neck with my other hand, forcing him to look at me. "Hey! You don't just lay down and take this shit!" I shouted. "Fight, you fucking idiot!"

But as his eyes slipped closed, I knew not even my words would save his life. He didn't have anything left inside him to give.

"Tired…" he murmured, his eyes slipping closed once again.

I turned around in my seat, only now aware that we were still under fire as Cash and Kavanaugh fought to get us out of there.

"Cash, get moving or we're going to lose him!"

The SUV jolted forward as Cash finally got us moving. I turned back to Sinner just as he called my name. "Take care…of Cara…"

He was breathing heavily, struggling to get out his last request. As much as I wanted to tell him to keep fighting, I had to make sure I knew what he wanted if he died.

"Love her," he whispered.

I pulled back and looked him in the eyes. Nodding, I gave him what he needed. "I will, Mark. I promise. Just hang on," I urged him. "You can tell her yourself."

He gave a slight nod, but then he closed his eyes and his head lolled to the side. I looked up at Eli, locking eyes with him. We both knew the chances of him surviving weren't great. He'd only been on our team for a few weeks, and now he was giving his life, all in the name of protecting a client.

6

FOX

Cash dragged the asshole that took Sinner back to the office. He thought he'd interrogate him and find out everything he knew, but it wouldn't be enough. Cash had this moral compass that always led him down the straight and narrow. Not that he wouldn't push the boundaries, but he didn't always have the conviction to take things further when needed. I had no such moral compass.

I looked in the rearview mirror at the dark eyes that stared back at me. I knew what the others saw—a man who was determined to do whatever it took. They only knew half of it. It wasn't the need for truth and justice that drove me. It was something deeper and darker that I couldn't always control. I had known it all my life. When the military realized they couldn't control me, they cut me loose. It would only be a matter of time before Cash figured it out, too.

I pulled into the parking lot and parked at the back. I shut off the truck and got out, storming around to the tailgate. Scottie Dog ran over to me, ready to help, but I turned and glared at him.

"I don't need any fucking help."

"Whatever, man. Should I get the door, or can you get that, too?" he said sarcastically.

"Sure, you can hold it open for me." I hauled the unconscious man over my shoulder and patted his back. "Unless that's too much work for you."

"Not at all. I have no problem holding doors for assholes." I stopped and glared at him. "Relax," he rolled his eyes. "I was talking about the fucker thrown over your shoulder."

I had a sort of love/hate relationship with nearly everyone I worked with. It wasn't that I didn't trust them. In fact, they were all very well-trained and I had great respect for all of them. Although, I could do without Scottie Dog's constant sarcasm.

I strode through the back door and down the steps to the basement. In this type of facility, talking with assholes like this wasn't ideal. I had a whole idea in my head about the type of facility I would use if I ever had the money to create such a place. As I flipped on the lights at the foot of the stairs, I shoved the door open and tossed the fucker on the ground. He groaned as his head smacked against the floor.

"We should probably try to keep him alive just a little bit longer," Scottie Dog retorted. "You know, in case you want to actually get answers out of him."

"I'll get answers out of him," I said calmly. "Are you staying, or is this too difficult for you to watch?"

"I think I'll be fine. I used to watch my sister rip the arms off her Barbie dolls. This shouldn't be too much different."

"Suit yourself," I said, turning away from him. I bent over, grabbing the man off the floor, and hoisting him up in the air. I couldn't kill. Yet. I had to get answers first, and that was hard to do if he was dead. Dragging him over to the wall, I hit the button, lowering the chain with the hook attached to it.

"Cliche," Scottie snorted. "I thought for sure you would have something better up your sleeve."

"Why mess with the classics?" I asked. As the chain lowered to the intended height, I hit the button to stop it and pulled the dead weight of the man back to where the hook now dangled. I grabbed him by the chin, forcing him to look at me. Though unfocused at the moment, that wouldn't last for long. "Don't worry, this is going to be very painful."

His head lolled back as I released his chin and hoisted him in the air, piercing the hook right below his collarbone. He screamed out as I shoved his body down on the piece of metal until his shoulder was resting in the curve of the hook. Taking a step back, I nodded at my handiwork.

"Not bad."

The man's screams died down until they were just whimpers. Stalking forward, I slapped him across the face to keep him awake. "Who sent you?"

The man didn't answer, snot dripping down his nose as he cried in front of me. I rolled my eyes, wishing just once I could hang a man who would actually have some balls about the situation he found himself in.

"Hey, we all know you're not the mastermind. Adams is behind this."

"Who?" he asked, genuinely confused.

"Adams, the man running this show."

He shook his head. "His name wasn't Adams."

"Then what was it?" I snapped.

The man squeezed his eyes shut, shaking his head. "You gotta take me down," he begged. "I'll tell you whatever you want to know. Just take me down."

I looked down at his feet, how they dangled on the ground as he tried to relieve the pressure. A stream of blood slid down his body, dripping onto the floor. "You'll tell me what I want to know either way. The question is, how long will you hold out before you can't take any more?"

"Please," he begged, spit flying from his mouth.

"Yeah, this is getting you really far," Scottie Dog laughed from behind me.

Slowly, I turned and shot him a nasty look. I hated when people questioned my methods. "Would you like to take over?"

"I'm not falling for that again," Scottie grinned. "The last time you let me take over, you nearly stabbed me just to get some fucking answers."

"That'll teach you to never intervene in an interrogation."

The man behind me cried out again. "Let me down! Please!"

"Tell me what I want to know and I'll make this not quite as bad as it could be."

"I don't know," he begged. But his eyes widened slightly and his lips parted. Sensing he had something to tell me, I moved closer. "He's like death."

"Got a name?"

He shook his head quickly. "He moves like a ghost. You'll never see him coming."

I grinned at that. He sounded like a worthy opponent, someone I really wanted to meet. I whistled one of my favorite songs, internally laughing at the confusion on his face. I turned and started to head for the door.

"What the fuck was that?" Scottie Dog asked, rushing forward. "Did you even get anything out of him?"

"Nah," I said, "It was a dead end."

"What about the guy hanging from the hook? Aren't you going to at least get rid of him?"

I slowly turned to Scottie Dog, a grin on my face as I started whistling the "Jet Song" from *West Side Story.* He rolled his eyes, shaking his head at me.

"Fuck, you're crazy, you know that?"

Whistling about being a Jet, I slid my knife out of my sheath. I grinned at Scottie Dog right before I threw the knife right past his head, lodging it in the base of the man's neck that was hanging behind him. With wide eyes, the death rattle left his lips, along with what breath was left in his body.

Scottie stared at me angrily. "I swear to God, Fox. You're a fucking psychopath."

And now I was at my favorite part, singing about how he was never alone. I tipped my hat as I walked out the door and headed upstairs with a smile on my face.

7

CASH

I walked out of Sinner's room, grateful he was alive. He looked like shit, but that was to be expected after what he went through. Driving to the hospital reminded me of waiting for a medevac while in the field. The whole time I was hoping I could get to the hospital in time, that he wouldn't die in the back of the SUV. But he was in bad condition, and none of us thought that he would pull through. I didn't even bother to argue with Sebastian when he demanded his team go in to see Sinner before me. I'd already been put in place by his girlfriend.

"How's he doing?" Sebastian asked as he walked up to me holding a cup of coffee.

"Didn't get any for me?" I asked.

"Oh, this is for you," he said as he continued to lift it to his mouth and drink it.

I smirked at him, knowing that was his way of telling me he was pissed off that Sinner was taken. "He's hanging in there, but he's in a lot of pain."

Sebastian nodded. "That's to be expected. Now that things have calmed down, do you want to tell me how the fuck this happened?"

"We caught it on the camera feed outside the building. He was talking on the phone. He didn't even see them coming."

"Sloppy," he said, taking another sip. But I knew he wasn't actually blaming Sinner. Not everyone could be on guard twenty-four seven, no matter how much we tried. "Did you get anything out of him?"

He was referring to the man we captured in the warehouse. He was trying to escape when Scottie's team intervened and captured him. They took him back to the office and tortured him until he gave in. "He's a nobody, just someone hired to do the job."

"Does he work for Adams?"

I shook my head. "I don't think so. It appears he works for someone else."

Sebastian cocked his head to the side. "So, Adams hired someone and then it was outsourced?"

"That's my best guess. I'm getting the feeling that whoever was hired by Adams is pretty dangerous. These guys…they were good, but just hired mercenaries. The real threat is still out there, and I'm guessing he's biding his time to make the perfect maneuver."

Sebastian sighed, running his hand across the scruff of his jaw. "Fuck, I need to find out what the hell is going on."

"Is Vanessa safe?"

"That's about the only thing that's going right at the moment," he grumbled. "What are we going to do about Sinner?"

"What do you mean?" I asked.

"Well, clearly, he needs to come back to Reed Security."

I barked out a laugh. "He left your ass and came to me."

"But his girlfriend lives by us."

"Then she can move out here," I challenged.

"Not gonna happen. You've seen her."

I had, and I wasn't giving up that easily. Sinner was a good employee, and I wasn't giving up. "I have, and I know that she'll do anything to be with him, including moving out to sunny California."

"But her family lives by me. Hell, Sinner's teammates, the same men he fought with in the military, are with me."

I grinned at him, seeing an opportunity opening up. "And I'll gladly take a few good extra men."

"Seeing as one of them is in a wheelchair and can't fucking walk,

I'm guessing he's not going anywhere. Not that I would let you have him anyway."

"Oh, you're not going to *let* me have him. I see how it is."

He pulled out his phone and held it out to me. "You're welcome to ask him yourself, but he's pretty fucking grumpy right now, you know, with the loss of his legs."

"He didn't lose his legs. He just needs to get them working again. I'll gladly hire him a physical therapist and get him moving again."

Sebastian sighed, shoving his phone in his pocket. "Look, what's it going to take for you to release Sinner from his contract?"

"Well, first, he has to tell me he's leaving."

"And second?"

I shook my head. "There's not a damn thing I want from you."

He tensed for a moment, then blew out a breath, staring at the ground. Whatever this was, it was personal, and I wasn't budging without a good reason.

"He's good friends with my—with Freckles."

"And who is Freckles?"

"She's my girlfriend…woman. Or she was. Freckles and Sinner have this connection that I don't fucking understand."

I grinned at him, finally understanding. "So, you fired Sinner because he was getting a little too friendly with your woman."

I could tell this was a sore subject for him, and even harder for him to admit the truth, so I waited.

"They're just friends, but it's different with them, so easy. I said some shit to Sinner, knowing it would set him off. He took a swing at me and I fired him. I told myself I was trying to protect Cara, but…" He shrugged, not looking at me. "It's my fault Cara broke things off with him. He was trying to protect her. And now, I'll never keep Freckles if he doesn't come home. So, I'm asking you as a personal favor to let Sinner out of his contract."

"Well, fuck," I sighed. "You had to go and make this personal."

"Is it working?" he smirked.

I wanted to say no, but I couldn't deny that his story hit me in the gut. He was trying to fix things, and if I held Sinner to his contract, this poor schlub would lose the woman he loved. It shouldn't matter, but I found myself liking Sebastian.

"If I let him go, you'll owe me big time."

He held out his hand. "I have no doubt you'll make me regret ever bringing Sinner home."

"And then some."

8

BETH

The landlord swung the door open to the studio apartment on the first floor of the building. I stepped inside through the puff of smoke that left her mouth. The cigarette dangling from her lips was making me nauseous, but it wasn't like I could be picky about what she did. I was getting this apartment for a steal. They let me pay cash and had a month-to-month lease.

I waved the smoke away, holding back a cough as I pushed on. The apartment wasn't much. The kitchen was to the right and there was enough space on the left side for a small table pushed up against the wall. Straight ahead was a single window that had bars over it. I wasn't exactly thrilled about that. I preferred to have a first floor apartment so I could escape if needed. I'd been moving around every two months for the past six months, trying not to stay in one place too long. This apartment was the worst of any of them. Between the water stains on the ceiling, the peeling paint, and the cockroach I saw on the counter, I wasn't at all impressed. But I could get some poison for the bugs, and hopefully, that would be enough.

I turned toward the lady, ready to say I would take it, but she already had her hand stretched out. I pulled out four hundred dollars and placed it in her hand, but she raised an eyebrow, shaking her head.

"Uh-uh, sweetie. You also have to pay the deposit."

"No," I said firmly. Based on the vacant apartments, she didn't have very many tenants, probably because this place was a dump. "There are multiple code violations, including the fact that you're smoking inside. If you want to get rid of the cockroaches and fix the ceiling, I'll gladly pay more. But until then, I'm not paying a dime over the monthly rate."

"I can kick you out on the street," she said snidely.

I snatched the money out of her hand and stormed past her. *One. Two.*

"Wait," the woman snapped. "You can stay, but if you're even a day late on next month's rent, you're out."

"Fine," I said, waiting for her to walk out. I grinned as she closed the door behind her. It wasn't that I particularly wanted to stay in this place, but I wasn't about to be swindled either. I set my purse on the counter, brushing off crumbs that were left behind. The place was disgusting and would need to be cleaned before I could really live here.

I rubbed at my shoulder, wincing at the ache that never really went away. The pain was a constant reminder of Art and all he sacrificed for me. When I closed my eyes, that day replayed in my mind over and over again. I'd never seen anyone killed before, and the fact that I knew Art made it more difficult to get past. I kept thinking about those last few days, wondering if I had just left earlier, if he would be okay. I never knew how they found us, but I assumed it had something to do with the men that attacked us in the alley.

I shook off the remnants of bad memories and got to work cleaning. There was garbage still in the apartment that had to be taken out. Once I finished that, I went down to the corner store and grabbed some cleaning supplies and poison. It took me a lot longer to clean than it should have, considering how small the apartment was. By the time I was finished, it looked brand new. Well, as brand new as a rundown apartment could.

I had a few things in my car that I took from one place to the next. It was a junker car that I bought a few months ago from a used car salesman. He wasn't too concerned about paperwork, and neither was

I. That was the only reason I bought it. It cost me half my savings, but made it easier to find jobs and move when it was time.

I grabbed the blowup mattress out of my car, along with my blankets. I had to make several trips since my left arm really couldn't hold any weight. I was pretty sure when Art's friend put my shoulder back in place, it wasn't done correctly, but beggars couldn't be choosers. I was grateful that I wasn't in constant pain.

After everything was put away, I ate my dinner and went to bed, but sleep never came easily for me. Demons from my past always haunted me, no matter how hard I tried to escape them. I tossed and turned as the nightmares infiltrated my head.

I hid under my blankets, sure that if I was quiet, he wouldn't come in here tonight. Every night was the same, I pulled the blankets up just over my nose so only my eyes were peeking out. It would be easier to hide completely, but I needed to see. Not knowing if he was coming was the hardest part.

Footsteps sounded outside my bedroom door. My heart started racing as they stopped right in front of my door. I wanted to squeeze my eyes shut, but was too terrified not to see it happening. My eyes narrowed in on the door handle as it slowly turned. I choked on my scream, knowing it would do me no good.

My eyes shot to my window. I'd always been too scared to run. When he was around me, his smell and size overwhelmed me until I was paralyzed. But as sickness swirled in my stomach, I decided I didn't want to stay here for one more minute. Flinging off the covers as he walked in, I stood there, heart pounding, as he grinned at me.

"Going somewhere, angel?"

My throat was so dry I couldn't speak. I stared at him, my legs shaking so hard I nearly collapsed. I opened my mouth to speak, but only a squeak came out. Slowly, he strode toward me. I glanced around the room, hoping to find something to protect myself with. I'd never attempted something like this before. I'd always been too weak, but today, I was finding courage from somewhere deep within.

It could end up costing me my life.

But not fighting back wouldn't do me any good either. I had spent the past two years terrified of the night, and all that did was give him all the power.

Shifting over to my desk, he watched me curiously. My hands grasped around behind me for a weapon, but it only amused him.

I watched the slow smirk spread across his face. "Oh, angel, I was hoping one day you would come out to play."

The bile in my throat threatened to spew over. This was all a game to him, but this was my life, as shitty as it was, and I couldn't deal with this anymore. Clutching a pen in my hand, I popped off the cap and prepared to defend myself.

But I had no training, and when he came at me, my attempt to stab him in the face was easily thwarted. He laughed at me as he held my arm in his thick hands. The evil in his eyes was brighter than ever as he shoved me hard against the wall. I hit the side of the desk, falling hard to the ground. Wincing, I was too slow for him as he came at me again. He hauled me up by my arms, his fingernails biting into the skin.

The evil look in his eyes made me wish I had never tried to fight back. He leaned in, his lips brushing my ear. "You'll regret that," he murmured. Then he smiled at me and jerked my body toward him. Then I was flying backward, my body hitting the cheap window and crashing through. I screamed as my body flew through the air as if in slow motion. The air whooshed out of me as I hit the ground, my whole body aching. I couldn't hear anything as I laid there, my body broken and bleeding. And as I stared up at my bedroom window, I saw his terrifying face staring down at me. In that moment, I knew I would never escape him.

I jolted upright in bed, my heart pounding out of control. I wiped the sweat from my forehead and closed my eyes as I breathed deeply. After all these years, I still couldn't escape. I got up from my air mattress and walked to the window. I stared outside at the dark sky and wondered when he would find me again.

"You'll be working the night shift," my new boss said, guiding me through the building. "There are quite a few employees that stay late working, and they don't like to be disturbed. Your shift will begin at nine o'clock, and it ends at five in the morning. If you finish early, you can leave early, but if I find that you're not doing everything required, I'll find someone to replace you."

I wasn't worried about the hours. Working at night meant that I could sleep during the day, which was always easier. I still had nightmares, but not as frequently. And it was easier to calm down when I woke up in daylight.

"I don't mind the hours," I answered as we made our way through the first floor.

"There are five floors in total. You'll be cleaning the third floor, which is the research department and the hardest to clean."

"Why is that?"

"Because everything has to be kept extremely clean. There are a lot of electronics, so we do a very thorough cleaning every night." We walked over to the elevator and stepped inside. My boss seemed to be a tad cross, but I could deal with that. I was used to angry people. I'd survived more than I cared to admit at the hands of people like her. Not that I could compare her to some of the other people from my past. Compared to them, she was a saint.

We stepped off onto the third floor and she took me room by room. "Most of these labs are connected to an office. You're never to touch the equipment other than to clean it."

"Understood."

"And every computer is password protected. If you enter the password wrong one time, you only have one more chance to enter it correctly. After that, the police are called."

My eyes widened as she narrowed her eyes at me like I would attempt that. "I'm not interested in what's on computers. I doubt I could even turn one on."

"Yeah, that's what they all say." She turned and walked down the hall. "There are cameras on every level, in every lab and office. If you attempt anything, we'll have evidence and you'll be prosecuted."

Geez, it was like I was working at a government research facility or something. "Can I ask why you hired me?"

I didn't have any identification, and I needed to be paid under the table. It didn't make sense that a place like this would hire just anyone off the streets. With all this technology, shouldn't they be hiring properly vetted people?

She turned to me with a fierce expression. "Do you want the job or not?"

"Of course I do," I answered. I just didn't understand why, if they were so wary about their technology, they would hire someone they didn't have information on.

"We have security in place. If you do anything, we'll know."

But somehow, I thought I was being set up. I couldn't be sure about it, but the pay was better than anything I'd made before, and the hours were ideal for me. So, against my better judgment, I accepted the job.

"You start tomorrow. You'll work with Rianne for the first week. Once she's sure you can do the job, you'll work on your own. Am I clear?"

"Yes."

"Good, be here tomorrow at 8:45."

9

CASH

I walked through the doors of OPS, still thinking about how Sinner was taken six months ago. It could have ended so much worse, and we were lucky that we only lost Sinner because he chose to go back to Reed Security, whatever Sebastian Reed thought of the situation. It bothered me that we could never find out who was behind the attacks on not only Vanessa, but one of our own. And in the months after Sinner left, Reed had been stonewalling me on what was happening.

Part of me thought it was because he blamed us for what happened to Sinner, but I got the feeling something else was going on that we weren't privy to. When Sinner was taken, it really shook everyone up, especially Red. He'd been the one to stick by Sinner's side as we got him to the hospital. After vowing to take care of Cara for Sinner, he wouldn't leave her side until he was sure she was okay.

"Boss," Rae said, running up to me. "Um, we might have a problem."

"Nope," I said, walking right past her. She ran beside me to keep up. Her short little legs made it easy for me to get away from her. Though she trained with our guys and could easily hold her own against them, that was in the ring. And I wasn't in the ring. I knew better than to go up against her. She was scrappy, using her small stature against all of us.

"What do you mean? You're the boss. If there's a problem, I come to you."

"Rae, it's not even eight o'clock in the morning. I got stuck in traffic behind a five-car pileup, I haven't had any coffee yet, and if you must know, I haven't gotten laid in weeks."

I pulled open my office door, determined to shut it in her face, but she easily blocked me and ducked under my arm to slip inside.

"I brought you coffee," she said, handing me a cup. "Just as you like it. Don't worry, I won't tell anyone you prefer lattes to black *man* coffee. I've also been tracking your phone, and I know you stopped by your ex-girlfriend's house, which I'm assuming is because, as you said, you haven't gotten laid in weeks. And since you're still in a grouchy mood, I'm guessing she didn't take you back just because you wanted sex. And it's actually now one minute past eight."

She stood there with a satisfied smirk on her face, waiting for me to say something. And she thought I would keep my mouth shut because that's what most guys did. I wasn't most guys.

"I actually did get laid this morning, if you must know. It was extremely satisfying in every way, but you're right. She still feels the same way as before. My job is too dangerous and the hours are too long. Not that I'm surprised she feels that way. Most women I dated while in the military couldn't handle it. I didn't expect much different after I got out. The military may have been an excuse at the time, but I'm still the same person with the same drive at work. And you're wrong on the lattes. I don't prefer them over black *man* coffee, as you suggest. I get them because you like them. And at some point during my morning, you always steal my coffee."

Her jaw dropped open and then her eyes flicked to my coffee. She snatched it out of my hands and drank it. "Well, since I know you do that, I'll expect one every morning."

"I thought you'd say that," I grinned. Walking around behind my desk, I set my things down. "So, what was so important you had to come chase me down?"

"Fox is back."

My head snapped up and I stared at her in question. "Is he…"

"Same. I really didn't think he would come back this time."

"Neither did I." Dropping what I was about to do, I stormed out of my office. "Where is he?"

"Where do you think?"

"I don't have time for his crap today," I muttered.

"Well, the guys aren't exactly encouraging him to leave."

"Of course not."

Fox had worked for me since I first started the company. The man was deadlier than anyone I knew, but I couldn't put him in the field. He was cunning, a quick thinker who was always ten steps ahead. But he could be very secretive also, which put his team in a dangerous position when they couldn't be sure he'd follow the strategy previously set out.

As I pushed open the doors of the training room, I shook my head at what I saw. Fox was standing behind the line at the target practice for knife throwing. Everyone was standing around watching as he picked up a knife and flipped it in his hand.

"These are a few of my favorite things," he sang, then grabbed the knife by the blade and flung it at the target, hitting it dead center. He moved on, continuing to sing. I rolled my eyes, walking over to where Jerrod Lockhart from Team One stood.

"How long has this been going on?"

"About half an hour," he grunted.

"And how many show tunes is he on now?"

He glanced at me out of the corner of his eye. "Well, we've been through "Steppin' Time" and "It's The Hard-Knock Life" so far. I'm expecting he'll start taking requests at any time."

"Christ, why today?" I grumbled.

"Is today not a good day for Fox to return?"

"Is any day?" I asked, instantly regretting it. I liked Fox. He was a good guy, if only a little eccentric. I didn't know a whole hell of a lot about him, other than he was very ruthless and really liked show tunes. Hell, that was really all anyone knew about him.

"Still haven't gotten his file?" Jerrod asked.

"I have his file," I muttered. I just wasn't sharing it. Everything about his military career was in there. It was his life before the military that had me questioning him.

"I take it that means you aren't sharing."

I shot him a side glance. "Do you want all your personal shit aired for everyone?"

He cleared his throat. "Maybe it's best to keep that locked down."

"That's what I thought."

"What do you want to do about this?"

I sighed, rubbing my hand over my eyes. "I'll handle this."

"Uh…you might want to approach carefully. Thumper nearly lost an eye when he tried to give him a hug."

I laughed at that. "He deserved it then. Who in their right mind would try to give Fox a hug?"

We both looked at each other and burst out laughing. "Thumper," we said at the same time. I walked over toward the table Fox had set up. "Hey!" I shouted, ducking when he spun on me, ready to throw his knife.

He grinned at me, shuffling his feet in some kind of dance move. "Oh, we got trouble," he grinned.

"This is not River City," I said, holding my hands out as I slowly stood. "And there are no pool tables in this building."

He pointed a knife at me, laughing loudly. Honestly, I couldn't believe I knew this much about musicals. It wasn't until I met Fox all those years ago and he dragged me off to the theater that I even knew what a show tune was. Every once in a while, I caught myself singing along without realizing what was happening until the room got quiet and everyone started staring at me.

"So, what made you decide to show up today?"

He shrugged, flipping a knife in his hand. "Got bored, I guess."

"With what?"

"You know."

I caught the glint in his eyes and knew exactly what he had been doing. Hunting. Fox was usually around when we needed him, but every once in a while, he would disappear without a trace. It usually meant he was onto something, whether personal or for business. None of us ever really knew, and I wasn't sure it was wise for us to find out.

"What have you got going on here?"

"Ah, I'm glad you asked," he grinned, flipping the knife back and forth in his hand.

This wasn't a tactical knife or a combat knife. Fox wouldn't bother with something like that for training. No, he loved his throwing knives, and every time I watched him, he seemed to get even better.

"I was just giving the boys a demonstration."

"You know we're not going to start carrying throwing knives," I said, crossing my arms over my chest.

"That's because you've never held one in your hands and felt the power of the beautiful mistress," he said, walking over to me and wrapping his arm around my shoulder. "Trust me, just one touch, and you'll fall in love."

He stopped in front of the table, finally taking his arm off my shoulder. I wasn't going to play into his games, but when he handed me one, I couldn't help the curiosity building inside. Sighing, I took the knife from him and attempted to hold it, but he laughed.

"No, it's all in the placement of your thumb. Now, at this distance, you should have your thumb in about the middle. The closer you are, slide your thumb down near the blade. For further away, choke up and hold it up here," he said, repositioning my hand. "This is a half spin."

"This is ridiculous," I grumbled. "Like I'm ever going to have a need for throwing knives."

"When wouldn't you want to use it?" he asked incredulously. "Trust me, this is something we need on our side."

"A bullet moves faster," I pointed out.

"Ah, yes. But you can't always rely on a gun, can you? Sometimes, stealth is more important. Trust me on this."

He positioned my body, then stepped back to watch. I let out a breath, then threw the knife, which bounced off the target. I tossed the other knives on the table, irritated with this.

"Look, I'm a sniper. I don't throw knives."

"You're not relaxing. It's just like using a sniper rifle. It's about deadly accuracy and focus. You can do this."

I took a deep breath and positioned my body the way he showed me, then focused on the target and flung it hard, shocked when it stuck. I couldn't believe how fun that was, but I was forgetting that I wasn't here to play.

"Right, well…we have shit to do."

He started to whistle, but I cut him off. "We're not performing right now. If you're back, get your ass in gear and start training." Spinning around, I faced the rest of the guys. "Lock, I have a job for your team. Let's meet in the conference room in twenty."

He nodded and headed off to the locker rooms, followed by his team, Edu, Rock, and Scottie Dog. Meanwhile, I headed back upstairs and pulled out their files, looking over their most recent jobs. I tried to rotate them when on assignment so they weren't always doing the same jobs. Some companies liked to keep a close protection agent the same at all times, but I always felt it was best to keep them on their toes. You never knew when someone would go down and another man would have to step into that position.

One by one, they filtered into the conference room and took their seats, all freshly showered and ready to get to work. I pulled out the file folders and passed them around the table.

"Alright, job of the day," I grinned, letting them know this was going to be an easy one. "Simple job."

"Yeah? Who's the princess?"

"*She* is a highly intelligent piece of equipment."

"We're guarding equipment?" Scottie asked.

"Scottie Thacker—" Cash started.

"Scottie Dog!" the rest of them shouted, pounding on the table.

I grinned at their raucous behavior. "You will be working close protection. You're in the air."

"Where to?"

I clicked the screen on, showing them the small plane that would be taking flight in just a few days. "This is a Cessna Caravan. You'll be riding shotgun while they test out their new equipment. Attached to the bottom of the plane is a new AI tracking system. It's a combination of machine learning, artificial intelligence, and computer vision."

Lock raised his hand. "What the fuck does that mean?"

I cleared my throat, staring down at the table. "Uh, well…it means…" I cleared my throat again when Rae walked in with a smirk on her face.

"Basically, it means that the facial recognition on your camera is now being used to identify weapons and combatants on the field. And through artificial intelligence and machine learning, it quickly processes the videos from the cameras. Machine learning teaches the computers to spot trends and anomalies in the data for us to understand."

Edu leaned back in his seat. "So, basically, a bunch of technological bullshit none of us understand."

I nodded. "Yeah, basically."

"Good, just say that next time."

"Anyway, Lock, you'll be on point. Rock, you're my eyes in the skies. As you know, small aircraft aren't required to file a flight plan. I want you in the tower, watching over those assholes and making sure the plane doesn't crash and burn with Scottie Dog inside."

"I would appreciate that also," Scottie raised his hand. "Not much for crashing and burning."

"And me?" Edu asked, lounging back in his seat.

"Perimeter security. We aren't anticipating any problems, but be vigilant as usual."

Rae sidled up to me, tucking her hand through my arm as she stared up at me with pouty eyes. "I don't suppose there's room on this security detail for me."

"Where do you suggest we stash you?"

"Stash? Boss, I'm insulted. I would be there to serve and protect. You know I'm more than capable, and as your head of IT, it's imperative that I oversee all details that involve my area of expertise."

I glanced around the table at the guys smirking at me. "Any objections to Rae tagging along?"

"Tagging along? Should we head to the ring and see exactly who is tagging along?"

The guys all shoved their chairs back, gathering up their folders.

"I'd better get on planning," Lock said quickly.

"Yeah, and I have to practice jumping out of a plane," Scottie Dog added. "You know…because I've never done a HALO jump out of a Cessna."

I really expected Edu to stand up to her, but the big black man almost seemed the most skittish of any of them. "I got…" he jerked his thumb over his shoulder, then cleared his throat. "Yeah, I'm out."

"Rock?" I asked, sure he wouldn't back down.

He smirked at me, looking between the two of us. "Yeah, have fun with that one."

He laughed as he walked out of the room, leaving me alone with Rae, who looked ready for the challenge.

"So, what's it going to be? Is the big, bad boss up for the challenge?"

I shook my head. "Nope, and it doesn't hurt my pride to admit that."

I walked out of the room with her calling after me. "You're all a bunch of pussies!"

10

BETH

My first few nights of work were uneventful. With all the sensors and cameras, I was sure that at any minute, someone would step off the elevator in some action movie scene, demanding I lead them to the secret weapon of the company. I was actually a little disappointed when that didn't happen. It wasn't that I needed more suspense and drama in my life. What I was dealing with was already enough. But every once in a while, I dreamed of a man who would come in with the capabilities to steal me away from this life.

I walked out of the grocery store with my meager groceries and walked down the sidewalk past the appliance center. I stopped when I saw a sign in the window, instantly intrigued. It was a class for self-defense and it was just down the street at the gym. Pulling out my pen and a piece of paper, I wrote down the hours and the phone number. I knew no one was coming to rescue me. I had to learn to defend myself so I never had to rely on anyone like I had with Art. I only got him killed in the end.

There was a class tonight, so I got in my car and drove home. I would be cutting it close, going to the class and then to work, but this was something I needed. After putting away my groceries, I went to sleep, not even bothering to eat first. Ever since Art died, my appetite was non-existent. I had to force-feed myself just to survive.

When my alarm went off, I wiped the sleep from my eyes and got to my feet. Every afternoon, my back ached from the cold that seeped into the air mattress. I stumbled into the kitchen and flung open the cabinet, staring at all the unappetizing food. I pulled down a bowl and some Cheerios, not even bothering with the milk. Per my usual routine, I flipped on my small TV and searched for any news on Art. Even all these months later, I was sure there would be a report one morning, telling of how he was murdered at the bus station.

After watching for a half hour and eating most of my cereal, I turned off the TV and stared out the window. Guilt ate at me constantly. Every day, I thought of Art's friend who helped me and wondered if he was okay. Had they gotten to him too? I was desperate for answers, but I was pretty sure I would never get them.

I showered and dressed for the self-defense class, unsure of what to wear. I didn't have anything other than jeans and T-shirts. It would have to do. I didn't have a lot of superfluous things. I allowed myself a TV only because I wanted the news, and it helped me calm down when I had nightmares.

I drove over to the class, watching from outside the building for a few minutes. What I saw inside was absolutely amazing. There were women inside that were performing moves I'd never seen before. I bit my lip, wishing that was me.

"Are you going in or are you going to stay out here the whole time?" a gruff voice came from behind me.

Startling, I spun around and pressed myself to the glass. My heart raced out of control as I stared into the darkness at the man standing in front of me. I closed my eyes for a brief moment, just long enough to remind myself that not everyone was out to kill me. When I opened them again, the man stepped into the light, the shadows still playing across his face.

He was tall, much taller than I imagined when I first saw him. With short hair, a thick scruff along his jaw, and dark eyes, a shroud of danger washed over me. I could tell he was muscular, even through his leather jacket. Everything in me screamed to run, but as he stepped closer to me, I found myself paralyzed.

"Are you here for the defense class?"

I glanced through the window again, stuttering my response. "Uh...yes. I should get in there."

I slipped past him, my arm brushing against his. For just a moment, I thought I felt something when we touched, maybe excitement, but it could have just as easily been dread. It had been so long since any man had elicited such a response from me that I wasn't sure I would recognize it if it slapped me in the face.

I hurried to the door and yanked it open, stepping inside before the man could say anything else to me. Unfortunately, he walked in right behind me, forcing me to step forward. I skittered off to the side, needing some space so I could regain my senses. In this light, the man didn't look nearly as terrifying. And as he saw someone across the gym, he smiled and waved to them. My body relaxed against the wall as air finally filled my lungs.

Maybe I wasn't really ready for this. I pulled my bag higher on my shoulder and turned for the door just as a woman came rushing over. "Hey! Are you here for the class?"

I looked around at the other students and shook my head. "I changed my mind."

"Are you sure? It's a great class."

I shook my head, ready to get out of there. "No, I just dropped by to see what it was all about."

"Well, why don't you let me show you a few moves? If you don't like it, you can leave."

"I don't have enough money," I said almost pleadingly. At this point, I just wanted to escape. I wasn't ready for this kind of action. My shoulder was still sore and the thought of fighting made me sick to my stomach.

"It's okay. The classes are free. Come on," she said, taking my hand without asking. I almost pulled back, but she was already dragging me across the gym. I felt people staring at me and I ducked my head, letting my curtain of blonde hair fall over my face.

"Here," the woman said, stopping and reaching for my bag. I

flinched back, clasping it tighter to me. She watched me warily like I was about to attack her. I swallowed hard, wanting to apologize for my reaction to her, but I couldn't seem to get the words out.

She walked closer and lowered her voice. "You don't have to be scared. I know this is new and there are a lot of people here. These men," she said, pointing around the room. "I work with all of them at a security company. They're all ex-military, which I know sounds scary, but they're born protectors. They would never hurt you."

My eyes flicked to the man I met outside. He was watching me from across the gym, his arms crossed over his chest. I dropped my eyes, not wanting him to see my curiosity…or fear. "That man…the one over there," I jerked my head. "Is he…"

She glanced over her shoulder, then turned back to me. "He's my boss and the best guy I know. However, he's a former sniper, so kind of a pussy when it comes to street fighting," she said teasingly. "I've been known to kick his ass a few times in the ring."

I knew she was telling me all that to make me feel better, though based on the way she moved, I wondered if she was telling the truth about kicking his ass. "I can only stay a few minutes."

A soft smile touched her lips, but I didn't believe she was soft at all. She looked like she kicked ass for fun. Deep down, I wished I could be her. "My name is Rae Dennon."

She held out her hand to me. I stared at it for a moment, then reluctantly held out my hand, shaking hers. "Beth."

"Let's get to work."

I followed her over to a mat, setting my bag just a few feet away. Glancing around the room, I watched as others continued with the class led by the other men. It seemed Rae was taking me aside to teach me separately. With even a small amount of their knowledge, I might actually be able to escape if those men ever came for me again. I gave as good as I could outside the diner, but it wouldn't have been enough. Though I was mostly healed, I still felt every punch and my life slowly slipping away.

"Alright, let's go through some basic maneuvers."

I nodded and followed along as she showed me how to put up my arms to block a punch, how to form a fist to punch, and how to protect my body. I moved through the motions, but I felt like an imposter. As she led me through a series of maneuvers, I felt like the whole room was watching me, laughing at how ridiculous I looked.

"You're doing great," she grinned.

"I look like an idiot."

"Well, in all fairness, we all look like idiots when we start out. Nobody is just born to do this stuff. It takes training and practice."

"Alright, let's try some easy defensive moves."

I frowned, not sure what she was saying. "You mean, like fighting you?"

"Not exactly. I'm going to pretend to attack you, and then I'll walk you through how to break the different holds and get away."

The thought of someone holding me down sent shivers over my skin. But she was here to help me. I had to push past this. Swallowing down my fear, I nodded and waited as she got in position. With her arms wrapped around me from behind, she closed her hand over my shoulder, squeezing just a tad too tight. I barely heard her instructions, but managed to do as she said and break the hold, though I gathered she let me go because she could tell I was uncomfortable.

We worked on it for well over a half hour. My declaration that I could only stay a few minutes was obviously a lie at this point. But I was actually learning something, even if I wasn't sure if I could put it to use. Maybe I could practice at home or something.

"Now, I want you to practice with Cash. He'll—"

"Cash?" I interrupted, turning around.

"My boss. It's fine to practice with another woman, but to get the feel of fighting off a man, you need the real deal."

I almost told her that I already knew what it was like to fight off a man, but I bit my tongue as he walked over. I looked up into his eyes for just a second before quickly averting my gaze. I couldn't control the shudder that washed over my body. I knew I shouldn't be attracted to this man, but my body had other ideas. But that all changed when he stepped closer to me. My brain was telling me to trust him, but my body was itching to run. When he stepped up behind me, I had to force myself not to react to him.

Fear threatened to overtake my body. My breathing picked up as his body pressed against mine. I nearly swayed on my feet as I remembered the men in the alley, punching and kicking me. The pain of my arm being torn from its socket flashed through my mind.

"You're not using your full range of motion," he said, taking my left hand in his and pulling my arm in an arcing motion that left me in a state of agony. I wasn't sure what happened, but it felt like that night when my shoulder was dislocated. I cried out, tearing my body from his grasp as I gripped my shoulder, squeezing my eyes shut to block out the pain.

"Are you okay?" he asked, starting toward me.

I stumbled for the edge of the mat, all too aware of the stares from the other students. I grabbed my bag and pulled it over my other shoulder as I raced for the entrance. I couldn't think of anything but getting out of there right this minute. Nausea overwhelmed me as I raced for the door. Gasping for air, I shoved the door open just as vomit rose in my throat and I threw up all over the sidewalk. I slumped against the brick wall, trying to get my bearings so I could make it home. But at the sound of a door opening, I spun around to defend myself, only to find everything going black.

11

CASH

I watched from across the gym as the new woman struggled to do any of the moves Rae was teaching her. I hated seeing women come in here, terrified to even try. It was obvious that she was one of the unlucky, a woman who had already suffered through something horrific.

We'd had a number of women like her in the past, but a lot of our students were just here to learn to defend themselves. They'd never dealt with anything horrible in their lives. They were the lucky ones.

Rae motioned me over, telling the woman I was going to step in her place. I wasn't sure that was a great idea, but if I could help her out, I gladly would. One of the things I noticed was that she wasn't really using her whole body. She was just going through the motions, but that would get her injured. I stepped up behind her and gently grabbed her arm, extending it fully.

"You're not using your full range of motion," I said, about to show her what I was talking about when she suddenly cried out and yanked her body away from me. I knew in an instant that she was injured, but she hid it well when she was working with Rae.

I was about to stop her when I saw the fear and pain in her eyes.

She ran for the door after grabbing her bag, but when she stumbled, I knew I couldn't let her leave.

"Dammit," I swore under my breath, chasing after her. As I ran around the corner, I saw her vomit all over the sidewalk, and as I shoved open the door, she spun, but her eyes rolled back in her head. I barely had time to catch her before she collapsed on the ground. Holding her in my arms, I adjusted my grip before hoisting her up.

Rae was already at the door, holding it open for me. "What happened?"

"She's injured," I said, stalking down the hallway to the medical room at the back of the gym. Rae hurried ahead of me and opened the door, flipping on the light. I laid the woman down on the table, then lifted her shirt to assess her injured shoulder. It was pulled from the socket, dangling there like a limp weed.

"Holy shit," Rae muttered.

"Did she say anything about a shoulder injury?"

"No, she didn't say a word. I definitely got the feeling she wasn't comfortable training, but that was it."

"Call Lock in here."

"Shouldn't we take her to the doctor?" Rae asked.

I stared down at the woman, knowing instinctively that's not what she would want. Until she woke up and I could talk to her, I wasn't taking her anywhere.

"No, go make the call. I'll stay with her."

"Boss—"

"Just do it!" I snapped over my shoulder.

I gritted my teeth, mentally berating myself for talking to Rae like that. I was always the calm one, cool and collected. Shit washed right off me, but staring down at this woman, my protective instincts were flaring, telling me something really shitty was going down.

Now that I had a moment to really look at her, I brushed the dirty blonde hair from her face and took in her features. With an angelic face and beautiful, tanned skin, I had a hard time figuring out why anyone would dare hurt this woman. I pulled her shirt back down, not wanting her to wake up in such a vulnerable position. As I was shifting her shirt, I noticed scarring on her stomach, wrapping around her back.

I bent over for a better look. She had a few jagged scars that ran along her waist, but I couldn't see how far they went without moving her. Taking a deep breath, I forced myself to calm down before I beat the shit out of someone. I pulled her shirt the rest of the way down and moved over to the sink, resting my hands on the edge as I breathed through the anger and hatred.

I'd seen enough shit in the military to make me want to kill every fucking man out there that even so much as looked like an asshole. But I'd locked that shit down long ago. I had a successful business and great friends. I would not ruin that all by exacting revenge on someone that I didn't even know. Even if I felt something stirring inside me when I looked at this woman.

A moan from behind me reminded me that whoever she was, I needed to use kid gloves with her. She was injured and scared, and my anger would only terrify her. I turned around, but stayed where I was, not wanting to make her even more uneasy. She winced as she tried to raise her arm, only to have it lay limply at her side.

"You dislocated it," I said more gruffly than I intended.

She flinched slightly, her eyes moving cautiously to meet mine. "What happened?"

"I was about to show you how to move when you cried out. Then—"

"I remember now," she interrupted me. She started to sit up and I rushed over, pressing my hand on her good shoulder.

"You don't want to do that."

"I need to leave. I have to work tonight."

"Not like this, you're not."

She glared at me, the first sign of some fight coming out in her. "I'll be fine. Please take your hands off me."

I gritted my teeth, but did as she asked, stepping back to give her space. With her good arm, she shoved herself into a sitting position. I didn't miss the hiss of pain or the way she bit her lip to keep from crying out. Luckily, the door opened and Lock walked in, followed by Rae.

The woman noticeably stiffened until Rae walked over and stood beside her. "Beth, this is Jerrod Lockhart, but you can call him Lock," she smiled. "He's a medic, and he's going to take a look at your arm."

She shook her head immediately. "No, it's fine."

"It's not fine," Lock said as he walked over to her, trying to get a better look. "You should go to the doctor. From what Rae told me, Cash barely touched you when your shoulder dislocated."

"It's an old injury," she confessed. "But I'll be fine."

"If it's an old injury, you might want to consider surgery."

"I can't," she said quickly. "I…don't have insurance."

Lie. She didn't have insurance, but that wasn't the reason she couldn't have surgery.

"How did you hurt it the first time?"

She bit her lip again, a dead giveaway she was trying to come up with an excuse. "Car accident."

Another lie.

I knew Lock wasn't buying it either, but he didn't call her on it. "Can I take a look at it?"

"No," she said quickly. "Like I said, it'll be fine."

Lock stood to his full height, crossing his arms over his chest. "I can imagine you're in a lot of pain right now. The only thing that's keeping you sitting upright is the adrenaline, but that's going to wear off, and the pain will become excruciating. If you don't let me set it, the pain is only going to get worse. Your arm will continue to swell up and—"

"Fine!" she snapped, refusing to look at any of us. "Just get it over with. I have to be at work soon."

"Call in sick," I demanded. "You shouldn't be working right now."

She didn't say anything, which told me she couldn't call off, either because she couldn't afford it or they would fire her.

"Beth," Rae said, sitting beside her.

I stopped listening as I watched the woman. The name Beth did not fit her at all. If I had to guess, this woman was in trouble, and was using a fake name. But I'd been around people like her before. After losing faith in other people, they were very unlikely to trust anyone else again.

"Can you just set it so I can be on my way?"

"You're not going to be able to drive," I pointed out. "But I'm guessing you already know that."

She raised her eyes to meet mine, almost like she was challenging me, but as soon as that spark shone in her eyes, it fizzled out. I wanted to tell her to fight me, to never let that spirit die, but now wasn't the time.

Lock turned to me, lowering his voice. "You should wait outside."

I frowned, wondering why he would ask that of me. "And why is that?"

"Because I need to examine her. It's good if Rae stays, but too many eyes…"

I looked over his shoulder at Beth and nodded. "I'll be outside. Let me know if you need me."

I let the door slam behind me as I stepped into the hallway and leaned against the wall. For the first time in my life, I felt uneasy. I'd seen all kinds of shit before, and it never affected me like this. When I saw those scars on her stomach, I wanted to puke. Normally, I could rationalize things in my head. I understood the circumstances and therefore, could accept the fate of a person. But with her, I couldn't do that. I couldn't look away or say I'd done all I could. Even if I took her to a clinic or helped her get away from whoever was hunting her, it still wouldn't ease the ache in my chest that said she needed more from me.

A sudden scream had me pushing off the wall and rushing to the door, but Rae beat me to it, opening the door and blocking me before I could step inside. She pressed a hand to my chest, glaring at me to back off. I watched over her shoulder as Lock worked on Beth, who was passed out on the table.

Frustrated, I stepped back as Rae followed me into the hallway. Running my hand over my head, I did my best not to lose my shit and punch the wall. "How bad is it?"

"Lock said it looked like it was never set right."

I nodded, blowing out a breath through my nose. "She didn't go to the hospital the first time it happened."

"Boss, it's not like it's your fault."

"I know that, but—"

"But what? You and I have seen this before. She needs help, and she obviously wasn't getting it. You can't force someone to get out of an abusive relationship."

I didn't even want to think about some shithead beating on her. I was wound up enough as it was.

"Boss, you need to let this go. You can offer her help, but in the end, she has to want to take it."

"I know," I said angrily. "What am I supposed to do with her tonight?"

"I don't think you should do anything. I'll take her home. She won't want you with her."

"No," I said fiercely. "Not gonna happen."

"Boss—"

"If she goes home to some asshole, who's going to protect her?"

"I'll take her home and make sure she's okay. I'm telling you, there's no way she's going home with you."

I didn't like it, but I knew she was right. "Fine, but I want to know everything the minute you leave her place."

"Tomorrow."

"Tonight," I argued.

"You can command me all you want, but unless she's in danger, it can wait until tomorrow. You need to chill the fuck out. Go beat up Fox. That should relieve some tension."

She turned and walked back into the room, leaving me to stew in the hallway. After much deliberation, I went back to the office and found the camera footage from inside the gym. I ran facial recognition software on her, but got nothing. She was a ghost.

12

BETH

"How are you feeling?" Rae asked as she drove me back to my apartment.

I kept glancing at the clock on the dashboard, willing her to hurry the fuck up. I needed her to get me home so I could turn around and get to work. I couldn't afford to lose this job. I'd looked around town. This was the best paying job. I was trying to save up some money so I could relax a little longer when I moved to the next place. Maybe I'd even consider moving further away.

"Beth?"

"Huh?" I asked, turning slightly to face her.

"I asked how you are."

"I'm fine. This really wasn't necessary."

She snorted slightly. "I would say passing out twice would constitute just a little bit of help."

"Or you could have just listened to me," I retorted angrily. It wasn't her fault. She was only trying to help, but that had never worked well for anyone.

"Look, I'm just taking you home. It's not a big deal. Is this it?" she asked, nodding to the apartment building.

"Home sweet home," I said sarcastically.

She grimaced as she shifted into park. "It's not exactly The Ritz, but it's not the worst I've seen."

"You haven't been inside," I muttered under my breath. I shoved the door open and grabbed my bag, digging inside the pocket for my keys. After getting them, I hauled the bag over my shoulder, surprised when she didn't hand me my keys.

"Boss's orders. I'm supposed to make sure you get inside okay."

"That's really not necessary—" I started, but she walked past me, her gaze flicking over the shadows of the parking lot. I watched the way she moved like she was always on guard and ready to take someone down. If I tried moving like that, I'd probably trip and fall on my face.

"So, is your husband home?" she asked.

"My— What are you talking about?"

"The guy that did that to you," she gestured at my arm after I caught up to her.

"I'm not married."

"Ex?"

"No."

She nodded like that explained everything. "You don't look like a Beth."

That's because it wasn't my real name. I hadn't used it since that fateful day. I wasn't sure I'd ever be the woman I used to be. "Sorry to disappoint."

"I'm just saying you can talk to me if you need to."

Her offer was nice, but that would never happen. I would never allow someone to get close to me again. Art hadn't even known my real name and he still ended up dead. If she knew what was really going on, she would be in danger, along with anyone who knew her. I couldn't carry that weight on my shoulders.

I opened the door to the apartment building, hearing her scoff of disgust as we walked through.

"Security here sucks."

"I don't think that was on the advertisement for this building."

I headed for my apartment, grateful it wasn't on a different floor. The idea of walking up stairs was daunting right now. When I approached my door, I paused, my heart thundering when I saw it was already open slightly. Rae shoved past me and pulled a gun. I stepped back, my eyes wide as I stared at the weapon in fear. Where the hell did she get that?

She put her finger up in front of her lips and slowly shoved open the door. I watched in amazement as she entered the apartment without fear, but then she stopped almost immediately as a man walked out of the bathroom as if he had every right to be there.

"Freeze, motherfucker."

The man stopped, raising his hands slightly. He was a slimy bastard with yellowing teeth and filthy clothes. The grin on his face said he didn't think she was a threat. That was just stupid. One look at Rae and I knew she could kick his ass. Still, he walked forward like he would intimidate her.

"I'd stop moving if I was you," she said, her voice not even shaking.

I was terrified and *she* was the one guarding *me*. I took a step toward the door, my back hitting the wall. My instincts told me to run, that I wasn't capable of winning this fight. I'd had enough of getting beat up in my lifetime, and now all I wanted to do was survive.

"Lady, do you even know how to use that?" the man asked, continuing to advance on Rae, who stood her ground.

"Well, I know there's this thingy here. I'm supposed to pull it, right?"

"You're going to hurt yourself."

Rae cocked her head to the side. "You mean, this is, like, dangerous or something?"

"Sweetheart, if you don't know how to use that, you should really put it down."

Rae glanced over her shoulder slightly and frowned. "I don't know. What do you think, Beth? Should I put it down?"

I didn't answer, and I didn't think she really wanted me to.

"I mean, it can't be that hard, right? Point and shoot?"

The gun fired without warning and the man screamed out in pain, clutching his knee as blood poured through his fingers. "Fuck! I told you not to use it!"

"Huh, that wasn't nearly as hard as I thought. I was aiming for your head, though. I guess my aim was a little off."

My lips twitched at her humor. There was no way she was aiming for his head. The large man suddenly stood to his full height and charged. Very calmly, almost as if she'd done this a million times, she fired off another shot, this time hitting him in the shoulder. He stopped instantly, clutching his shoulder as he cried out in pain.

"Damn, I was really hoping that would hit him in the head. Maybe I should just keep firing until I get it right. How many pew pew things does this hold?" she asked, looking at the gun funnily.

"Pew pew things?" the man shouted. "Lady, that's a deadly weapon!"

"Is it? I thought it was just really badass looking."

The man stood, ready to charge, and she quickly turned the gun back on him, the look on her face deadly serious now.

"I would rethink your next move. If you thought the last two shots hurt, I can guarantee this next one will end your life."

This time, he seemed to finally get the message that she wasn't screwing around. He slowly raised his arms and shuffled for the door. I moved out of the way, skittering to the far side of the kitchen while she kept her gun trained on him as he exited the apartment. Once he was out, she shoved the door closed and locked it, not that it would keep anyone out.

"Pack your shit. We're leaving."

"Excuse me?"

"You heard me. You're not staying here," she said, shoving her gun into the back of her pants. She looked around the apartment, shaking her head. "The boss will flip if he sees this place," she muttered to herself.

"I'm not leaving. This is the only place I have."

"And now you're coming to stay with me."

I immediately started to panic. "No," I shook my head wildly, backing up as my heart thudded in my chest. She may be a great shot, but there was no way she could fight off the men after me. She would be killed, and I would not repay her kindness in that way.

"Beth, whoever you're running from, I can protect you."

"Protect me?" I laughed, tears spilling down my cheeks. "Are you insane?"

"Beth—"

"Get out," I demanded.

"Beth—"

"No, you don't get to come in here, insult me for where I live, and then force me out of my place."

"A man was in your apartment," she argued. "He would have killed you or done some other not so nice things that I don't think you even want to think about."

She had no idea how much I already knew about the bad things men could do. I'd grown up with evil. It was ingrained in my brain. I would never forget what could happen. But I also wouldn't put others in danger.

"Leave now. I didn't ask you to come here."

"You also didn't ask me to get rid of the asshole, but I did that."

"Who do you think you are?" I yelled. It was so out of character for me. But I think I knew deep down that she wouldn't hurt me, and that gave me the confidence I needed to stand up for myself. "You shoved your way into my life when I didn't ask for it. I don't need to be saved."

"It sure doesn't look that way to me," she retorted. "How would you have taken that asshole down with one working arm?"

I didn't have an answer for that, so I kept my mouth shut.

"Look, my boss wanted me to look out for you—"

"Your boss? The guy that hurt my arm?" I scoffed.

"He didn't do that, and we both know it."

I did know it, but that didn't mean I trusted him. I didn't trust anyone, not anymore. I was hanging on by a thread, and as nice as it would be to just let someone swoop in and take care of me, I knew that would only end badly. So, against everything inside me begging for help, I made her leave.

"You're trespassing, and if you don't leave, I'll call the police."

Sighing, she finally turned for the door, but not before setting a card on the counter. "When you finally decide you need some help, give me a call. Not everyone is evil, Beth."

She unlocked the door and walked out, closing the door with a soft snick. I stared at the card on the counter, wanting to take it and run toward someone who might be able to help. But I refused to watch another person die because of me. I snatched the card and tore it into pieces, tossing it in the garbage.

13

CASH

Rae finally walked through the doors at seven-forty-five. I rushed over, ready to berate her for taking so damn long when she held up her hand, stopping me from starting my barrage of questions.

"She kicked me out."

"What?"

"Yep, there was a guy in her apartment, obviously not supposed to be there, and she kicked me out after I shot him."

I paused for a moment, thinking that through. "Did she kick you out because you shot him?"

"No, you would think maybe that was the reason. She doesn't want anyone interfering in her life. Whatever's going on, you're not finding out anytime soon."

"Was the guy living there?"

"Don't think so. She lives in a shitty building. It looks like he broke in."

"And you left her there?" I asked accusingly.

"Boss, she's a grown woman. What exactly do you want me to do?"

"Your fucking job," I seethed.

"Oh, I'm sorry. Is she my job now? Because last I checked, she didn't come to us for help."

"Sometimes we help people when they don't want it," I argued.

"No, in fact, I don't think we've ever done that." She got in my face, forcing me to stand down. "The problem is, you like this woman for whatever reason, and you think you can save her."

"I can," I argued.

"No, you really can't. Based on what I know—"

"Which you haven't told me jack shit."

She rolled her eyes at me. "She's running from someone, which I assume you already know. She's basically living out of a bag. Her apartment is a monthly rental, and she has traps out for rodents. It's a real charming place to live. But even with all that, she seems proud of it, which would lead me to believe that despite everything, she's fought to stay alive for a long time. She's not going to let you step in and take over, which is why I left."

"Wait," I grabbed her arm as she started walking away. "That's it? You just left her?"

"Well, yeah, boss. When a woman yells at you to get the fuck out, you listen."

I ran my hand over my head, frustration building by the minute. I couldn't even fucking sleep last night because of this woman. I didn't know what it was about her, but I felt like she would play some important role in my life.

"Boss, there's nothing you can do. She doesn't want help, so let it go."

"I can't," I seethed. I was so fucking pissed right now. If things were different, if I wasn't juggling so much shit right now, I would march over there and demand she let me help her. I'd bang on her door and…and what? Scare the living shit out of her. I was losing my fucking mind. I'd been around women like her enough to know that going in with that kind of attitude would only push her further away.

Hell, I didn't know anything about her. I didn't know if she'd be sticking around. She could already be gone, for all I knew. And with women like her, when they felt their safety was at risk, they didn't wait for the other shoe to drop. They ran and never looked back. Chances were, I would never see her again. And something about that really pissed me off. I had to let this go.

I had a business to run, and chasing after a woman was not part of the agenda for the day. Rae was right, I needed to forget about her. If I saw her again, I might be able to help her out, but for now, I had shit to take care of. Until I found out more information about my mystery woman, I had to move on with my day.

"Get Lock's team in the conference room. We have to finish planning for the job tonight."

We pulled into the airport just before dusk. The job should be fairly easy, though I had the feeling Scottie Dog was feeling anything but at ease. He looked like he was going to puke in the seat beside me.

"I fucking hate planes," he grumbled beside me.

"You're a fucking pilot," I retorted.

"*Was*," he corrected. "Just because I have my pilot's license doesn't mean it's something I want to do on a daily basis."

"This isn't a daily basis. This is literally only for one day," I corrected. "Not even a whole day. It'll be an hour tops."

He snorted. "Yeah, that's what they all say right before they crash and burn."

Lock leaned forward between the seats. "If you hate flying so much, why didn't you say something when we were planning shit out?"

"Because I thought I could handle it," he grumbled. "I really don't think I should be the guy in the sky. I already feel a little queasy from lunch. I think I ate something bad."

"Suddenly, you ate something bad?" Edu laughed.

"It's not sudden," Scottie argued. "I've been feeling it coming on all afternoon."

Rock handed something up between the seats to Scottie. "Here, just in case."

"A barf bag?"

"Actually," Rock grinned. "I was thinking in case it came out the other end. People are used to seeing puke. Shit, on the other hand, isn't something you can come back from."

Scottie Dog glared at Rock. "Don't you have a salon to go to or something?"

I looked in the mirror at Rock, who nervously ran his hand through his perfectly mussed hair. Brock Patton, or Rock as we called him, cared just a little too much about his appearance—and for that reason, we felt he needed a more manly name. Hence…Rock. For a former military man, he almost looked too pretty to be in the field. If I hired based on appearance, the man never would have made the cut. Luckily, his skills more than outweighed his handsome looks.

"I don't hear you complaining about my appearance when I'm the close protection agent."

"Can we focus on the job at hand?" I asked as I pulled to a stop near the hangar. We all got out, Scottie barely holding back the urge to spew the contents of his stomach on the pavement. I clasped him on the shoulder. "You got this. You're Scottie Dog."

Rock walked past him, slapping him hard on the back. Scottie braced himself against the truck, letting out a loud belch that could have easily turned into something else. We moved around to the back of the truck and loaded up with our gear. It shouldn't be necessary for a job like this, but I never took chances.

"Here, Scottie Dog," Rock grinned, shoving more barf bags at him. "You should take these up with you."

Scottie snatched them out of his hands with a glare, then tucked them into his vest for safekeeping. "You're all assholes," he muttered.

I chuckled, pulling on my vest and strapping on my guns. Our clients were due to arrive in three hours. "Let's do a sweep of the airport before Grady and Evers arrive. I want cameras in place. Make sure we're live-streaming back at the office. I want Rae to watch every minute of this. Rock, you're with me. Let's go check the tower."

Lock, Edu, and Scottie split off to check out the airport. Rock and I headed over to the tower. Knocking on the door, I showed my credentials before they opened the door. I also had paperwork for them, proving we were working security today.

I glanced at the name tag on the man's uniform. Mallick. He checked over the paperwork and nodded, handing it back. "Looks good. What can I do for you?"

"I'd like Rock in the tower with you. He'll stay out of your way. It's more of a precaution, but we need to be in contact with the aircraft at all times."

"Do you have the flight plan?"

I frowned at that. "They haven't filed with you?"

"It's not unusual," he said, looking over the paperwork. "Small aircraft flying under eighteen thousand feet don't necessarily have to file. I'll need to see the paperwork when they arrive."

I hoped that didn't mean there would be any delays in the flight. I finished up in the tower, leaving Rock to take over, then headed back down to check in with the team.

"Lock, how are we looking?"

"Everything's secure, and our clients are pulling in now."

A car pulled in and three men got out, unloading some cargo. "Need a hand?" I asked them.

"No, we're good. Sensitive instrumentation," one of them said. "Are you Cash Owens?" I nodded. "Elliott Grady."

"Good to meet you," I shook his hand. A second vehicle pulled up with two more men. "Are they with you?"

"That's my pilot and co-pilot."

"One of my men will be going up as well."

"That's really not necessary," he said quickly.

"If you want our services, it's the only option," I clarified.

"Fine, but he stays out of the way."

I nodded in agreement, but Scottie wouldn't be staying out of the way. Grady didn't need to know that, though. "We've checked out the airport. Everything's clear. The tower mentioned you hadn't filed a flight plan."

I wasn't sure why, but that made me uneasy. Whether or not they were required to file, it seemed that on a job like this, they would want a flight plan filed.

"Honestly, to test this, it has to be on the fly. We need the targeting system to do its thing and allow the computer to work in conjunction with it. If we plan a specific route, the data will be skewed. We need to know that the equipment can work on its own."

I nodded, glancing over at Lock. It made sense, but something still seemed off. Maybe it was all that time in the military that made me suspicious of anyone who didn't follow every last procedure to the letter.

"Scottie Dog, go make sure the plane passes all inspections and... shit."

He gave me a sardonic smile before saluting and heading off to the plane. I didn't know shit about planes, but I knew they had to be cleared before takeoff.

"Mr. Grady," I said, turning to the man beside me, "How long until testing begins?"

His brows furrowed as he pulled out his laptop. "I need to get set up. Calculations have to be very precise to get an accurate reading and ensure everything goes according to plan."

Crossing my arms over my chest, I watched him warily. "And where are you planning on flying?"

"Over the general vicinity."

Lock and I exchanged looks, not liking this guy's idea of a plan. "Sir, in order to ensure your safety, and that of your equipment, we have to have some idea of what you're doing."

"Mr. Owens, I think we have our wires crossed when it comes to what exactly your job is. I hired you for protection of the equipment. It's not the plane I'm worried about as much as the programming. I can rebuild the equipment on the plane, but the software is something that can't fall into the wrong hands."

I knew this was a delicate situation, but he was making this sound like some kind of terrorist threat.

"Mr. Grady, if you want my people involved, you're going to have to be a little clearer about what's going on here. You made it sound like you were testing equipment. Why do I get the feeling that this is armageddon-style programming."

He looked at me, his eyes hardening slightly. "Because it is."

He glanced around and placed his hand on my shoulder, guiding me further from prying ears. "Mr. Owens, there are things I'm not at liberty to say without my employer's permission. However, let me paint you a picture. You have a phone with facial recognition, correct?"

"Yes."

"And that's supposed to be private to you, but the technology in your phone makes it possible for others to use that data to find you anywhere, anytime, and use that information against you. It's your ID, but only so long as you control how it's being used. Now imagine that technology like that was used on other things, more dangerous things…weapons. And in the right hands, that's a powerful tool, but in the wrong hands, it means war. Believe me when I tell you, this is only the tip of what this technology is capable of. *That* is why I need you here, to protect the software which, if in the wrong hands, has the potential to start World War III, and tilt the odds against all of us."

I gave him a stiff nod as he walked back to his laptop and got to work. I motioned Lock over, not trusting this guy one bit. "Something about this feels very wrong," I said, crossing my arms over my chest as I looked out at the plane where Scottie was checking things over. "He's testing something more dangerous than what he first implied. I want all eyes on him and his crew at all times."

"You want to go through with the job?" he asked, not accusing, but curious.

"I'm not sure what his angle is yet. If he's truly just testing this for the technology of using it in war, why isn't he working with the military on this?"

"Because he knows damn well that the military would take over and seize all his prototypes and software. This is the government we're talking about."

I knew that was true, but still, this didn't sit right with me. "Tell everyone to be on guard. If something goes wrong, it's our asses on the line. I'm calling in Team Two. We need all the help we can get if something goes wrong."

"Gotcha, boss."

He ran off to let the others know as I called Thumper—Tate Parsons, the team leader for Team Two. As the phone rang, I discreetly watched Grady and the rest of his team. I knew he would be ready for takeoff at any moment. We didn't have long to get another team here to have our backs.

"Go for Thumper," Parsons said.

"Get your team together on the double. I need them at the private airfield on the edge of town ASAP."

"Gotcha, boss. We're out in five."

My eyes narrowed as a man walked toward the plane carrying something. I couldn't see what it was, but the way he quickly strode toward the plane set off alarms in my head. I moved closer to him, trying to see what was in his hand, but I was too far away.

"Boss," Thumper said like he was repeating himself.

Unease trickled down my spine as the man looked around quickly before lowering himself to the ground by the luggage compartment at the belly of the plane.

"Haul ass over here. We've got a situation."

I hung up and pressed my hand to my ear. "Scottie, you copy?"

"Scottie Dog here, prepared for takeoff."

"Do you have everyone on board and accounted for?"

"Roger that. I'm still willing to trade if anyone's up for it."

"Do *not* allow takeoff. Do you read me?"

"Affirmative. Anything I should know about, boss?"

"When I know, you'll know."

"Edu," I barked through comms, moving closer, but keeping Grady in my sights. "We've got a target under the plane. Can you identify him?"

"Checking now…"

I waited, my eyes flicking back to Grady. This was wrong. I quickly made my way over to him. "Who's the man by the plane?"

"Excuse me?" Grady said, his fingers flying faster over his keyboard.

I grabbed him by the shoulder and spun him to face me. "Who the fuck is that man by the plane? He didn't come in with you, and my guys didn't let him in."

His eyes flicked up to the plane as sweat beaded on his brow. "He works for me."

"Then how the fuck did he get in here?" I asked angrily.

His jaw clenched hard. "He's installing a vital piece of equipment."

"That plane isn't leaving the ground, not until we've checked it out."

"This is my project. I hired you!" he shouted as I walked away.

I started running from the edge of the hangar over to where the plane was parked. "Edu!"

He grabbed the guy by the collar, hauling him out from under the plane just as the man grabbed the metal container he was holding and swung it at Edu's head. He flopped back on the ground, out cold as I pulled my gun and aimed at the man, but he disappeared to the other side of the plane where I couldn't get a good angle.

Suddenly, the engine started, kicking up dirt and rocks right into my face. I ducked, trying to avoid the debris as I ran closer to get Edu out of the line of fire.

"Scottie! Stop that fucking plane!"

I grabbed Edu and hauled him away from the plane, wincing at the gash across his forehead. The mystery man was back under the plane, attaching the canister to the belly. Whatever the fuck was in there, it wasn't any good. I ran flat out to the plane as it started to move, shouting into my comm system as I pressed the push-to-talk button on my vest.

"Scottie! Do you read me? Do not let that plane take off!"

But he still didn't answer.

"Rock, tell the tower the Cessna is not clear for takeoff!"

"On it!"

Lock was running from across the lot, trying to catch up to the plane with me. I got close enough to see the canister, but then the plane picked up speed and left me in its dust. Swearing, Lock and I turned back to the hangar to where Grady was waiting. He looked up, grabbed something from the table he was working at, and ran for the other end of the hangar.

"Do we shoot him?" Lock shouted.

"Not until we know what the fuck is on that plane!"

A crash at the gates had us both spinning, drawing our weapons and ready to fire. Black SUVs drove straight at us, then turned and headed for the hangar, squealing to a stop right where Grady had been set up. We ran straight for them, not sure if they were friendly. When they stepped out and pointed their weapons at us, their intent became pretty damn clear.

"Take cover!" I shouted, zigzagging to avoid being hit.

"By what?" Lock shouted. "Do you see a magic fucking boulder somewhere?"

Gunfire erupted, keeping us from our intended target and cutting us off from Edu, who was behind enemy lines all on his own.

"Rock, get your ass down here!" I shouted.

"The plane took off," he shouted. "What the fuck is going on?"

The men continued to fire at us as I hid behind a concrete barrier. Peeking over the edge, I saw them racing over to Grady, firing on him also.

"Who the fuck are they shooting at?"

"Who are *we* shooting at?" Lock asked. "This is more fucked up than a soup sandwich!"

14

SCOTTIE

I turned to the pilots, scrutinizing them. Upon closer inspection, they both looked nervous, like they were getting ready for something they weren't sure they wanted to do.

"Anyone know where to get good tacos around here?" I asked nonchalantly, watching as they prepared for takeoff.

"What?" the pilot asked.

"Tacos, you know, meat in a shell with all the good stuff. Lettuce, tomatoes, cheese..." I pulled my gun out of my holster, keeping it at my side, out of sight. "Sour cream," I continued.

"Uh...I'm not from around here."

"Really? I'm surprised Grady didn't hire locally for this job. Isn't that kind of important when you're flying so low...over tall buildings that you could potentially crash into at any moment? Now I definitely want a taco."

"It'll be fine," the pilot said, but he was facing the co-pilot like he was trying to reassure him.

"Yeah, I mean, as long as you watch out for the birds. I swear, it's like an Alfred Hitchcock film out here some days. Seagulls, sparrows, quail, woodpeckers, hummingbirds..."

"Hummingbirds?" the pilot asked. "I think we'll be fine."

"Sure," I snorted. "Until one of them zips in front of you and scares the shit out of you. Have I mentioned I'm not a great flier?"

The pilot turned around, shooting me a dirty look. "Then what the fuck are you doing up here?"

I raised my gun, pointing right at his head. "Keeping you from taking off. Get the fuck out of that seat."

"What are you talking about? We're clear for takeoff."

I shook my head. "Not what my boss says. Now, if you'd kindly remove yourself from the pilot's seat, we can figure out what the fuck is going on."

He slowly raised his hands and nodded to the co-pilot. I backed up, keeping distance between us, but unfortunately, on a plane this size, there wasn't much room to maneuver. Out of the corner of my eye, I saw another man approaching the stairs. I knew he wasn't anyone on my team. They would have announced themselves. Quickly looking over, I knew I was fucked when the guy walking up the steps pulled out a knife.

Spinning, I knocked the knife out of his hand, then slammed his hand against the frame of the door. With a swift kick to the chest, I knocked him down the stairs and out of the plane. Unfortunately, the pilot took that opportunity to hit me hard on the back of the head, and everything went dark.

I wasn't sure how long I was out, but the screaming in my ear let on that I was pretty much fucked and had screwed up the job. Squinting in the dark, I tried to see where we were, but it didn't really matter. My stomach was pretty much announcing that we were in flight, and it wasn't too happy with me about that.

Making as little noise as possible, I looked up at where my wrists were bound with duct tape to the base of the seat. Shifting slightly, I glanced into the cockpit, but the pilots were clearly distracted by whatever they were doing. I wiggled between the seats until my wrists were near hip level. With a deep breath, I yanked both wrists toward my chest, tearing the tape. I also hit myself in the face, but that was something I'd keep to myself when I landed this fucking plane.

I pressed my finger to my ear, shoving the comm back in. Reaching for the comm switch, I hoped it still worked. "Cash," I whispered. "You copy?"

"Scottie, what the fuck are you doing up there, taking a nap?"

"You aren't completely wrong on that," I grumbled, keeping my voice low. "What the fuck is going on?"

"They attached something to the bottom of the plane, Scottie. Whatever their target is, you have to stop it."

"So, save the world and die in the process. Cool."

"It was in a small metal canister attached to the luggage compartment. There's no way for you to reach it."

"How do they trigger it?"

"We don't know!" he shouted, grunting something as he breathed heavily.

"What the fuck is going on down there?" I asked, glancing back up at the front.

"Fucking war," he breathed. "You have to stop the plane!"

"Sure, no problem," I grumbled, shifting to my knees. I glanced around the plane, trying to find my gun, but it wasn't anywhere I could see. The pilot probably grabbed it, not that it would be a good idea to use it anyway.

"Over there!" the co-pilot shouted, pointing out the right side of the plane. I sat up a little, looking out the window.

"Holy shit," I whispered. Laying back down, I called for Cash again. "Cash, do you copy?"

"What the fuck is it? I'm kinda busy down here."

"They're going after an electrical substation. Do you copy that?"

"Fuck!" he grunted. "Do not let them fly over it."

"Or into it," I retorted. "I'll just use my wits."

"Why don't you just shoot them? You're a fucking pilot."

"Right, and a gun in a plane, flying over a substation would be an excellent option. How about I just jump out of the plane and kill myself now?"

"Would you just fucking take care of it?"

"Alright, alright. Shit, don't get your panties in a twist," I hissed. Letting go of the push-to-talk, I prepared myself for the task ahead of me. "Don't let that plane leave, Scottie. Use your gun, Scottie. Don't eat those tacos, Scottie. Just fucking once, I'd like to do things my way."

I looked around quickly for something to use to defend myself, but the only thing I found was a flare gun, and that was a hard no where I was concerned.

"Fuck this," I muttered, jumping to my feet and racing toward the cabin. Without hesitation, I wrapped my arm around the pilot's neck and squeezed.

"Fuck!" the co-pilot scrambled for control, tilting the plane to try and throw me off balance. I stuck my foot out to brace myself against the cabin wall. The pilot was reaching up for me, trying to poke my eyes out.

"Didn't your mother ever teach you to keep your hands to yourself?" I shouted. I slapped his hands away with my free hand, then hit him in the face a few times. "How do you like it?"

The co-pilot tilted the nose of the plane down, sending me flying forward into the instrument panel, making me lose my grip on the pilot. He slammed his fist into my face, but I blocked his second hit, kicking out my foot and catching him in the face. I turned just in time to duck as the co-pilot raised his gun and fired.

The bullet went right through the windshield, luckily only leaving a small hole. "What the fuck is wrong with you?" I shouted. "Are you trying to kill us all?"

"You're attacking us," he retorted.

"Because I *am* trying to kill you," I snapped, leaning forward just enough to slam my fist into his face. Then I pressed the button to release his seat belt and pulled him from his seat, not even stopping when his arm got caught in the belt. Tossing him to the back of the plane, I turned just as the pilot regained control and steered us back toward the substation with a hard right. I tumbled into the wall, my stomach revolting at the sudden movement.

The co-pilot stood, holding the flare gun in his hand. I held out my hand, covering my mouth with the other. He looked at me funny, and I held up a finger. It was coming up one way or another. Better on him than me. I stumbled forward and vomited all over him as I snatched the flare gun from his hand before he could fire. He tried to step back, but I spun the gun around and slammed the butt of it right into his head, hitting him several times until he was down and out.

Wiping the vomit from my mouth on my sleeve, I spit on the guy. "That's what we like to call tactical vomit."

I turned and rushed to the front of the plane, slamming my fist into the side of the pilot's head. He tried to fend me off as I pressed the button on his belt. He turned his face toward me and bit down on my arm, breaking the skin as he raked his teeth over my skin.

"Son of a bitch!" I shouted. "I haven't had my rabies shot in fucking years!"

"Scottie!" Cash shouted in my ear. "You're headed straight for the fucking substation! Quit fucking around!"

Looking up, I stared in sheer terror as we approached the electrical station. Tearing the pilot from his seat, I jumped into the pilot's seat, taking the yoke and pulling back to increase the altitude. The pilot grabbed me from behind, trying to choke me unsuccessfully.

"What are you even doing?" I asked, fighting to keep his arm away from me. "Are you trying to choke me or give me a massage?"

"You're gonna die!"

"Highly unlikely," I argued, grabbing his arm and twisting it as I fought to control the yoke. I slammed my elbow back, catching him in the face and giving myself just a few seconds to gain control again. But I froze at the sound of a gun being racked.

"Scottie, something dropped from the plane. Get the fuck out of there!" Cash shouted.

"You need to get out of that seat," the man holding my own fucking gun against my head said.

I gritted my teeth, my fists tightening on the yoke. "Is that my gun?"

"You shouldn't have brought it on board."

"Ya know...I really fucking hate it when someone takes my gun."

I jerked the yoke, causing him to fall to the side. He fired the gun, the shot missing me by inches. I glanced back quickly, knowing if I didn't get that gun from him, he would take the fucking plane down. A few small holes wouldn't cause us to crash, but if he shot out the windshield, we'd both be sucked out of the plane.

Pulling back the yoke, I screamed through gritted teeth as we climbed higher in the sky until we were almost vertical. "I really fucking hate flying!" I shouted. I planted my feet against anything I could as I prepared to roll us. Glancing back, I could see the pilot hanging on for dear life. When we turned upside down, I heard him slam into something and then again when we started to nosedive. The engine alarm sounded as I tried to pull out of the dive. I screamed again, cursing Cash for making me do this.

I finally pulled us out of the dive, only to see I was headed straight for a building. "I really don't feel so good," I said right before I puked.

15

CASH

The plane turned at the last minute, avoiding flying directly over the electrical substation. From this distance, I couldn't tell what was happening, but as the plane flew away from the substation, something else caught my attention. Even this far away, I could see the sparks fly into the sky, and then everything started to go black just a moment later.

"Scottie!" I shouted, but got no response.

It was as if time stood still as the lights of the city slowly shut down one grid at a time. The cascade effect was both amazing and terrifying to watch. If the electrical grid went down, that would affect so much more than any of us could even imagine. Street lights would cease to operate, causing multiple pile-ups and effectively stopping movement around the city. Cell towers could go down, hospitals wouldn't be able to provide life-saving measures, access to clean water would be limited...the possibilities were endless.

I looked back over at Grady, working in the hangar. As everyone else was watching the destruction of the city, he was still working from his laptop. Sprinting from where I was taking cover, I knew I had to reach Grady and find out what exactly he was doing. But I barely made it twenty feet before gunfire erupted around me.

"I gotcha, boss!" Rock shouted in my ear. Ignoring the bullets flying around me, I ran until I reached the safety of the hangar. Grady looked up at the last minute and saw me coming, pulling out a weapon I didn't even know he had. I came to a screeching halt, holding my own weapon on him.

"Grady, put the fucking gun down," I commanded. Based on the way he was holding his gun, I knew he wasn't a serious threat. But a madman with a weapon and no knowledge how to use it could be just as dangerous as a man fully trained.

"You have no idea what you're messing with," he laughed.

"Because you fucking lied about your true intentions. You wanted to take down the power grid. Why?"

"You're so blind. All of you have no vision. You stand there with your gun and think you're doing something for your country. It's pathetic."

"And what are you doing? You're a domestic terrorist."

He threw his head back and laughed. "Your vision is so narrow."

"Step away from the computer," I growled, irritated with this bullshit.

"Boss!" Rock shouted through comms. "We've got more company!"

I shifted until I could see the front gate out of the corner of my eye while still keeping Grady in my sights. More vehicles pulled into the private airfield. Men poured out of the vehicles, all in tactical gear and armed to the teeth. I didn't know who exactly I was supposed to be protecting right now, our team or Grady. If he was right, and this equipment was really as dangerous as he said, then the obvious choice was to protect him for the time being.

But as I swung my gaze back to Grady, my overwhelming instinct was to take him down at all costs. He'd already taken out a power grid. Grady's gaze flicked over to the men, and that's when I made my move, shooting him in the bicep. As he went down with the hit, I raced toward him, leaping over his work table and pinning him to the ground. I yanked out my zip ties, pulling his hands behind his back for good measure.

He screamed as I wrenched the arm that I'd just lodged a bullet in. Blood poured from his wound, and I pulled out my packet of combat gauze— a fine, white clay we used in combat to stop bleeding. It burned like hell, but he'd survive. Spinning around, I grabbed his computer to protect it from any potential damage.

Edu, who was hanging out on his lazy ass in the corner after being struck with a metal canister, was finally starting to rouse. "Edu! I'm coming to you. Get your ass up!"

"Fuck, my head feels like a fucking boulder."

"Maybe that'll teach you to watch your surroundings," I huffed, grabbing Grady by the shirt and dragging him across the floor. I shoved the laptop into Edu's arms. "Don't fucking lose this. Looks like Fox needs to do some work with you."

"Fuck, I hate that guy," he grumbled, stumbling to his feet as he grabbed his weapon.

Gunfire could be heard from outside the hangar, but as I moved further back, I couldn't see what was happening. "Rock, check in," I commanded.

"Friendlies finally arrived. I think we need to have a talk with Thumper about his tardiness."

"Fuck off, I had to change my shirt," Thumper said, joining our conversation.

"How many fucking times do I have to tell you not to wear pink?" Lock asked. "You're a fucking target in the field."

I snorted at that. Thumper was anything but subtle. In Afghanistan, he lost the lower part of his left leg, but now had a fucking bionic foot. He was a workhorse, but insisted on wearing fucking bright colors to draw attention to himself. Almost as if he was daring someone to fuck with him.

"It's pitch fucking black out. Who the hell is going to notice I'm wearing pink?"

"Edu is taking a nap," I responded, getting back on track. "I need to get Grady out of here now."

"We're still protecting his ass?" Lock asked.

"Right now, he's our only lead on finding out what the fuck is going on. I need cover fire."

A few seconds later, two dark figures came running in, weapons drawn as they approached. They looked like ours, but the hangar was dark, and I wasn't about to assume anything. I kept low, protecting Edu with my body. As they got closer, I recognized the way they moved as our own. Slider and IRIS nodded as they passed, clearing the rest of the hangar before returning to me.

"Sitrep," I snapped as IRIS approached.

He huffed out a laugh. "FUBAR, boss. FUBAR."

"Fuck, why couldn't this have been a simple job?"

"What would be the fun in that?" Slider asked.

"Lock's holding them off, but we need to beat feet," IRIS said quickly.

I nodded. "Slider, you've got Edu. IRIS, take the lead. I've got this prick," I nodded to Grady.

Flipping the switch on comms, I spoke to the rest of the team. "Lock, Thumper, Rock…we're making a break for it. We need cover fire to get out of this clusterfuck."

"Gotcha covered, boss," Rock answered.

I nodded to Slider, waiting for him to help Edu up. I grabbed Grady by the shirt, hauling him to his feet. He was awake, though he wanted to pretend he wasn't.

"I know you're awake, asshole. Pretending to be asleep will only get you killed. If you want to stay alive, I suggest you move with me."

"You can't stop it, you know," he grumbled, struggling to his feet.

"I may not be able to stop this, but I can sure as fuck keep you from doing anything else you had planned. Trust me, you're going to wish you were dead by the time I'm done with you."

I jerked him forward by the arm, keeping my gun trained on my surroundings. We got to the end of the hangar where IRIS held up his fist to stop our movement.

"Rock, sending Edu and Slider to you," he murmured.

"In position," Rock answered.

He turned to Slider, giving him a slight nod, then turned back, taking a deep breath as he started firing at the men taking cover behind their vehicles blocking the gates. Slider took off with Edu, racing across the vast open space, returning fire to keep from getting their nuts shot off. Edu was struggling to stay upright.

"Any ideas how to get out of here, boss?" IRIS asked over his shoulder.

Looking into the fray of chaos, I couldn't see any clear way out of this. The gate was blocked, and that was our only way out. "Anyone got a few grenades on them?" I asked.

"I didn't exactly think this was a grenade situation, boss," Rock responded. He shouted out, swearing under his breath. "Goddamn, son of a bitch!"

"Rock, check in!"

"Yeah," he groaned. "I'm good. Nothing a little morphine won't fix."

I saw a dark figure move across the landing strip, but recognized his movements. "Lock, you got him?"

"He's a fucking pussy. It's just a leg wound. The bullet didn't even strike his femoral artery."

"Then tell him to get the fuck up and slap a bandaid on it," I retorted.

"They don't give out chest candy for leg wounds," I heard him tell Rock.

"Hate to tell you, but they don't hand those out after you leave the military." Chuckling, I turned my attention back to the situation at hand. "Alright, let's pull a Charlie Rogers and get the fuck out of here."

"On it," Lock grunted. "But I'm not being Charlie this time. I nearly got my ass shot off last time."

"I've got this," IRIS said, laughing at the situation.

He would laugh at a time like this, I thought. That's how he got his nickname.

"Boss, I'm gonna need the keys to the SUV."

I groaned, shaking my head. "No, we're not doing that."

"We're totally doing it. Keys."

Sighing, I handed them over, knowing I was never going to see that vehicle again. I shoved Grady up against the wall and pointed at him. "Stay, or I'll fucking shoot you."

I switched positions with IRIS, ready to lay down cover fire for him.

"You got it?" he asked.

"In position. Haul ass."

As soon as he took off, all of us were firing at the enemy as he sprinted across the landing strip to where the SUV was hidden off to the side. I was running dangerously low on ammo at this point, and if he didn't hurry the fuck up, I was going to be a sitting duck.

"Get your ass moving!" I shouted.

"Geez, you're so cranky when things don't turn out the way you want," IRIS huffed as he finally reached the vehicle. "Give me two minutes."

"You've got thirty seconds," I answered, firing off another few shots. It was nearly impossible to see in the dark, but it was even worse with the lights of the city completely gone. Something was happening by the gate, but I couldn't tell what exactly. Men were moving around, getting into different positions, but it was unclear right now what they were trying to achieve.

"Time to burn some rubber!" IRIS said a little too gleefully.

"Did you get my lucky charm?" I asked, worried that he was going to burn the very thing I always carried with me in any vehicle.

"Relax, I've got Betty," IRIS answered. The SUV came barreling out from where I'd parked it, the wheels squealing as IRIS yipped loudly, shouting as he picked up speed and drove straight for the vehicles blocking the gate.

"Now, IRIS!" I shouted.

"One more minute," he said gleefully.

"You don't have a fucking minute!"

"You have no faith in me, boss. Oops."

"Oops? What the fuck is oops?"

"I dropped Betty. Don't worry, boss. I won't leave her behind."

I watched as the SUV careened out of control for just a moment. Enemy fire was raining down hard on him, but the windshield should hold. Then I saw the trunk pop and IRIS jumped out the back, rolling a few times before jumping to his feet and hauling ass out of there. The SUV crashed into the first vehicle going at least sixty miles an hour. Men scattered as the SUV flipped, taking out another vehicle in its path, effectively flushing them out for us.

Grinning, I was ready to move out of position when I heard the rack of a gun behind me.

There are those times in your life where you look back on things that just happened and wonder how the hell you missed something so big. Here I stood, gun in hand and hardly any bullets left, and I had a fucking gun to my head. This was what I did for a living, yet I somehow managed to fuck this up.

"On your feet, Grady," the voice snapped from behind me.

Even without looking, I knew who this asshole was. He was throwing his voice on purpose, trying to keep me off his scent, but I'd know him anywhere. Turning, I smirked at him, daring him to fucking shoot me.

"He's not going anywhere with you."

The man stood before me, covered from head to toe in black. He even wore a mask—like that would keep his identity a secret. "You're outnumbered. I'd say you don't have a fucking choice in the matter."

"If you had just picked up the fucking phone, none of this would have happened. We could have worked together," I argued.

"Yeah, but you know me, I don't really work well with others."

I grabbed Grady off the ground, holding him against my body. "You have no fucking clue what I just went through with this asshole. There's no way I'm handing him over to you."

"You also have no fucking clue what you're dealing with," he retorted.

"Then tell me why the NSA is involved."

"I'd think that'd be pretty fucking obvious, but I'm not exactly here on their behalf."

"Yeah? Whose side are you on now?"

I could see the smirk on his face beneath the mask. "Let's just say it's need to know."

"And I don't fucking need to know," I finished for him.

"Boss, what the fuck is going on?" Rock asked.

I clicked on the mic to speak to my team. "Hold your positions."

"I just fucking told you this doesn't concern you," the asshole said.

"And you think I'm going to hand over a national security threat without seeing some fucking identification?"

With his gun still pointed at me, he slowly reached into his pocket and pulled out his badge. I took it from him, squinting in the dark to try and read it, but it was nearly impossible. I pulled out my phone and flipped on the flashlight, snorting when I saw the badge. "Special Division?" I flicked the badge back to him. "Is that supposed to mean something to me?"

"I could give you a number to call in, but then you're basically fucked for interfering in a government operation."

"You wouldn't even have him right now if it weren't for my team."

"And who do you think is going to be held responsible when my boss finds out you allowed a plane to deploy a graphite bomb over a fucking electrical substation?"

Chills raced down my spine as I finally understood just how fucking serious this was. I imagined it was a terrorist threat, but a graphite bomb unleashed over a substation would have catastrophic effects.

I yanked Grady closer, shaking my head at this asshole. "He stays with me. Until I see some fucking paperwork, I'm not releasing him to anyone. He's a fucking terrorist and I'm not risking him getting away."

I could tell the man wasn't happy about my decision, but he could fuck off. Either that, or he'd have to physically remove him from my custody, which neither of us had the time for at this moment.

"You and I need to work together if we're going to figure out the bigger picture."

"Fine," he bit out. "You have an office?"

"You fucking know I do," I shot back.

"Boss? Scottie Dog just landed the fucking plane."

"On my way." I dragged Grady behind me, well aware of the looming presence at my back. "Don't fucking shoot anyone else," I told my team. "We've got alphabets with us."

"Alphabets?" Grady asked.

I sneered at him. "Government agencies," I said, not bothering to explain further. Lock walked up to me, eyeing the company at my back. I shoved Grady to him. "Lock him up. Nobody goes near him."

"Got it, boss."

"I'll accompany him," the asshole remarked. "After all, if we're going to work together, I need full access."

"Who is this guy?" Lock asked.

I clenched my jaw, refusing to give away that knowledge. It was for everyone's benefit. "Just another government asshole."

I strode away from them, then started running for the plane. Edu and Rock had already limped their way over there. I watched as Scottie stumbled out of the plane, gripping it for support. I ran up to him, catching him just as he was about to collapse.

"What happened? Are you hit?"

He shook his head. "Just nauseous as hell."

I instantly released him, letting him drop to the ground. Rock leaned his head inside and grimaced. "Holy mother of God, what is that smell?"

"I had to make some tactical maneuvers up there to save my ass. Guns are a no-no."

I shot him a look of disgust. "You threw up on him to gain control of the plane?"

He shrugged slightly. "I had to get creative."

"Jesus, it's like you were on the Vomit Comet. I swear, there's not a fucking inch of that plane that's not covered in puke."

"I almost flew into a building," Scottie defended himself. "You weren't up there. You don't know what it was like."

"I know if I was about to die, I wouldn't throw up and risk ruining the control panel that could save my goddamn life," I said.

"Hey, I landed in one piece. I would prefer you just say, *Thank you, Scottie. I appreciate that you didn't fly into the fucking substation and create a massive explosion that would have wiped out everyone in a one-mile radius.*"

"I could, but we have bigger problems on our hands right now than you using puke as a tactical weapon."

"Like what?"

"Like the fact that this power grid failure appears to be only the start of our problems."

16

BETH

The thing I hated most about my job was walking around in the basement. The lighting wasn't very good, and the shadows had me jumping out of my skin constantly. I hurried over to my cleaning cart and loaded up what I needed. Everything around me stirred like it was coming to life. A strange feeling washed over me like something else was going on. But as I looked around, nothing seemed out of the ordinary. One of the other girls pushed her cart over to the elevator, taking it up without waiting for me to join her.

Sighing, I stood outside the elevator, my back pressed to the wall as I waited for it to return to the basement level. I scanned the area, sure that at any moment someone would jump out at me. Finally, I heard the ding of the elevator, but at that moment, I caught sight of five men walking my way. They were coming from the other end of the basement, but I had no idea how they got in.

My eyes widened in surprise, not only at seeing them, but the long trench coats they wore. Everything about them screamed danger. One of them seemed to hesitate as he drew nearer. He leaned over and whispered something to the man beside him, who gave a quick jerk of his head. While the others scattered, this man walked straight for me.

As the doors slid open, I shoved my cart inside, quickly pressing the button to take me to the third floor.

When the doors didn't immediately shut, I pressed the button to close them. Relief flooded me as the light from the basement slowly faded with metal blocking the light. But then a hand shot out, stopping the door from closing. Swallowing hard, I pressed myself back into the corner, putting the cart between this man and myself. He stepped on as the doors opened, his dark eyes boring into me as they roamed over my body.

A sick wave of disgust rolled over me, making me wish I had some way to defend myself. He slowly raised his hand, hitting the button for the third floor again. I nearly choked on my panic, my heart hammering in my chest as I was once again put in a situation I didn't know how to get out of.

He's not here for you, I told myself. I watched as he slowly reached inside his coat. My eyes narrowed in on his movements, waiting for whatever weapon he would pull out. I tried to formulate a plan, to think of some brilliant move I could make that would keep him as far away from me as possible. I lowered my good arm and gently pried the spray bottle filled with cleaner out of the basket, praying he didn't see what I was doing. I wasn't sure if it would work, but if he came after me, I would spray him in the face until I could get out of here.

His eyes flicked up to mine as he pulled out…a keycard. With a slight smirk, he attached it to his jacket. I slumped back against the wall, sure I was about to throw up from the stress and excitement of nearly dying over a piece of plastic. The elevator finally started to move, but I kept my gaze averted from him, watching the numbers as we rose in the building.

But my hope of escaping this man was cut short when the lights flickered off and the elevator stopped with a sudden jolt. My harsh, panicked breaths filled the elevator quickly as my brain started forming ideas of all the ways I could die in the next five minutes.

A hand clamped on my arm and I screamed, terrified I was about to be murdered.

"Hey, it's okay. It's just me, the man that got on the elevator."

That didn't help me calm down. If anything, my panic increased tenfold. I shoved myself as far into the wall as possible, wishing it could swallow me up. I grabbed the handle of the cart, trying to box myself into the corner and prevent this man from coming near me.

"I'm not gonna hurt you," he said, but his voice sent me back to a time where terror was a daily feeling for me, one that I could never escape.

His crooked smile sent chills down my spine. As my mother stood there, introducing me to her newest boyfriend, I instinctually knew this one was different. His smile was leering and the way he reached down to adjust himself with no concern for the fact that I could see him nearly made me run out of the room. But that wouldn't do me any good. Not with my mother standing there, expecting me to behave myself. I knew all too well what happened when I didn't behave the way she wanted.

He strolled forward and held out his hand, but I refused to take it. I stared in disgust at his outstretched hand, wishing I could run away and never come back. Deep down, I knew this wasn't going to end well for me.

"Hey, I'm not gonna hurt you," he said with a teasing grin as he waited for me to respond. As I slipped my hand into his, my hands turned clammy and my stomach revolted.

"Just calm down," the man whispered.

I came back to the present, my breathing so ragged that it was all I could hear. I knew I was losing it, on the verge of passing out if I couldn't get my breathing under control.

"I know this is scary, but the power will come back on. We just have to wait it out."

Except, I didn't have time to wait it out. For years, I'd worked past the demons that haunted me, but recent events had made it nearly impossible for me to keep those negative thoughts at bay. It was bad enough to deal with the nightmares, but now this...

A slight chuckle filled the air and I heard the man move to the opposite corner of the elevator. I thought he shifted to sit down, but it was hard to tell in the dark. "I actually hate confined spaces. This damn tie feels like it's strangling me right now."

I swallowed again, breathing deep through my nose to calm myself.

"When I was a kid, I got stuck on a Ferris wheel at the top. The ride broke down, and I was just dangling up there, knowing that at any moment, I could crash to the ground. And even with the fresh air blowing around me, all I had was that fucking box to keep me safe."

I licked my lips, finding his story slightly distracting from my own fear. "How long were you up there?" I croaked out.

"Five hours. It was the longest damn day of my life."

"And you chose to get on an elevator?"

He laughed again. "You have to conquer your fears, right?"

I told myself that all the time. That didn't mean I believed it actually worked.

"How are you not panicking?" I asked.

"Believe me, I may seem calm, but my heart is racing out of control. If you could see me, I probably look as pale as a ghost and have sweat beaded on my forehead. It's like a fucking sauna in here for me."

Slowly, I slid down the wall, putting my head down between my knees. I closed my eyes and focused more on my breathing. If I could just clear my head, I could think of something else to take my mind off my growing concerns, like why he followed me on the elevator. He may be trying to calm me down, but I was pretty sure he wasn't supposed to be in the building right now. Then again, he had an employee badge.

"Do you hate small spaces too?" he asked.

I nodded, realizing he couldn't actually see me. "Something like that."

It was so much more than small spaces. It was being in here with a man twice my size. It was knowing that I was injured and couldn't possibly fight back. And then there was the fact that if this elevator gave out, I would die a horrible death, crashing at the bottom of the shaft. No one would know or care that I was dead. I would never experience life to the fullest, get married, or have kids. The thoughts racing through my mind at a million miles a minute were just a small part of the panic inside me.

"We'll get out soon."

"You don't know that," I snapped. "Who are you, anyway?"

He was quiet for a moment. "I work in the Chicago office. I came in for a visit, and I was supposed to pick up some equipment for the return trip home."

I had no idea if he was lying or not. I hadn't looked into the company enough to know if there was a Chicago office. I knew people worked late, but I'd never seen one of the employees in the basement. That was reserved for the underlings—the unimportant employees of the company. We were seen and not heard, and frankly, that's how I preferred it.

"Are you new here?" he asked.

"Yes," I responded, not sure how that information could be used against me in any way. What would it hurt for him to know? I didn't cause the power outage or for the elevator to stop.

"Shitty way to start a new job."

I had to agree with him there. I thought I was taking a simple job that would provide me stability and a larger income until I moved on. After tonight, I wasn't sure I'd ever be able to get on another elevator again.

A screeching noise above us had me covering my ears. I wasn't sure what the noise was, but it felt like nails on the chalkboard.

"Seth!" a voice shouted.

"Yeah, I'm here!" the man on the other side of the elevator responded. He lowered his voice so only I could hear. "I guess I should have introduced myself earlier. Seth."

I bit my lip, almost holding back. "Beth," I said hesitantly. Again, it was just my first name. I couldn't see the harm in telling him. And if we were going to be stuck in the elevator, it would be nice to not call him *Man in the elevator.*

I heard more noises from above and then a loud thump on the top of the car. I gasped, looking up into the darkness as metal scratched against metal. I couldn't tell exactly where the noise was coming from until something moved. Then a flashlight was shining down into the elevator. Seth stood from the other side and moved underneath the opening.

"Give me your hand. I'll haul you up," the man on top said. Seth looked down at me, almost pitifully, then held his hand out. As he grasped the man's hand, he hoisted himself up, using the cart for leverage. Once his upper half was through the hole, he used his upper body strength to pull himself the rest of the way up. I stared at him, waiting for him to turn around and offer to help me, but instead, he started to move away.

I stood suddenly, realizing he was leaving me behind. Where I was terrified of him just five minutes ago, now the thought of being totally alone was more than I could take. My voice squeaked as I tried to call out to him. A new kind of panic washed over me, one where I considered the thought that if he left me, I might never be found.

"Seth," I finally croaked out.

He turned back and looked at me, a sad look on his face.

"Please," I whispered. It may have been quiet, but the plea in my voice was evident.

Sighing, he bent down and shoved his hand through the opening.

"What are you doing, man?"

"I'm not going to leave her in the elevator," Seth said over his shoulder.

When he turned back to me, I knew something else was going on, but I wasn't about to question it when I finally had a way out. After I escaped this death trap, I'd walk away and leave them to their business.

I reached up and clasped my hand with his. I wasn't expecting him to suddenly lift me so easily. I scrambled to grab onto something, relieved when I laid my elbow on the top of the elevator. But the pressure was too much for my injured shoulder and I cried out, nearly blacking out from the pain.

"Are you alright?" he asked as he pulled me the rest of the way out.

I nodded, biting down on my lip to keep from crying. I knew with time the pain would ease. "Let's just get out of here."

I looked up where the elevator doors were open just a few feet above us. In the darkness stood the other three men, and they were staring at me like they needed to get rid of me. I found myself pressing my body closer to Seth's. Better the devil you know, and all that. His hand rested on my lower back, then shifted to my hip as he gave a slight squeeze. I didn't normally like men touching me so freely, but in the presence of the rest of these men, it was a comfort more than anything else.

"Let's get moving. We have shit to do," the other man on the elevator said.

He was the first out as he easily hauled himself up through the doors. Seth guided me over, but I couldn't go up to those other men alone. I needed Seth there first. Maybe that was insane, but I felt more comfortable with him, and the rest of them seemed…harder and more dangerous.

"I'll go up first," he said, as if sensing my unease. "I'll pull you up."

I nodded in the harsh light of the flashlights and waited for him to get up there. When he turned back to me, I had a creepy feeling that this might not end well for me. None of these men were friendly, and I got the distinct impression that they would like nothing more than to get rid of me, whether that meant leaving me in the elevator or disposing of my body.

"Give me your hand."

I walked forward, but realized at the last minute how useless I was. With my shoulder injured, I was going to have a hell of a time getting out. "Um…my shoulder…"

"It's okay. I'll be careful."

Taking a deep breath, I raised my hand to meet his and allowed him to start pulling up my dead weight. I winced at the pulling on my shoulder, even though it was just dangling there. One of the other men reached for me, his arms wrapping around my arm to help. I cried out as he barely touched me, and he immediately backed off. When I was finally on my knees outside the elevator, I scrambled away from them, shoving myself against the wall as I cradled my injured arm.

They all stared at me strangely, but it was Seth who finally walked over. "We just need to grab a few things. After that, we can get you out of here."

"I can take the stairs," I said numbly, just wanting to get away from them.

They all exchanged looks, then stared at me again. "It's best if you come with us," one of them said. "If something happened to you, no one would know it."

I didn't want to go with, but it didn't seem like they were giving me a choice. I swallowed hard and shoved to my feet. If I complied, I should be fine. And Seth seemed to genuinely care about me in some way, so as long as I stuck by him, I should be fine.

The leader walked down the hall, leaving us all to follow. They went to a research lab, opening the doors with no problem since the power was out. Seth stayed with me outside while the others went in. I studied his badge a little more closely now that he was holding a flashlight. It looked exactly like mine.

"You said you work in the Chicago office?"

"Research division," he clarified. "We came specifically to pick up a project, but our flight arrived later than expected, and we're supposed to return on the midnight flight," he said smoothly.

I nodded and glanced toward the window at the end of the hall. That's when I noticed the whole city was dark. It wasn't just our building. "I don't think you're going anywhere. Look," I pointed outside.

He looked out the window and cursed. "Well, that's going to make it difficult to leave."

"What will you do?" I asked.

He thought about it a moment. "Maybe drive to another city. Whatever caused this blackout, I have no idea how long it will take for them to restore power. And our project is time-sensitive."

I nodded, feeling more at ease by the moment. Maybe I had them all wrong. If they were working on a time-sensitive project, it could be that it was classified, and they were worried about me knowing. I wouldn't say a word. I wasn't about to draw more attention to myself.

"Well, I hope you're able to get what you need."

The other men returned a moment later and we moved down the hall to another door. This one didn't have any signs indicating what was stored inside. Again, I waited with Seth in the hallway.

"I'm assuming you'll go home after this," he said casually.

"Yeah, there's no point in me staying to work when the power's out."

"Do you live far from here?"

I looked at him warily. I didn't know him, even if I did feel comfortable with him, and I wouldn't be giving up that information.

"I'm only asking because it'll be hard to get a ride at this time of night with the city shut down."

"I'll be fine," I said stiffly, though the idea of walking alone at night sent shivers down my spine.

The men returned again and the leader jerked his head to the stairwell. I followed behind them, unsure of what else to do. I briefly thought that maybe I should report this in the morning, but I wasn't even sure if anyone would be in tomorrow. With the whole city dark, it was unlikely they would get power restored in just a few hours.

Once we reached the lobby, my fight or flight instincts kicked into high gear. Something seemed very wrong, but what was I going to do against five men? Even if what Seth said was correct, I didn't want to be around them any longer than I had to be.

"Thank you for helping me out of the elevator," I said to Seth.

"No problem. You're sure you can make it home safe?"

"Yes," I said confidently, though I was feeling anything but. I just wanted to get away from it all.

We all walked out of the building together, but when they turned right, I turned left. Unease trickled down my spine with every step I took. I forced myself not to look over my shoulder. I listened intently for any sounds of footsteps behind me, but didn't hear a thing. When I got to the end of the block, I turned the corner and then quickly pressed myself against the building. Peeking around the corner, I saw the men get in a car and drive off. I slumped against the building in relief. I had worked myself up for nothing. They were gone, and I would go home and forget this night ever happened.

17

CASH

"You need a shower as soon as we get inside," Lock ordered Scottie.

He sighed loudly as if he was irritated with all of us. "You know, you're all acting like I didn't just save your asses from a massive explosion."

I strode ahead of them to the door. I wanted to get inside before our guests showed up, and they were pulling in right now. "Everyone inside. You don't say a word to our new friends. Scottie, go take a fucking shower. None of us need to smell that."

"You know, a simple thank you would be nice. After all, I did just—"

"Yeah, yeah. I got it. You saved our asses from hell and brimstone."

Scottie huffed as he turned away from us. "That's all I'm saying," he said over his shoulder. "It would be nice to be acknowledged for my sacrifice."

The generators were running, but only necessary systems were running. We couldn't risk draining all the power by firing up everything we would need to do a proper investigation into the clusterfuck that just happened. Rubbing my hand over my face, I reorganized my thoughts. "Is Grady on lockdown?"

"Put him in the cellar, boss," Edu answered.

"Good. Go get your head checked out."

His dark skin paled as he stared at me. "You're sending me to the hospital?"

He actually sounded offended that I would suggest he take care of himself. "You got hit in the head with a metal canister and you were out cold for way too fucking long. Yeah, I'm saying go get fucking checked out."

"But…Lock's here."

"Yes, and he's a medic. You need a fucking doctor."

Edu straightened, standing taller. "No, I refuse medical treatment."

"Edu, it's a fucking checkup—"

"Not gonna happen."

"And if you fall over?"

He shrugged, looking away. "Then I guess it's my fucking fault."

I glanced at Lock, wondering if he knew more than me. He shook his head, telling me not to push it. "Fine, go with Lock and get checked out." The door opened and the ABC men strode in as if they owned the place. "Rock, make our guests comfortable in the conference room. Make sure they don't touch anything."

They all dispersed while I went in search of Rae. She was in the IT room as expected, laying under the desk. It wasn't something I had seen before, but these were strange times.

"What are you doing?"

"Trying to get some extra power to the system. Do you know how hard it is to use only one computer?"

I quirked an eyebrow at her in the dim light. "Do you know how hard it would be for me to even attempt to use two computers at once?"

She slid out from under the desk, brushing herself off as she stood. "What do you need from me?"

"I have some guests with me."

"Guests, good? Or guests that you're going to beat up?"

"A little of both," I grinned. "And we'll have to see how the rest of the day goes."

"What do you need from me?"

"A background check on everyone that walks through that door. Except Rafe," I added quickly.

"Rafe?"

"Tall guy in charge. Trust me, you'll know him when you meet him."

She looked at me inquisitively, already smelling trouble. "And why am I not running background on him?"

"Because I already know him, and that information stays with me."

Amusement filled her gaze, along with a hint of curiosity. "Anything you say, boss. But how do you want me to get that information? I don't exactly have a lot to run on right now. And with the power outage, who knows how long it will take to get up and running again."

"For now, I want you to join us in the conference room and do your thing."

She nodded, understanding what I wasn't saying. Rae had a bit of a gift, one that we all possessed on some level, but Rae was fucking great at it. She read people like a book, picked up on their ticks, and could almost always tell when they were lying.

"Without technology to help us out at the moment, we're going to have to do things the old-fashioned way."

"Pens and paper. Got it, boss."

I stopped by my office and walked over to my wall safe, pulling out my pen. It was actually a recording device, something I didn't think I'd ever have to use with today's technology, but now would come in very handy. I grabbed another magazine, emptying the one loaded in my gun. This shutdown left me feeling unprepared, so I was going into that conference room loaded with anything to make me feel more at ease. The only thing left for me to do was take Sally in with me, but bringing a sniper rifle into a meeting probably wouldn't put people at ease.

I walked into the conference room, ready to get this meeting over with. I smirked as my guys all lounged around the table, not leaving a single chair empty for the newcomers. I took the head chair, sitting down to face my teams.

"As you all know, we picked up some ABCs at the hangar. For now," I said, looking pointedly at their leader, "we're working together to figure out if Grady's target was only the substation or if he had a bigger plot in mind. Rafe, care to fill us in on what you know?"

The tall asshole at the center of the pack stepped forward. Still wearing his mask and all his gear, he looked like he was prepared to go to battle. "We've had our eye on Grady for some time now. Various intel suggests that he's not the mastermind behind the operation, but the man charged with carrying out the plan."

"Various intel?" Slider asked. "What does that even fucking mean?"

"It means it's above your pay grade," Rafe retorted.

"It's funny because I thought we were working together," Thumper answered with a smirk. "But I guess this is one of those situations when government assholes need our help, but won't give anything in return."

Not only did my guys have it pegged, they were getting under Rafe's skin. And I knew the next hit would set him off.

"Why is it that you're still wearing that mask?" IRIS asked. "Something you're hiding besides every fucking government secret that would allow us to help in some sort of way instead of sitting here with our thumbs up our asses?"

To his credit, Rafe didn't flinch like I expected him to. He was somewhat of an enigma. He despised working for the government, but also realized that in order to have the intelligence he needed, sacrifices had to be made. He was Special Ops in the military for years, until he was recruited for special assignment from the higher-ups. Somehow, he got dragged into his current position, and I knew it ate at him that he didn't get out sooner before they had their claws in him permanently.

"We have a fucking terrorist in your basement, and the man he's working for is still out there. I don't give a fuck if you like working with me or not. You don't like it? There's the door. Walk out and don't come back." He looked around at all of us, but no one moved. "We have bigger problems right now than just this terrorist threat. We need to work with the city to restore power. As of right now, the power failure has spread along the entire West Coast. It could take weeks to repair. In the meantime, the city is failing. We were lucky this occurred at night when hardly anyone was on the streets. If this had happened during the day, we would have had massive pile-ups on every single road. However, we still have major issues with hospitals working on backup generators. The current standard for backup generators at a hospital is ninety-six hours. That buys us a few days, but we need to figure out a way to buy them more time. Fuel trucks to replenish the supply will be in high demand and—"

"Hold on a minute," I interrupted. "We have a terrorist in the basement and you want us to focus on the city?"

"This is the current threat. My team will handle Grady—"

"Like hell you will," I threatened. "If it weren't for us, you wouldn't have gotten to him in time. We're not stepping back. The city needs the fucking National Guard, not a security company."

"I think you're misunderstanding," he said in a low voice. "This isn't a joint operation. Your job ended the minute you allowed Grady to put that fucking bomb on the plane."

"Maybe if the government shared intel, we could have prevented it from ever happening," I snarled.

Rafe scoffed at that. "You know I can't share intel. It's classified. And even if I could share it, what would you have done about it? You're just a security company."

I stood, shoving my chair back along with every other person on my teams. "Just a security company, highly trained by the very government you work for," I said through clenched teeth. "Where the fuck has keeping secrets ever gotten us?"

"You want to talk about secrets?" he shot back. "Why don't we tell everyone in the room how we know each other?"

Silence filled the room as my guys all turned and looked at me, but I was still staring down Rafe. "Everyone get the fuck out, now!"

The room cleared out so fast it was like no one was ever there. Even his men beat feet to get away from the shitstorm brewing. Rafe walked over to me, his eyes gleaming in the dim light of the room.

"Do you really want to go there? After all we've gone through to keep our connection a secret, you want to throw it all away now?"

"I never fucking said that," I snapped. "You knew this was happening in my city. You could have contacted me."

"You know I can't do that!" he shouted. "Fuck, don't you think I would have if I could?"

"No, I don't think you would have."

"You don't trust me?" he said, flinching back slightly.

"Tell me, when was the last time you gave me a reason to."

I watched as he tensed, his jaw ticking hard under his mask. Tensions were running so high it was suffocating. But I knew him. He wouldn't yield. Nothing would stop him from finishing a job, not even me. It didn't matter what my team could offer. Right now, we were shoved into the back seat, left to only help clean up the mess.

"I'll get in contact with the mayor's office and fill them in on what's happening. I'm going to request they work with your office to make sure the city is secure. I don't have the time or manpower to take over operational control."

"And Grady?" I snarled.

"I'm taking him with me. Don't fucking try to stop me, Cash. It won't end well for you."

He stomped past me out of the room. I knew I had lost that round. It didn't matter what my team did to stop the threat, the repercussions of not succeeding just slapped us in the face.

I watched as Rafe and his team frogmarched Grady out of our facility. Anger welled up inside me, but there was nothing I could do. If the government came in and took over, you were basically fucked. I could go through old contacts and try to worm my way back in, but in the end, Rafe would shut me down, just like he always did.

"Boss, are we really letting this happen?" Scottie asked.

"We don't have a choice."

"Then what the fuck did I risk my life for?" he scowled.

As much as Scottie loved to jest, he really did hate flying and that took a lot for him to take control under the circumstances. Between narrowly avoiding crashing into the substation and then again when he almost flew into a building, he was lucky to be alive.

But I was his boss, and sometimes, I had to put my men back in place. Turning to him, I became the hard ass he knew me to be. "You risked your life because it's your fucking job. You prevented a major disaster and helped bring down Grady and his men. We might not get the win, but we sure as fuck brought them to their knees."

He gave a swift nod, backing down immediately. "Message received."

"Good." Turning, I addressed everyone. "Rafe is tasking us with operational control for getting the city back on track over the next few weeks. As soon as we receive our orders, we'll get in contact with the Mayor's office. In the meantime, I want all of you working on potential problems from the power outage. Break up into teams and strategize how to best handle the situation. I want us prepared when we meet with the Mayor's office. No doubt they'll already have plans in place. Let's make sure we've covered all angles."

They all nodded and started to walk away. Rae hung back, though, knowing I would want her take on recent events. I nodded toward my office, then shut the door after she walked in. I hit the lights, remembering afterward that we didn't have the power to waste.

"What did you get?" I asked, taking my seat behind my desk. She sat across from me as she started her account of our new enemy allies.

"Unfortunately, none of the other asswipes said anything, so that's a bit of a dead end. It does tell us that they follow Rafe completely. None of them showed any signs of unease around him. They're not going to help us out in any way. Any information we want, we're going to have to get ourselves."

"Can you do that?"

She snorted in amusement. "Right now? Not a chance. I do have some contacts I can reach out to. I'm not sure they'll be any help with this situation."

"Dammit," I swore. "We need information as to what's happening."

"I thought we were letting it go."

I shot her a funny look. "When have you ever known me to just let something go? No, we need to stay on top of this as best we can."

"I have some friends that might be able to help. I can't say it would be strictly legal."

"Do I want to know?"

"Not even a little."

I grinned at her. "Do it, but be careful. The last thing we need is anything to do with a terrorist threat coming back on us."

"And Rafe?" she asked after giving a tight nod.

I shuffled some things around on my desk, refusing to look at her immediately. Rafe was a touchy subject, and as I feared, she saw too much. "What about him?"

She cocked her head to the side, giving me a knowing look. "You didn't ask about him."

"I think you already know that I am aware of who Rafe is."

"Yes, but you never said how close you really are with him."

"And you think you know."

A slight smile curved her lips. She was having fun with this, knowing she had me in a tight spot. "He's important to you. You deferred to him, even when you didn't mean to. And that either means that you have a personal relationship or you owe him. You never back down to anyone, but you did to him."

"It's the government," I countered. "They sort of outrank me."

"Yes, but that's never stopped you before. In the past, you would have complied to keep them happy, then turned around and stabbed them in the back."

"Who says I'm not doing that now?"

"I do, and remember, I see everything. That's part of the reason you hired me."

"Very true," I grinned.

"So?"

"So what?" I asked, refusing to give even an inch. My secrets were mine for a reason. I wouldn't give them up to even her.

"Fine, be that way." She stood from her chair and headed for the door. "I'll get started on gathering intel on Grady. Let me know if our new friend gives you anything else."

"You know he won't."

She pulled the door open, glancing back at me one last time. "Are you sure about that?"

Then she disappeared into the dark hallway.

18

BETH

I waited all night long for someone to show up at my door. Despite the fact that everything was normal on my way home, I was sure that it wouldn't be the last time I ran into Seth. I sat in the corner of my studio apartment waiting for the door to be broken in. My muscles were strung so tight that I could hardly get up to use the bathroom.

When daylight finally broke, relief surged through me. I debated what to do with the knowledge I had. Something was definitely off about last night. Even though those men had badges to get in, I knew instinctually that they weren't supposed to be there.

In a snap decision, I headed back to the research building. I was tired and needed to get some sleep, but I also had to figure out if I was supposed to show up to work tonight. The minute I stepped outside, I knew life was going to be very different for the foreseeable future. Cars were lined up on the streets, honking at the intersection for their chance to get past the non-functioning street lights. It was chaos.

Pulling my jacket closed, I hurried down the sidewalk. It was a half-hour walk back to the building, and I was usually fine with making it, but today was different. Everyone was on edge. I watched as people across the street gathered, talking in hushed whispers. I could feel the growing panic in the air as people spread gossip about why there was a power outage and when it would be restored.

"I heard the entire West Coast was affected," one woman spoke as I passed.

I slowed my steps to try and hear more.

"My son said it was an earthquake."

"That's ridiculous. We would have felt an earthquake that strong."

I kept walking, a million thoughts running through my mind. Up ahead, a traffic cop was doing his best to keep cars moving through the intersection. I felt terrible for him as people shouted at him, cursing him for not being able to control the odd vehicle that didn't pay attention to his instructions.

I turned the corner and kept walking, quickening my steps. The sooner I got to my work, the better I would be. After what felt like hours, I finally arrived outside the main entrance to the research facility. When I tried to open the doors, a security guard came forward.

"The building is closed," he said gruffly.

"I work here."

"Like I said, the building is closed today."

I almost turned and walked away, but found myself rooted to the spot. Whoever was in charge needed to know what happened last night. "I was working last night when the power went off. There are things I need to speak with the boss about."

"Such as?"

"Some men showed up here." I left it at that, hoping he understood that I wasn't comfortable saying more than that at this time. He scrutinized me for another moment before nodding and allowing me to enter.

"Parker!" the man shouted to another guard. "Take this woman up to the main office. She has information for Mr. Hayes."

The other security officer nodded and motioned for me to follow him. We walked over to the stairwell together, then climbed the stairs to the top floor. It felt odd to be following him, when any other day I would be going about my job.

"Right through here," he said, opening a door for me. It led to a waiting room outside another office. He walked over and knocked on the door, opening it when someone on the other side answered. "I have a lady here who says she has information for you."

"Send her in," the deep voice answered.

I found myself suddenly terrified to go into the office. This guy sounded like a grouchy old man who didn't like anyone. Still, I came this far, so I walked through the doors, surprised when I saw a man no more than thirty-five years old. He wore dark-rimmed glasses, and his short hair flopped just over his forehead giving him a haphazard look. He was dressed oddly, wearing a plaid shirt and dress pants with tennis shoes. I expected a man in a suit with white hair and a grouchy face. This man just looked tired.

"Yes?" he asked, his voice rough and gritty.

"Um…I work on the night crew," I said slowly. "I came into work last night and was filling my cleaning cart when five men walked in through the basement."

He sat up at the mention of these men, his attention laser-focused on me. "They walked in through the basement," he repeated.

I nodded, glancing at the security guard. "Yes, I found it odd. Four of them broke off in another direction, but one of them got on the elevator with me."

"And you didn't think to report this?" he snapped.

I swallowed hard, fighting the panic rising in me. This wasn't my fault, I had to remind myself. "I was going to, but the power went out while we were in the elevator."

"But why didn't you call from downstairs?"

"Because five men were walking toward me," I laughed incredulously. "I was alone in the basement with five men who were all twice my size. My only thought was getting away from them."

"I'm sorry," he immediately apologized. "You're right. What happened after that?"

"Like I said, the power went out and the elevator stopped. We were stuck for…I don't know how long. The man who came on the elevator with me was able to keep me calm. Then the other men showed up and got us out through the top of the elevator. We had stopped just shy of the third floor."

"And they pried the doors open and got you out?"

"Yes."

"What happened after that?"

I fidgeted as I considered how much to tell him. For some reason, I felt loyal to Seth despite the fact that he was part of this gang of men. "I got the feeling that they were there to do something bad," I said slowly. "I was going to go down the stairwell by myself to leave, but they insisted I go with them. I didn't really feel I had a choice in the matter."

"Where did they take you?"

"Outside one of the research labs. Um…5B, I think."

Something darkened in his eyes for a moment before he nodded. "Anywhere else?"

"Yes, we went further down the hall to an office. There was no name on it, so I assumed it was empty."

He shifted in his chair, staring out the window for a moment. I couldn't tell if he was angry with me or not, but something in him had definitely changed. "Did they say anything about why they were here?"

"Yes, they said they were from the Chicago office to collect something. They had badges with them. They looked so real, but I had this bad feeling."

His jaw clenched hard as he stared down at his desk. He looked like he was seriously trying to rein in his anger.

"I'm so sorry, but I didn't know if what they were saying was real. I had no idea if there was even a Chicago branch." I was silent for a minute, waiting for him to speak. When he didn't, I continued. "I hope nothing bad happened."

He finally looked up at me, a tight smile on his face. "It's fine. I'm sure anyone would have thought it real, given the situation you were in. I appreciate you coming forward with this information. Now we can do a security sweep and see if anything was taken."

I nodded, not sure what else to do. "Would you like me to come into work tonight?"

He glanced up, lost in thought for a moment as he stared at me. "No, without the power on, there's no point."

"Do…do I still have a job?"

"Of course." It sounded sincere, but I had the feeling he was very angry with me. Then again, maybe I just found it hard to trust anyone. "Did you drive?"

"No, I walked."

"Let me have a driver take you home."

"I think it would be faster to walk. Traffic is backed up outside."

He gave a polite nod as he walked around his desk, gripping me lightly by the elbow. He steered me to the door, opening it for me. "I'm not sure how long it will take to get the power back on. Why don't you assume that until the power's on, it's best just to stay home. Do we have your phone number on file?"

"I…I don't have a phone," I admitted weakly. I didn't want to admit that I couldn't afford to just take off for an extended amount of time. That wasn't his problem, and they were probably losing money every day the power was out, but I also couldn't afford to be proud right now. "If anything comes up that I can help with, I'd be glad for the work."

"Come by tomorrow. We'll see what we can do."

Relief filled me as my shoulders sagged. "Thank you."

"You're welcome…" He trailed off, not knowing my name.

"Beth."

"Beth. I'm Adam." He held out his hand, gripping my small hand in his larger one. Warmth flooded me as he watched me intently. For the first time in years, I felt something when I looked at him, but that wasn't really a good thing. I wouldn't be sticking around long enough to be attached to anyone.

19

CASH

"Mayor Kinsley," I said, shaking his hand as he walked into our offices. He had a team of five people with him—not enough, in my opinion, but that wasn't for me to decide.

"Mr. Owens, I was told you're leading operational control on this disaster."

His tone was friendly enough, but there was a hint of disgust or hate in his voice. Probably because we had been tasked with controlling the situation. "Sir, we'll do everything we can to get the city up and running again."

"I heard you were there, that you allowed it to happen."

"No, we were there, but we weren't aware of Grady's plans. When we realized something was off, we did everything in our power to stop his plans. Unfortunately, it was too late."

"Yes, well, let's make sure the citizens can function as close to normal as soon as possible."

"That's our goal, sir."

I nodded to Eli, who was waiting by the conference room. He opened the door and walked inside, waiting for the rest of the group to join. After we were all seated around the table, I made introductions.

"I'm Cash Owens, owner of this company. I have Eli Brant, Red

Warren, and Bradford Kavanaugh with me today to help navigate this situation."

"Is your father Senator Walter Kavanaugh?" the mayor asked, leaning forward curiously.

Kavanaugh bit back the sarcastic retort that I knew was waiting on the tip of his tongue. This wasn't the time or place to say what he thought of his old man. "Yes, sir."

"Good man," the mayor grinned.

Kavanaugh nodded, but said nothing further. It was clear the mayor was going to try and use Kavanaugh to further his own career. Little did he know that Brad didn't even speak to his father.

"Mayor, let's get this meeting started," I said, trying to push the meeting along.

He stood, buttoning his jacket as he pointed around the room. "I've brought the city engineer, Mark Sampson with me, along with the police and fire chief, the medical director at the local hospital, and my public relations liaison."

I nodded to them, taking my own seat. "Mark, tell us what you can."

Mark cleared his throat, pulling out paper maps and unrolling them on the table. It was like we'd gone back forty years in time. "For those of you who don't know, a graphite bomb is basically a metal canister filled with spools of graphite filament and an explosive device. When the explosive detonates, it breaks the filament into very fine pieces which are ejected from the canister in a gas-like plume. If the bomb had gone off over a power line, there would have been outages, but power would have been restored more quickly. However, because a substation was attacked, the power was instantly transferred to a brother substation," he said, pointing to another substation on the map, "but it couldn't take the overload of power and also failed. The power stations started falling like dominos, each one unable to hold the surge in transfer of power, which is why there's a power outage on the entire West Coast."

"What time frame are we looking at to get power restored?" I asked.

Mark glanced at the mayor, blowing out a harsh breath. "Best guess is six weeks. It could be more or less. It's hard to tell right now."

I leaned back in my seat, shocked by how long it would take to get everything up and running again. "What can we do in the meantime to help people out?"

"What I'd like to do is go around the city to larger buildings that have backup generators. We can reverse the flow of power back into the city."

"Will the city be fully functioning?" the mayor asked.

"No, it'll power bare essentials. However, if we can start reversing the flow by grid, most sections of the city will have at least a little power. It's all we can do at this point."

"That means having fuel trucks designated just for driving around and refilling generators," the fire chief stated.

"We'll have to block off roads to keep a path clear for them."

"How are the hospitals doing?" I asked the medical director.

"I've been in contact with the two hospitals in the area. They're doing okay for the time being, but as you would expect, things are strained. There are blocked roads preventing staff from reaching the hospital. And the conditions aren't ideal for running a hospital. If we can, we need to get more power to the hospitals so they can function at full capacity."

"We also have the issue of getting people clean water," Mark spoke up.

"Not to mention food," the police chief spoke up. "We live in a society where cash is used less and less. Everyone swipes a card now. But you can't use a bank card if the entire system is down. There'll be a run on the banks."

"People won't have cash for long if they don't have jobs to go to. What are people supposed to do when the money runs out?"

I stood from my seat, needing to put an end to the endless stream of problems. "Alright, these are all valid points. I've already had my team working on some solutions. The governor has ordered the National Guard to come in, but they'll be stretched thin as they aid the entire West Coast. Let's put together our best solutions for the most urgent problems. Red, I want you to contact other cities. Find out what they're doing. Let's make sure we share information. Eli, go with Mark and give him whatever help he needs to start reversing the power into the city. The National Guard should be arriving in the next six to twelve hours. Kavanaugh, let's make sure we're ready for them. Work with the mayor's office to find mobile locations to set up."

"I'll have my office set up a news conference to set the public's mind at ease," the mayor spoke up.

"How are we going to do that with no power?"

The mayor sighed. "I guess we'll send people around to news outlets and have them gather in front of city hall. I'll just have to talk really loud."

"It's going to be like going back to the 1800s," I muttered. Running my hand through my hair, I gave a funny look. "Anyone know where we can find an old printing press?"

After hours of meetings, I broke away for five minutes to check in with Rae. I despised the fact that Rafe put me in charge of operational controls. The last thing I wanted to do was deal with the Mayor, the Governor, and everyone underneath. Not to mention that because of the lack of power, we were practically living in the stone age. I had to find satellite phones so we could stay in communication with members of the city, but even those would eventually lose power.

"What have you found out?" I asked Rae.

"Well, considering I'm having to go through dark channels, and try to communicate with people halfway around the country when we have no power, and—"

"Yeah, I got it, Rae. The situation sucks. Do you have anything," I said slowly, emphasizing each word. I was already running low on patience.

"Not a lot yet. Grady works for a company called VTS—Vogt Technological Solutions. My guy did a deep dive on the company, but so far, he can't find a single thing they actually produce."

"Grady made it sound like they were a research company."

She shook her head, keeping her voice low as she looked to the IT door to make sure no one was listening. "There was nothing on research either. Whatever they're doing, they're hiding it well. They don't want anyone to know what they're really doing."

"What about other known associates?"

"We're working on that." She sighed in annoyance. "I could really use a computer right now."

"We're running on bare essentials right now," I reminded her.

"A computer is a bare essential to me. It's my lifeline."

"What about our friend, Rafe? Any idea what he's up to?"

"He's off the grid. Whatever he's doing—"

"He doesn't want anyone to know either," I finished. "Does anyone do anything transparent anymore? Fuck, this is annoying."

"Well, it doesn't help that we're basically working in the Stone Age. You wouldn't be willing to send me out of state, would you?"

"For what reason?"

"Because I could find out things a lot faster if I wasn't restricted to digging through state records. Give me a company vehicle, and I'll set up in freaking Kansas or something."

I wasn't sure I wanted to lose any manpower, but since she was already working solely on this, I couldn't really argue that this wouldn't be valuable. "Fine, but you're taking Fox with you."

Her face dropped and she groaned, covering her face with her hands. "Not Fox. Anyone but Fox."

"He's fucking crazy as hell. You know I can't let him deal with people. He'll end up killing someone."

"So, you're sending him with me?" she asked incredulously. "All you're going to end up with is another dead body, and it won't be mine."

"If you want to go, you take him with you. But if you leave, you keep a tight grip on him. We don't need more alphabets coming after us."

"Fine," she grumbled. "But know that I'm taking him with me under duress."

I sighed heavily, pinching the bridge of my nose. "You know what? Don't take Fox. Take New Guy."

"Excuse me? I'm not taking him," she said quickly.

"You didn't want to take Fox, so now you're taking New Guy."

"Boss," she groaned.

"I don't want to hear it. You have to break him in at some point."

She flipped me off as I turned and walked out of the room. I really needed some fucking coffee, but I wasn't even sure how to make coffee without a fucking coffee pot. I headed into the kitchen, staring at the coffee pot and willing it to brew me just a single cup.

"Can't we turn it on just long enough to brew a few pots of coffee?" Scottie asked.

"Until we are sure we can get a fuel truck out here, we have to conserve as much power as possible," I muttered, wishing I could say differently.

"What if we boil the water?"

I turned to him, curious at his suggestion. "Do you know how to make coffee from boiled water?"

He rushed over to the cabinets, digging around inside. Finally, he pulled out a silver pot of some kind. "This is an espresso machine."

I pointed at it, my eyebrows raised. "I've seen an espresso machine. That's just a hunk of metal."

"No, see, you put the coffee grounds in…" He unscrewed the middle and pulled out a sieve. "In here, and then you pour the water in the…um…well, it might take some experimenting, but I'll figure it out."

"And where are you going to get boiled water?"

He frowned, thinking that over. "The training center. I'll build a fire and put the machine over the flame."

"Great, so we might get coffee in an hour?"

"Do you want coffee or not?"

I weighed my options, which were pretty much go without coffee or risk burning down the building with Lock's crazy idea. "I need coffee."

He grinned, grabbing the rest of the supplies.

"You know, if you were IRIS, there's no way I would let you do this!" I shouted as he ran out of the room.

20

BETH

That dreaded feeling in the pit of my stomach had returned. Ever since I went to work yesterday, I felt like someone was watching me. The whole way home, the hairs on the back of my neck were prickling, but every time I looked over my shoulder, I only saw regular people. If someone was following me, they were doing a damn good job of blending in.

I looked through the slats of my blinds, studying everyone on the street. There were so many people out there, walking now instead of driving. I hadn't heard any more about how long this power outage was going to last, but earlier, I could have sworn I saw military vehicles driving a few streets over.

Dropping the blinds, I paced around the living room. Adam—Mr. Hayes— said to stop by today, and hanging around the apartment wasn't doing me any good. Grabbing my purse, I decided it was now or never. I locked up and made the long walk back to work, practically running at times because I could feel eyes on me. I bumped into someone just as I was rounding the corner to the building, nearly falling over until someone grabbed my arm and steadied me.

"Hey—" I was ready to snap until I looked up into the eyes of my boss. "Oh, sorry. I didn't see you."

"It's fine. I'm actually glad you came by today."

"You are?" I asked in surprise.

"Yes, I was hoping you could describe the men you were with."

For some reason, that made me uneasy…because of Seth. I didn't want to give him away. It was so ridiculous. If he was there doing something wrong, then I should definitely tell Mr. Hayes what he looked like. On the other hand, he was really good to me, helping me out of my panicked mind when anyone else might have ignored me. And if I gave his description and he got in trouble, he would just be another one of my casualties.

"Beth?"

I was lost in my thoughts, not even paying attention to my boss. "Um…I'm not sure I got a good look at them. It was dark," I said dumbly.

"Any description would help."

He took me by the elbow, directing me around the corner to the entrance of the building. He nodded to the guard as we passed, noting there were now several more security guards than yesterday. "Did you have any luck finding out what they took?"

"I thought you said you didn't know if they took anything," he said, side-eyeing me as we headed for the stairwell. He opened the door for me, still gripping my elbow as we started to climb.

"Oh, well, I guess I don't know. I just assumed if they were here and they weren't supposed to be, then they took something."

Feeling uncomfortable with how he was holding me, I gently pried myself from his grip, giving a tight smile as I moved further away from him. Except, when I stepped back, I forgot we were on stairs and I nearly fell backward. Adam's hand shot out, grabbing me before I could take a deadly tumble. He pulled me close to his body, holding me tight as my heart pounded in my chest. Like yesterday, I felt something when I was with him. My skin felt flush when he touched me, and everything around me seemed to stand still for a moment.

His hand slid up my arm, brushing gently over the curve of my neck. There was an intimacy to the way he was holding me like he needed to touch me. My eyes dropped to his lips, and for just a moment, I wondered what it would be like to have a man's lips on mine. It had been so long, and I was tired of being alone. But Art's death was a stark reminder that it wasn't safe for anyone to be close to me.

Clearing my throat, I pulled back from him, pushing my hair behind my ear as I attempted to do something with my hands as a distraction. I could feel my face flush bright red, but thankfully, he didn't say anything about it.

"We should head to my office." His voice was a gruff rumble that made me wish for things I couldn't have. Pulling myself together, I followed him upstairs and into his office. Thankfully, he took the seat behind his desk, putting some distance between us as I sat on the other side.

"So, what can you tell me about the men that were here?"

I shifted in my chair as Seth's face flashed in my mind. "They wore trench coats."

"Anything else?"

"Um...They were tall." I could see the frustration building on his face. I didn't want to disappoint him, but I felt like I was trapped in something I didn't want any part of. I was supposed to be keeping a low profile, and here I was being dragged into a mystery.

I stood suddenly, feeling too uncomfortable with all of this. "You know, I think I should actually go."

"But you said you were interested in working."

"Yes, but the power's still out. What would I even do?"

"Then at least let me take you home."

I wasn't sure if he wanted to grill me more about the men or if this was about our moment on the stairs. Either way, I needed to leave before this got out of hand.

"That's really not necessary. I actually have to make a stop anyway."

"Where?" he asked, almost an accusation, but then schooled his features. "Sorry, that was rude."

I was so shocked by the outburst that I turned on my heel and walked out of the room. I thought I heard him following me, so I ran for the stairwell and hurried down the stairs. Things were getting stranger by the moment. I burst out onto the street and ran to the corner, slipping around the edge of the building. Once pressed against it, I let my heart calm before peeking around the edge. Adam stood on the sidewalk, looking in both directions. Another man walked up to him and they seemed to argue, then Adam pointed in my direction. I quickly pulled back, afraid I had been caught. After a moment, I looked around the corner again, only to find the man hurrying in my direction.

I took off down the sidewalk, racing through the crowd quickly building the further I got down the street. Glancing over my shoulder, fear skittered down my spine when I saw the man still following me. And when our eyes locked, he started running toward me. I didn't even pay attention to my surroundings when I ran across the street, narrowly avoiding cars and trucks to get to safety on the other side.

Luckily, he didn't have the ease of crossing the street, and ended up nearly crushed by a vehicle he ran in front of. I ducked inside an open door, running up the stairs and praying I could hide out for a while. I didn't even bother to check out my surroundings as I found a dark corner to sit in. I stayed there for what felt like hours until, finally, my heart calmed. When no one came, I took a chance and exited my hiding spot.

With my hand gliding along the wall, I slowly made my way downstairs, watching for the man who chased me. But he wasn't there or anywhere on the street that I could see. Yet, I still felt eyes on me the entire way home. The question was, who was following me? Was it the man from work, or was it someone from my past?

21

CASH

"How are we looking?" I asked Mark as he showed me the grid where they'd been able to reverse engineer the power. "We're looking good. We've already started in some of the grids, but this particular grid is a problem."

I looked closer at it. "What's going on?"

"These five buildings, all of them have generators, but none of them kicked in when the power failed."

"Just on this grid?"

"Exactly. It doesn't make any sense. When the power went out, the generator would automatically kick in and take over, but that's not what happened here." He stared at the grid curiously, but I could tell there was something else on his mind.

"Whatever it is, just say it."

He finally turned to me, his face serious. "Look, in order for the backup generators not to kick in, they would have to be out of fuel. But what's the likelihood that happened to five buildings on the same block?"

I knew exactly how that might happen. "It could if the backup power was cut."

"Who would do that?" he said in a low voice. "It's gotta be a coincidence."

"I don't believe in coincidences." I grabbed the sheet with the grid information on it. "Keep working on this. I'm going to run down a few things."

Stalking out of the office, I headed to find Rae, only remembering when I entered the IT room that she had already left with New Guy. "Shit," I muttered.

"Need something, boss?" Dash asked as he walked into the room.

He was another IT guy, but also worked in the training center with Fox. Rae was my mastermind, but Dash grew up a computer nerd, so he switched on and off when needed. Fortunately, he could hold his own in the ring with everyone else, including Rae. "I need to find some footage."

He snorted. "There was a blackout. What kind of footage are you hoping to find?"

"I think we might have a lead on why the blackout happened, but it's a long shot."

"I love a good long shot," he grinned. "Where are we going?"

He grabbed his jacket off the back of the chair and pulled it on before I even answered. I waited to answer until we were completely alone. I didn't want too many conspiracy theories floating around until I had more evidence.

We got in my truck, and only then did I reveal what I thought might have happened. "You know we've been working on reverse engineering the power back to the city from larger generators around the city."

"Yeah."

"Well, one block is completely black. Five buildings, all with generators, failed to kick in during the power outage."

"That sounds like more than a coincidence."

"That's what I thought. So, we have a massive power outage with no explanation."

"You mean, other than the fact that they've fucked the entire West Coast. Boss, it's a domestic terrorist attack."

"Yes, but there's always a purpose behind it. What would that be? To teach us a lesson?"

He frowned, glancing away from me. "To cause disruption to the system."

"No, I don't buy it. And if it had been one failed generator, I would have believed it was just that, but five is excessive, and all on one block? Somebody purposely killed the backup power to those buildings."

"To hide the true target," he added.

"Exactly. Maybe they were hoping in the chaos nobody would notice, or maybe they just wanted to buy some time."

"But like you said, if they only cut the backup power to one building, nobody would think anything of it. Why take out the whole block?"

"I'm guessing so the target didn't realize they were a target. If there was a failure on the entire block, somebody else might not put two and two together."

"But you're not just somebody, boss."

"Aw, you flatter me."

"Well, someone's got to hold that gigantic head on your shoulders."

"It's gigantic for a reason. There are brains behind all these muscles."

"Didn't realize your muscles were in your head," he retorted.

"Your brain is a fucking muscle, moron."

I knew I walked right into it, but I couldn't help it. Sometimes, it was just too easy to bait Dash. "The brain itself is not a muscle. It contains blood vessels and nerves, including neurons and glial cells—"

I tuned him out as I parked the truck across the street from the grid where all the power went out. Dash was still rattling on about the brain as I looked at the buildings in front of us.

"You start with the far building," I interrupted, pointing to the building on the corner. "I'll start at the other end. As far as they're concerned, you're looking into how to get their backup generators working so we can use them for this grid."

"Got it, boss."

He shoved his door open at the same time as me and we went our separate ways. The first two buildings were a bust. The first was an office building. They didn't seem to be affected by the outage at all. There were security guards posted in the lobby, and they didn't report anything suspicious happening. The second building was much the same. There were no security guards, but the boss seemed wholly unconcerned about the actual outage. His only concern was how much money he was losing with his employees at home.

I walked into the third building on my list, not very hopeful that I would get anything out of them. That is, until I saw the extreme number of security guards in the lobby.

"I don't care about your excuses!" a man yelled from across the lobby. I couldn't tell who he was yelling at because the other figure was in the stairwell. The man turned and stomped toward me, his pace slowing when he saw me.

"Excuse me," I said, walking up to him with my hand held out. "My name is Cash Owens. I'm working with the city."

He eyed me speculatively. "You don't look like you work for the city."

I glanced down at my jeans, black jacket, and black boots, then back up to him. "It's laundry day, and that's not really an option right now."

He nodded, his hands fisting at his sides. He seemed agitated as he stood in front of me. He was eager to get somewhere, but he didn't want to appear rude. Either that, or he didn't want me to know that he wanted to get away from me as quickly as possible.

"What can I help you with?"

"Well, we're trying to reverse power from larger generators, such as the one you have, but it seems like this entire block lost its backup generators."

"As you can see, we're still in the dark," he said, holding his hands up, motioning to the darkness of the building even in broad daylight.

"Any idea what might have caused the backup to fail?" His eyes narrowed on me. "So we can fix the issue," I added. "We're eager to get as much power back to the city as possible."

"Since it's my generator, I think the power should be fed back into my building, not the city," he countered.

"Except, this is a coast-wide issue. Millions are without power."

"And that's my problem, why? I'm the one that pays for this building, the generator, and the fuel that runs it."

I smirked at him, glancing around the lobby again. "Is there some reason you need the power for this building more than others?"

"This is a research facility, Mr. Owens. We have many projects that are kept under lock and key. Electronic locks, that is. Without power, all our research is vulnerable."

I nodded to him. "Did anything go missing?"

He hesitated, his eyes flicking to the security guards before a smooth smile filled his face. "Not at all, but that doesn't mean I want something just up and walking out the door."

"Well, we can have some men out here later today to have a look at the generators and make sure they're running in no time."

"It's fine," he cut in. "I already hired men to work on it."

"Then I'll leave you to it."

I turned and walked out, ready to call my team, when I remembered my phone wasn't working. Swearing, I glanced up and noticed the cameras at the building across the street. Rushing across the street, I yanked the door open and headed to the security office. It was very unlikely they had any security footage from the day of the outage, but I'd take a slim chance over nothing.

As luck would have it, the security guard was in. "Can I help you?"

"Yeah, I'm Cash Owens. I'm working with the city on restoring power, and we noticed the buildings on the other side of the street were having some trouble with their generators. I was hoping I could see your security feed from that night to see if I can piece together what happened."

"Owens, you said?"

"Yes, sir."

He grinned. "Yeah, I know you. Owens Protective Services."

"That's correct."

"Yeah, my nephew works for your company."

"Really? Who's your nephew?"

"Brian Wilson," he said proudly.

I pretended I knew who the fuck that was. His nephew was obviously lying to him, probably because he didn't want to let him down. That meant he was trouble, and his uncle would know that.

"Brian, yeah, he's a real ball buster."

"That kid has been in so much trouble. I'm just happy someone finally gave him a shot."

"We're lucky to have him."

He waved me into his office. "So, you need security feed?"

"Yes, I know the feed probably turned off when the power went out, but I was hoping I might find something helpful."

"A couple of years ago, we had the power go out. Someone broke in and trashed the lobby. After that, the bosses had the security tied into the backup generator to kick in right away. I should be able to get you what you need."

"Perfect."

"I'll make a copy for you. Just give me a minute."

After a half hour and ten stories about his nephew, I finally had the footage in my hand. I walked out of there, shaking his hand and promising to keep his nephew on the right track.

"Hey, any luck?" Dash asked as he leaned against my truck.

"Possibly. What about you?"

"Nothing. Unless you think the power outage had to do with modern art or wine that can no longer be kept at the precise temperature needed."

I snorted and headed to my truck. "Let's go. I think I have something better than chilled wine."

"Is it beer? Because I could really go for a beer right now."

"Only if it's made in a research lab."

I walked through the doors of the office, eager to get to the sat phone to call Rae. Suddenly, the lights flickered on and the air kicked in. I stopped and looked around, wondering if power was fully restored, but noticed we still weren't running at full strength yet.

Mark walked out of the conference room with a grin on his face. "The mayor agreed that as the central location of operation, your office needed to get fuel right away so we could actually use some equipment to help us get the city online."

"Does this mean we get coffee?" Dash asked.

"After the disaster with Scottie, I really hope so. I don't think any of us can handle another open flame in the building. Mark, I'll join you in a little bit. I have a few things to catch up on."

"No problem."

After he walked away, I turned back to Dash. "Let's get the computers up and running right away. I want to see what's on this footage."

"Right away, boss."

He headed to the IT room as I went to my office for the sat phone to call Rae.

"Miss me already, boss?"

"Please tell me you're by a computer."

"I happen to have one right in front of me. Why?"

"We've got power restored, and I think I've found something. I need you to look into a research facility for me. I'll send you the address."

"What am I looking for?"

"I don't know, but they've got tight security. The man I spoke with said they have electronic locks and a lot of research that they can't allow to slip out."

"That sounds ominous."

"I could be wrong about this, but there were five buildings on that block that lost backup power."

"You think that was on purpose?"

"Almost positive. Dash and I checked it out. All the other businesses seemed perfectly normal, but this one…the man was panicked."

"Do you have a name?"

"No, but I'm sure you'll be able to figure it out."

"I'll let you know when I have something."

"Thanks, Rae."

I hung up and headed to the IT room. Dash already had one computer up and running, and was booting up the rest of the systems.

"I'm just pulling up the feed. What exactly are we looking for?"

"Anything that tells us why five backup generators went out."

He started scrolling through the feed from earlier in the day. We watched as hours of the day passed without anything suspicious occurring.

"I'm not sure if we're going to find anything," Dash sighed. "All someone would have to do is shut the valve for the fuel on the backup."

"There's got to be something," I muttered.

"Yeah, but we're looking at one camera angle. We can't even see all the buildings on the block."

"Just keep searching."

The footage ran until the power outage and the feed cut off, but popped up again five minutes later.

"Wait, stop there," I snapped, pointing at the people walking out of the building. "Can you zoom in or something?"

"The faces will most likely be distorted, but let's see if we get any hits."

He rewound the video and zoomed in as best he could. What I saw stopped me in my tracks. It wasn't the five men walking out of the building, looking very much like they didn't belong. It was the woman's face. I'd recognize her anywhere.

"What is it, boss?"

"I know her. She came into the gym just a few days ago." In that moment, I hated myself. I was sucked in with her sad demeanor, thinking she was a victim, but all along, she was hiding a very different kind of secret.

"Did you get a name?"

"Beth. That's all I have."

"Not really a lot to go on."

"I don't need any more than that. I know where she lives," I said just before I ran out the door. With my sat phone still in hand, I called Rae back.

"Geez, boss. It's been like fifteen minutes. Give me a little more time."

"I need something else. The woman you brought home the other night, Beth…"

"Yeah, what about her?"

I rushed over to my truck and yanked the door open before sliding inside. "She was on the video feed outside the research facility."

"Whoa, you think she was involved in this?"

"What are the chances she's not?"

"Uh, pretty good. Boss, she was terrified."

"Maybe of who she worked for. I need anything you can find on her."

"I only have her first name."

"But you know where she lives."

She sighed heavily over the phone. "I'm guessing you're on the way to her now?"

"She's involved in this. I know it."

"Remember how scared she was. She may not be a willing participant in what's going on."

"If not, then she's involved in something that could get her killed."

"I'll find out what I can. Just take it easy on her. Remember, women like men who don't yell at them."

"I know how to talk to women," I scoffed.

"When was the last time you had a date?" she asked, amusement lacing her voice.

"I…It was…"

"Yeah, that's what I figured. Be nice and try not to scare her. Maybe try being her friend."

"You want me to be her friend?"

"Without growling at her or accusing her of being a terrorist," she added quickly. "You catch more bees with honey."

"I'm not looking for honey. I'm looking for answers, and my gun works pretty well for that situation."

"I'm telling you, boss, she's not who you think she is. You hired me for a reason. Now listen to me before you scare off the only possible lead we have."

"Fine," I grumbled. "But I reserve the right to use my gun if necessary."

22

BETH

There was no way I was going back to my old job. There was definitely something off about Adam Hayes, but I knew that before he sent his man after me. Whatever he wanted from me, I wasn't giving it. I never should have gone back to work to report what happened the night of the blackout. Now, I wasn't even sure if it was safe to stay in the city. But I needed a plan. The last time I ran without having one, I ended up losing most of my money. In the meantime, I needed another job to tide me over until I could get out of town.

The first thing I did was grab a box of hair dye from the local pharmacy. They were barely operating with no power, so I had to fumble my way through the dark to find what I was looking for. When I was done, I headed back to my apartment, using a meager amount of water to take care of my hair. It wasn't the best dye job, but it would do for now, leaving my hair more of a strawberry blonde. I would need to go in for a cut soon, but that could wait a little while longer. I was hoping to change my look just enough to blend in and not draw attention to myself. Black stood out in a crowd. I always noticed people that dyed their hair such a dark color.

With that taken care of, I walked to the diner just a few blocks from my apartment to see if I could get a job. I was just turning the corner when I ran into what felt like a giant slab of meat. Then something hot soaked through my shirt, instantly heating my skin.

"Shit!" I cried out, pulling my shirt away from my chest.

"Crap. I'm so sorry."

I looked up instantly at the familiar voice, taking in his brown eyes and clean-shaven face. It was the man from the gym. I swallowed hard, taking a step back as he advanced on me, only to stop when he saw me move.

He watched me for a moment, his brows furrowed as he studied my face. I took the opportunity to stare back at him. I wasn't sure why I was being so bold. I didn't trust this man any more than the next, but the way he cared for me after I hurt my arm rang through my mind. I just couldn't make up my mind if this man was good or bad.

"I know you, right?"

I wasn't sure if that meant I had a forgettable face or if my dye job worked. "Um…I don't think so."

"You look so familiar. Maybe it's just one of those faces," he grinned, but his eyes were still scanning me. "The gym," he said suddenly. "That's where I know you from."

"I don't know what you're talking about."

I wanted to walk away, but I felt rooted to the spot. I didn't miss the way he stood in front of me, using his body to block everyone else from getting close. I would have guessed that was just a coincidence, but when a man tried to walk between us, he inserted himself in the way, his large frame keeping the man at bay. The way he stood beside me, tall and strong, made me feel protected. But then I remembered how Adam seemed nice at first, too. I thought maybe he was just interested in me, but the truth was, he wanted information from me.

"I remember you now," he grinned. "You were kicking ass."

"I puked," I stated bluntly.

"You were in pain." His eyes flicked to my shoulder. "How's your arm?"

I glanced down, realizing I was cradling my forearm. "It's fine," I said, quickly releasing my basically useless arm. "I took some painkillers and was fine."

His knowing expression said it all, but he didn't call me on my bullshit. "I wish I could say we'll be running more classes soon, but with this power outage, that's not very likely unless we hold them in the park."

"That must be bad for business."

He shook his head, glancing down the street. "I'm actually working with the mayor to get the city running again."

"That sounds like a big job." I glanced around, suddenly feeling like I was being watched again. My eyes darted around in search of the man who chased me the other day, but I couldn't find him anywhere.

"Is something wrong?" he asked, his gaze quickly shifting to our surroundings. He stepped closer to me, his arm nearly wrapping around me as his other hand went to his hip. My eyes widened at the sight of his gun, and he must have noticed my body tense because he quickly explained.

"I run a security company. I never go anywhere without my gun."

I gave a tight nod, but I knew all too well how guns were used, and it was never in my favor. "I have to go," I said in a rush.

"I'll walk with you," he answered, leaving no room for argument. I almost told him I didn't need the assistance, but then I noticed he hadn't stopped watching our surroundings. Was someone else really out there? Maybe he had seen something I hadn't.

My nerves were getting the better of me, and the only way I knew to help that was to talk. "Can I buy you another cup of coffee?"

He laughed slightly. "I should be asking if I can buy you another shirt. I hope you're not on your way somewhere important."

"I was actually going down to the diner to see if I could get a job."

I could feel the weight of his stare as we continued to walk. "The other night you said you had to go to work. They didn't fire you, did they?"

"No, I just…left for personal reasons."

"Well, I doubt the diner is hiring. Most businesses are shut down right now. We're diverting power from generators, but it wouldn't be enough to run the diner."

I stopped with a sigh. What was the point in continuing to walk if they weren't open? Maybe I should just consider picking up and moving out of town. After everything that had happened over the past few days, it didn't seem like the city wanted me here.

"Look, if you need a job, I might be able to help."

My eyes snapped to his face as I warred with my emotions. Relief, disbelief, but most of all…hope. "What kind of job?"

"It's not much. We just lost an employee not too long ago. She was sort of our janitor."

"That's perfect," I said in a rush. "That's actually what I did at my last job."

"Really," he answered, that fact taking him by surprise. "Where was that, if you don't mind me asking?"

"Um…it was a research facility."

"And you cleaned there?"

"Yes, at night."

"Were you the only employee?"

I was almost going to not answer, but these were sort of standard questions. "No, there were a few other girls that worked there also."

He nodded again, but looked almost uncomfortable. "Look, I really hate to ask this, but I do run a security firm. Can you tell me why you left your last job?"

Because my boss turned into a psycho? Because something bad went down there and I didn't want to be involved? "The hours were really cut back with the power outage. I just didn't see it working out long term, especially since nobody knows how long this will last."

"Fair enough. Do you want to come back to the office now and look around?"

"Wait, we haven't talked about hours or pay."

"Well, hours are pretty much whatever works best for you. We have men in and out of training all day long. All the offices need to be cleaned, but since we're a security company, there's always someone in the building. Honestly, I would feel better if you worked days. I don't like the thought of someone like you there all alone."

"Someone like me?" I asked, cocking my head in question.

"Well…untrained. Everyone that works at my company is highly trained in hand to hand combat, as well as with weapons. And since you were taking a self-defense class, I'm guessing you're not trained in either."

He had a point, and I hated that I was considered a liability, but that brought up a second point. "You don't actually have people come after you at your business, do you?"

"No," he laughed. "Nothing like that, but better safe than sorry."

"I guess," I said with a frown. "Um…I just have one other question. I sort of lost my ID and I know I need one to work, but I haven't had time to get a new one. And now, with the power outage—"

He waved me off. "Don't worry about it right now. It'll be a long time before anything starts working again, and then there'll be a backlog of things that businesses need to catch up on. We'll cross that bridge when we get there. But then I'm going to do a deep dive on you."

"A what?"

"Dig into your life and find out every last secret you have."

I must have looked horrified because he instantly started laughing. "I'm kidding. It's just a little security humor. Come on, let's go."

He continued walking, leaving me to follow. I wasn't sure that this was the smartest idea, but what other choice did I have at the moment?

23

CASH

I drove back to the office, remembering what Rae said about the way I needed to talk to Beth. This woman was holding a lot of secrets, and the interrogator inside me wanted to grill the information out of her. The other part of me wanted to believe that she wasn't involved in this, because if she was, that meant my instincts were far off base. I actually felt bad for her, felt a need to protect her. I was worried about her and wanted to be there for her, only to find out that she was involved in this. Now, this was personal. Yeah, I could see that she'd dealt with some shit in her life, but that was no reason to deal with terrorists. Now, I just had to prove that.

I glanced over at her, wondering what was going through her mind right now. There was one thing I could never quite wrap my mind around, and that was how the criminal mind worked. There were good citizens out there who followed the law and never did anything wrong. And then there were criminals who repeatedly broke the law without a care about the repercussions. I'd seen it over and over again —men and women who ended up in jail, served their time, only to be released and commit another crime. How did someone live like that? How did one decide that helping terrorists was a good idea? What was she getting out of this?

I would normally assume she was in it for the money, but she was searching for a job. Maybe she didn't get a dime out of them. It could be that she got on someone's bad side, and she had to go along with their scheme to stay alive. Whatever the reason, I was going to get to the bottom of it. For now, I had to be civil. Once I got her back to the office, all bets were off.

"So, are you from around here?"

"Uh…no, I moved here about six months ago."

I nodded, pretending to be really interested. "That's cool. Where are you from?"

"Around," she said vaguely.

It was clear I was going to have to really work for her trust. "I'm originally from Kansas. California is a far cry from that," I grinned, glancing over at her.

She was frowning as she stared out the window. Was I boring her? Christ, it was like pulling teeth to get her to talk. I'd been in this situation before, where I needed to get a client to trust me, but this was different. Usually, I didn't hate my clients, which made my job easier.

I pulled into the parking lot and pocketed Betty, who was hanging from my mirror. She was my good luck charm, and I really needed all I could get right now.

"What's that?" she asked, nodding to my pocket.

"Oh…good luck charm. I've had her since I enlisted."

"Betty Boop is your good luck charm?" She looked at me like I was insane.

"We all have something. She's always been mine."

She hesitated a moment, her eyes still on my pocket. "Does she work?"

"She got me out of some of the biggest fights of my life. Yeah, I'd say she works."

She chewed on her lip thoughtfully, her gaze still riveted to my pocket. If she even thought about touching Betty, I'd break her fucking fingers. I got out and slammed the door, my eyes scanning the parking lot.

I was on higher alert than normal. With the power being down and a domestic terrorist on the loose, I wanted nothing more than to pull

IN THE TRENCHES

my gun just to scare off anyone who came near me. Ever since Sinner was attacked out here, I'd been thinking of where we could relocate. I needed someplace outside the city, where I could put more security features in place. I hated feeling so exposed.

I walked around to Beth's side of the truck and opened the door for her. Placing my hand on her lower back, I noticed how she stiffened under my touch. "Just stay by my side," I said quietly.

"Why?" She stopped suddenly, looking around the parking lot. "What's going on?"

"Nothing." But my eyes never stopped scanning. "Let's get inside."

She did as I said, but I could feel the panic coming off her in waves. My chest tightened as I watched her try to hide her fear. I hated that I felt something, knowing she was so scared. The last thing I should feel for her is pity.

Unless...I couldn't forget what Rae said, that she was a victim. What if she was right and I was wrong? That would be a huge coincidence. Grady hired me weeks ago. He could have been scheming with Beth all along. Maybe she came in to check me out in the gym, and then reported back to Grady that I was a good guy. That would have made him more willing to work with me, knowing that it might be easy to pull one over on me.

I yanked the door open and ushered her inside. Dash was just coming out of the IT room down the hall when he spotted me, his eyes going wide as he looked at Beth.

"Uh...what's going on, boss?"

"Dash, this is Beth. She's going to be working for us."

His brows furrowed as he looked from me and then back to her. "Um..."

"Beth, can you wait out here for a minute? I just need to talk with Dash about a job. I'll only be a minute."

She must have caught on to the tension, but she nodded and took a seat in the lobby. I walked into my office followed by Dash, who shut the door before he laid into me.

"What the fuck are you doing, boss? You suspect her of working with terrorists, so you brought her back to the home base?"

"You know what they say, *Keep your friends close and your enemies closer.*"

"Sure, when you're talking about high school friends. This…this is bigger than any high school bullshit. You don't bring a suspected terrorist into the fold just because she has a nice ass."

I cocked an eyebrow at him. "I didn't realize you were watching her ass."

"I was. I mean, I wasn't, but it was there."

"Yes, it was there, along with the rest of her body. Are you going to be able to function around her?"

"Me?" His eyebrows shot up. "You're the one that knows this chick."

"Yes," I admitted, then pulled Betty out of my pocket and set her on the tiny pedestal on my desk.

"Oh shit," Dash muttered. "Boss, tell me you're not doing it."

"You know exactly what I'm doing. We have a suspected terrorist out in the lobby, and there's no way I'm letting her walk out of here until I have answers."

"You don't even know if she's actually involved."

"You've seen the tapes," I argued. "You saw who she was with."

"But she didn't leave with them. They parted ways."

"And all that proves is that the job was over."

"Then let me talk to her," he said quickly.

"Not a chance in hell. This one's mine."

The door swung open and Lock strolled in. "Who's the chick in the lobby?" he asked, shutting the door behind him.

"A suspected terrorist," I answered, ready to get this show on the road.

"She was caught on video leaving the research facility," Dash filled him in.

"Oh, that chick. So, what's she doing here?"

Dash sighed. "He put Betty on the pedestal."

Lock's face dropped. "Oh fuck. The pedestal? Really, boss?"

"I'm just doing what I have to do."

"You don't have to do this. She doesn't deserve to be interrogated unless you're sure."

"I am."

"You've known her all of five seconds," Dash pointed out. "Can't you try the easier route?"

I grinned at him, walking over to my safe. "This is the easier route." I unlocked it and pulled out a few of my favorite interrogation devices, shoving them in my pockets.

"Boss, if you take her down there, and she knows nothing, you'll be torturing an innocent woman," Lock pointed out.

I cocked my head at him. "Who said anything about torturing? We're just going to have a little chat."

Dash tried again. "Yeah, after you put Betty on the pedestal. We all fucking know what that means."

"Besides, we were given strict instructions from Rafe. Do you really want to take this up with the alphabets? We could lose the whole goddamn business by going against the alphabets."

"It's not a problem," I said, shoving my knife into the sheath.

"Yeah, because you apparently have some relationship with this Rafe guy, one that none of the rest of us know."

"Are you saying you don't trust me?" I asked Lock. "Should I be looking for a new team leader?"

"Of course, we trust you, and don't ever threaten my fucking job again. I just think you're too close to this. You don't need to interrogate her to get information from her. She just needs to be talked to like a lady."

I nodded my head from side to side in thought. "I can be charming when I want to be."

"Sure, when you're talking to Sally."

"Hey, leave my girl out of this."

"Boss, the only good relationship with a woman that you've ever had is with that rifle. And you killed people with that. I'm not sure Sally is going to be much help right now."

"Women are all the same, Dash. They get feisty and locked up sometimes. You just have to give them a good rubdown and clean them up, make them feel special."

"Are you really comparing seducing a woman to cleaning your rifle?"

"It's the same principle," I said, trying my best not to roll my eyes at the man.

"It's not the same at all. I guarantee, if you go out there and treat her like you treat Sally, this is going to end with you in prison and me coming to visit you once a month. And you'll have a big friend named Greaser, who will make sure *you* get treated just like Sally. When was the last time you had a rub down?"

Alright, he might have a point there. "Fine, I won't treat her like Sally."

He scoffed, walking away from me. "You and your women. One of these days, you'll find a real woman to keep you safe."

"It's the other way around," I argued. "I keep them safe."

"Then why do you kiss them and worship the ground they walk on?" he asked as he yanked the door open.

"Dash," I called out to him. "I want a folder on the desk right away."

He rolled his eyes at me and walked out of the room. I followed him into the hallway and motioned for Beth to come with me. Now that I had her in the building, I just had to get her to willingly follow me downstairs.

"So, these are the offices. We take care of these on our own, so you won't need to clean these."

"Where does this door lead?" she asked, pointing at the one I just passed.

"Oh, that's the medic room." Best not to let her in there either. "We take care of that one, too."

I shoved the stairwell door open and headed downstairs. "Down here is the training center, along with the locker rooms. Everyone comes and goes at all hours, so you won't have a lot of luck during the day."

"And this one?" she asked, pointing to our interrogation room.

I glanced at the interrogation room door just as Fox walked out of the training center with Dash and Lock. "Why don't I show you?"

I stepped forward just as Dash ran over to me, inserting himself between me and the door. "Hey, boss. I was just talking with Mark. He needs you upstairs."

"It can wait," I said, stepping past him.

"Rafe is on the phone," he added quickly. "Something about an update on the situation." His eyes flicked to Beth's for just a moment. I knew he was stalling, but if Rafe really was on the phone and I ignored him, I could be missing vital intel.

"Fine," I took a step back. "I'll be right back." Turning to Beth, I gave her a trusting smile. "I'll only be a minute."

She nodded as I turned on my heel and headed upstairs. I was prepared to walk into that room and find out that this was all a ploy to get me away from Beth, but when I walked inside, Mark waved me over, handing me the phone.

"Cash," I barked.

"About fucking time. Don't you have a working phone on you?"

"We're still in the dark ages here."

"Not from what I heard. Get a fucking phone and keep it on you."

I huffed out a laugh. "I wasn't aware you were into sharing information now."

"Listen to me," he said sternly. "Grady isn't behind this."

"I could have fucking told you that," I retorted.

"Then why didn't you?"

"Oh, I don't know. You didn't seem too interested in sharing information."

"Goddamnit, Cash! This is fucking serious."

"I'm aware of that, which is why I have someone in custody right fucking now."

"What are you talking about?"

"The graphite bomb that was set off was only a distraction."

"For what?"

"If you want to know, you have to include me in this investigation. I'm not playing second fiddle when I'm the one with all the information."

I knew he didn't want to play this my way, but he didn't have a choice if he wanted answers. "I can't get down there for two days."

"Then I'll continue as planned and you can catch up when you get here," I said, hanging up the phone.

I walked downstairs, but Beth wasn't outside the interrogation room like I thought. I heard raucous laughter coming from inside the training room and shoved the doors open. Fox was stuck in a climbing rope after what I deduced was another one of his experiments. Lock and Dash were laughing with him, and a few of the other guys had joined him.

"Beth!" I shouted just a tad too loudly.

She jumped, spinning on her heel to face me. Her face was red as she scurried back over to me. The rest of the guys were glaring at me, a few of them shaking their heads at me.

"We should continue with our tour."

"Sure."

I glared at each of them as I turned and guided her back through the door and over to the interrogation room. Opening the door, she stiffened immediately when she saw the table and chairs. Stepping right up behind her, I gave her no choice but to walk inside.

"What is this?" she asked, turning on me and backing away.

"I want to ask you a few questions."

"This is not why you said you were bringing me here."

"I lied," I said smoothly. "Just as I'm guessing you are."

"What…what are you talking about?" she shook her head in confusion.

"I'm talking about the fact that you're hiding information, things that I need to know, and I'm going to find out what that is."

"I—"

"I don't have time for lies, Beth. You either know exactly what you're doing, or you've gotten yourself wrapped up in something that could get you killed. Either way, I don't give a shit. I need information, and you're going to give it to me."

My sat phone rang and I pulled it out, glancing at Beth quickly. "I'll just be a moment." Turning away from her, I took the call.

"Boss, your girl is a ghost."

"Really? Why does that not surprise me?" I asked, looking back at Beth, who looked absolutely terrified.

"I've run her name and even talked to the research facility. She gave the name Beth Williams, but there's not a single hit on her name. I've checked all the databases, online and all social media. She doesn't have a presence on any of them. And there are a ton of Beth Williams out there, but none that match her age or profile in any way. If Beth Williams is really her name, she's going to great lengths to keep it a secret. You need to find out why."

"I intend to," I said, just before hanging up.

I walked over to the table and pulled out a chair, sitting down as I motioned for her to do the same. She hesitantly took a seat, shifting uncomfortably beside me. "So, Beth…can I call you that?"

"What else would you call me?" she retorted, her gaze flicking around uncomfortably.

I leaned back in my chair, taking a casual approach to the interview for the moment. We'd get to her involvement in a minute. For now, I wanted to know who I was dealing with.

"I just got a call from Rae. You remember her, right? She was the one that worked with you at the gym."

She gave a stiff nod.

"She says that Beth Williams doesn't exist."

"How did you—" She said quickly, cutting herself off before she said too much.

"How did I get your name? Rae got it from your previous employer. It's strange that you gave him the same excuse you gave me, that you lost your ID and you were in the process of getting it. It's strange how that worked out for you."

"I don't understand why you're asking me these things. I don't know anything!"

I nodded, then grabbed the folder I'd asked Dash to leave on the desk before I went in search of Beth. Opening it up, I spun it around to show the photos of her leaving the research facility with five hulking men.

"Do you recognize these men?"

Her face paled, but she quickly averted her eyes. Her breathing sped up and her hand rubbed at her wounded shoulder. She was definitely nervous.

"Look a little closer at them."

I spread the photos out, all of them zoomed in on the faces of the men she walked out of the building with, and one that was farther away, but still clearly her.

"See, in this one, you seem pretty close with this man. What was his name?"

Her eyes flicked back to his face, but she refused to say anything. But she studied the photo, her eyes taking in every last detail. Something about this man was the key to everything that was happening.

"I don't know who they are," she finally said.

"Really? You're walking out of the building with them."

"I walk out of a lot of buildings at the same time as other people."

"Yes, but this man has his hand on the small of your back. I don't know many strangers that touch so intimately. Who is he?" I asked, tapping his face with my finger.

"I don't know," she nearly shouted.

"Then tell me why you were with them in the middle of the night. The whole building was shut down aside from the cleaning crew, yet you walked out with them."

Her mouth opened, then shut quickly.

"I know you went your separate ways after you left. Was the job over?"

"Job?" She finally looked up at me, her eyes pinched in confusion. "What are you talking about?"

"You tell me. The power goes out in the city. This building is on a backup generator, yet it never came on. Then you walk out of this building with five men, and let's face it, none of them are good guys. So, why were you with them?"

"I wasn't with them," she reiterated. "It's just a picture. It doesn't tell you anything!"

I leaned forward, a smirk on my face. "Actually, it tells me a lot. I can tell from these photos by your stance that you're very uncomfortable. You're waiting to get away from them." I pulled out a photo that I hadn't yet shown her. She was at the end of the block, but I could see her peeking around the corner looking at them. "And this one tells me that you wanted to make sure they left. Why?"

"I don't know what you're getting at."

"Why did you need to make sure they left? Did you have someone else to report to?"

"No," she said incredulously. "I didn't know any of them!"

I slammed my hand down on the table, getting angrier by the second. "Then tell me what you were doing with them!"

"I was just in the building! I cleaned the third floor. That's it," she said, her voice shaking. "One of them got stuck in an elevator with me when the power went out."

I watched her carefully, then pulled out the photo of her with the man that touched her. "This man?" She swallowed hard, her eyes locked on his face. "What's so important about this man?"

"Nothing," she said quietly. "He…he was in the elevator with me and he kept me calm. That's all that happened."

I narrowed my eyes at her, leaning back in my seat as I assessed her. Part of her story was true. I could see it in her eyes, but the rest of her body language screamed that she was holding back. She blinked too often, and her fingers pulled at the hem of her shirt. She bit her lip like she was trying to hold something back. She definitely knew this man, and she was protecting him. But why?

"Who is he to you?"

"I just met him that night. I swear."

"Why do I not believe you?"

Something washed over her at that moment. Her spine stiffened and she finally met my eyes. She was shutting down. "I don't care what you believe or don't believe. I don't know that man or any of the rest of them. I met them that night, we walked out together, and I went home."

"Then why did you stop and stare at them?"

She faltered for just a moment, but then resigned herself to holding firm. "I want to go home."

"Well, that's just too damn bad. You're involved in a domestic terror threat, and until you provide proof otherwise, you're not going anywhere."

I stood and walked out the door, slamming it behind me.

24

BETH

I was stupid to follow him here, to think that he could protect me. And now he was accusing me of being part of some domestic terror threat. I paced the small room, chewing my nails as I tried to figure out what I was going to do. I briefly thought about telling them what I knew about the men, but wouldn't that make me complicit? I had followed them around the building. I knew they were bad men, yet I didn't do a thing about it. And when my boss wanted more information, I didn't tell him either.

The problem was, my boss was hiding something too. Maybe it was sensitive information that he didn't want getting out, but I couldn't be sure. Every person I ran into seemed to want something from me, and I couldn't figure out which was the right side to be on.

The door swung open and another man walked inside, the same man that got himself tangled in the ropes of the training center. "Ma'am," he said, tipping his imaginary hat.

I stared at him warily. He was smiling at me, and that made me uneasy. Was he here to kill me? I stepped away from him, sure I was about to be killed. "What do you want?"

"Me?" he asked, pointing to himself. "I'm just here to break you out."

I looked past him to the door, sure this was some kind of a joke. "You're going to let me walk out of here?"

"Oh, hell no. It wouldn't do any good anyway. Cash knows where you live. He'd only drag you back here."

"Then how are you breaking me out? You're going to put me on a bus or something?"

He shook his head, chuckling slightly. "Nope, not that either. Trust me, I'd like to see you run, but I'm afraid that would get my ass in trouble. However, I can show you some nicer accommodations."

"No, thanks," I spat, not liking the idea that I'd be sent to some other room that was just like this one, a prison.

"Are you sure? I've got food and drinks…movies," he smiled, his eyes twinkling.

I couldn't figure out this man. He looked kind of psycho. With dark hair and this half-serious, half-deadly look, I couldn't figure out if he was a good guy or a bad guy. He wasn't as big as some of the other guys around here. He was lean and muscled for sure, but something about the glint in his eyes led me to believe that he had pent-up aggression that was simmering under the surface, ready to be unleashed.

"What's your name again?"

"Fox," he grinned.

"What's your last name?"

"Don't have one," he answered with a shrug.

"So, you're like Cher or Madonna?"

He actually looked offended by that. "I would actually consider myself more like Liberace."

Liberace…Where did this guy come up with this stuff?

"Come on," he almost sang. "You know you want to do this."

"I actually think I'd prefer to stay here."

"In this cold room with the hard chairs?" He glanced over his shoulder quickly. "Look, I've got the perfect place for us to hide out. No one will think to look for you there."

"And why would I go with you? Being with you doesn't make me any safer."

"Honey, I could kill anyone that even tried to get next to you."

"Which means you could also kill me or do other…things."

He tossed his head back and laughed. "That's a good one."

"What is?"

"That I would do other things to you."

Now it was my turn to be slightly offended, though I wasn't sure why. "That means you'd still kill me."

Quirking an eyebrow at me, he turned the tables on me. "Are you a terrorist?"

"No."

"Have you ever helped a terrorist?"

"Not knowingly."

He shrugged. "Then I have no reason to kill you. That is, unless you're planning to kill me. Are you some secret assassin?"

I thought of my bum arm and laughed. "I wish I could claim that."

He watched me thoughtfully for a moment. "Well, we'll get to that one, but first things first. We need a TV, popcorn, Reese's Pieces, and someplace comfy to sit."

"You make it sound like we're going to the movies."

"Only the best. I'm telling you, you're gonna love this," he said, his grin stretching across his face, once again making me feel like the danger lurked inside him.

He walked over to the door and peeked outside before waving me over. I was conflicted about going with him. This could very well be a trap. There was every possibility that he had some other reason for wanting me out of this room. I was constantly getting myself into bad situations with men. Why couldn't I find a gaggle of women to hang out with? But if I stayed, I would be alone for hours or longer. I was hungry, and while popcorn wasn't the most appealing thing when I was so hungry, I couldn't deny that, at this point, anything would do.

As he walked out into the hall, I followed, keeping my distance from him. He instantly pulled me right behind him, almost as if he was hiding my body with his. We crept down the hallway until he led me to a second set of stairs that was hidden in a dark corner of the basement. Following him up the stairs, I kept looking behind me, thinking I would see someone chasing after us at some point.

When we got to the top, he motioned me to follow him down a

series of hallways. I had no idea where we were. This definitely wasn't anywhere near the main entrance. Cash hadn't said anything about this on his tour, and when Fox opened the door, I realized why. It was a bedroom.

"These are my private quarters."

"You live here?"

"Hell no," he scoffed. "But sometimes we work jobs that require some of us to be on standby. Technically, it's not just mine, but nobody wants to share with me."

"Why?" I asked, not sure that I wanted the answer to that question.

"Well, they all think I'm psycho," he said with a sadistic smile.

"Are you?"

He cocked his head to the side. "Why don't you spend some time with me, and I'll let you make up your own mind."

"That doesn't sound like something I want to do."

"Well, you could always go back to the interrogation room. However, this room has a nice bed. And let me tell you, it's a really comfy bed—big enough for both of us."

"I'm not sharing a bed with you," I said quickly, the thought making shivers roll over my body. I squeezed my eyes closed and pushed out the images, just like I'd done a hundred times before.

"No problem. The chair is just as comfy. Now, you stay here while I get the snacks."

He headed for the door, just leaving me behind. "How do you know I won't run?"

"Well...you could, but you'd most likely end up shot. Everyone knows you're here, and if you run, they won't hesitate to pull the trigger."

That didn't make me feel any calmer. In fact, it scared the shit out of me. "Then you can't leave me here! If one of them walks in, they'll assume I tried to escape!"

"To a comfy room with a bed? I don't think so. But, on the off chance that this becomes a problem, just tell them Fox brought you here. That should solve the problem."

Without another word, he walked out of the room, leaving me all alone. I hugged my arms to my chest, wondering what to do now. I didn't feel safe here, but strangely, this was preferable to my own apartment. Moving to the corner of the room, I slid down the wall, tucking my legs up against my chest.

Even though my heart was pounding and my mind was on the verge of breaking down, this was not the worst situation I'd been in, and that brought me some comfort. When five minutes later, the door opened again, I found myself ducking down further, hoping to escape notice.

"If you were hoping to hide from me, you should have chosen a better spot. The first place I would look is the most obvious choice."

Slowly rising from my spot, I tried not to let his build and dark, gleaming eyes frighten me. "Where would you suggest I hide?" I asked.

"Behind the door, of course," he said as if I was stupid.

"Then again, I would suspect that too."

I huffed in frustration as he walked over to me, handing me a bucket of popcorn. "You know, I think you might be one of the most infuriating people I've ever met."

He grinned widely at me. "Give it time. You might find someone worse than me."

"Like your boss?" I asked before thinking better of it.

His brows pinched together in thought. "Well…I suppose some might say he is."

"What would *you* say?"

"I'd say Cash is the most calculating guy I know. He's always thinking ten steps ahead. His instincts are very unlikely to be wrong, with the rare exception," he said, nodding to me.

"You believe me?"

He plopped down on the bed, kicking his feet up, not bothering to take off his shoes. "I believe you weren't involved, but lady, you have more secrets than the CIA."

Pursing my lips, I continued to stare at his boots. "Your shoes are on the bed."

He glanced down, then looked up at me in surprise. "What do ya know? They are!"

"You don't have to be an ass."

"It's my bed. I can do what I want. Besides, you should never take off your shoes. It makes it harder to run from the baddies."

I shook my head at that, trying to make heads or tails of what he just said. "You never take off your shoes?"

"Well, everyone has to change their socks."

"But…you always sleep with them on?"

He rolled his head on the pillow, looking over at me. "Why? Do you think that's weird?"

"Don't your feet hurt? You never let them breathe."

"I suppose I could always poke some holes in them."

"What about when you take a shower?"

He shrugged. "They dry eventually."

I couldn't figure this guy out. He had to be messing with me. "What are baddies?"

"Bad guys," he said slowly. "I thought that was self-explanatory."

"Not to me," I grumbled.

He passed me some pop. "Drink, you need the sugar to keep you level."

"Sugar hypes you up," I pointed out.

"Right, but you've been through an interrogation. You're scared, or you were until I came along and charmed the crap out of you," he grinned. "Now that you're feeling a little safer, the adrenaline is going to crash down and you're going to wish you had some sugar in your system."

I couldn't exactly argue with that statement, so I grabbed the drink and sucked on the straw. Surprisingly, it did make me feel better.

"Here, have some Reese's Pieces with it. Breakfast of champions."

"Candy?"

"Not just any candy. Reese's Pieces is the end all, be all of the candy world, much like M & Ms."

"Because they're small?" I asked. That was the only correlation I saw.

"Because they're—" He glanced over at me and snorted. "First of all, you get more in this bag than in any candy bar. See, the way I see it, a candy bar is gone in a few bites, but with Reese's, you tend to eat them slower, savoring the little bits of goodness. Therefore, it lasts longer and makes the overall enjoyment better."

I took the bag from him. "Oddly, that makes sense."

"Of course it does. I said it. Now, what are we going to watch?"

"Uh, anything but a disaster movie. Or a bang, bang movie."

He rolled his head toward me again and grinned. "I like the way you think." He pulled the gun from the small of his back and set it on the nightstand. "This is loaded with pew pews, so don't think about touching it. I don't want my brains shot out."

"And pew pews are bullets?" I guessed.

"See? You're getting the hang of it. We'll make you into an agent yet."

"No thanks," I muttered under my breath. "I just want to get out of here and live my life like a normal person. If that was possible."

He looked at me strangely, then turned on the TV and flipped through his video catalog. It had been so long since I'd seen something like this. In all the places I stayed, I watched whatever the antennae allowed, which usually wasn't much.

"Ah, here we go."

The cursor landed on *Oklahoma*. I glanced over at him, sure he was joking. "What is this?"

"*Oklahoma*. Don't tell me you've never seen it."

"I have, but what I don't understand is why *you've* seen it."

"It's a classic. I've seen this at least ten times on the stage."

I gaped at the man laying beside me. How could a man like this, who looked like he killed people for fun, go to the theater? I scooted a little further on the bed.

"What was the last show you saw?"

"*White Christmas*. I dragged Cash to it," he grinned. "Yeah, he pretended not to like it, but I caught him singing along in the truck on the way home."

"Seriously?"

"Yep," he laughed. "What about you? Last show you ever saw?"

I shook my head. "I never went."

His jaw dropped in shock. "Never? That's terrible. Didn't your mom ever try to take you to one?"

I shoved some candy in my mouth to avoid answering his question, but the weight of his stare told me he wasn't turning on the movie until he had an answer.

"Let's just say my mother wasn't exactly a great mother. There were no theaters—movie or otherwise—and the only reason I saw Oklahoma was because I had to spend the night at my friend's house whenever she had over—"

I shut my mouth, almost forgetting for a minute where I was. Fox wasn't my friend, even if he was pretending to be. Whatever this was, Cash probably sent him in here to soften me up. I was nothing more than a tool he needed, just like with Adam.

"Are we going to watch this or not?" I asked, sitting back against the pillows.

"The first one that sings along has to sleep in the chair," he said, not bothering to face me.

"That should be easy since you love musicals so much."

"Ah, but I have a high pain tolerance."

"What does pain have to do with this?"

He shook his head like I was stupid. "Because it's literally painful for me to not sing along. I thought that was obvious."

This was going to be a long night. He started the movie, which I hadn't seen in a long time. It wasn't hard for me not to sing along because I hardly remembered any of it. But I was instantly lost in the music, almost like I was in another reality. One in which I had a boyfriend and this was a regular Friday night for us. We'd be snuggled up in bed as a movie played. We'd eat popcorn and laugh at the movie, and everything would be perfectly normal.

I was so wrapped up in the movie that I hadn't realized I moved to the end of the bed, laying on my belly and watching intently as Judd tried to burn Curly to death on a haystack. I sipped the last of my Coke, sad when it was all gone. I sat up in excitement when Judd died, thinking of a few people I'd like to give the same treatment.

"This is my favorite part," Fox said, sitting on the edge of the bed with me. "Come on, sing with me."

"I don't remember the words," I laughed.

"It's not hard. It's literally a song about Oklahoma. You can spell, right?"

He started singing along, making me laugh. He even sang the women's parts, pitching his voice for every line. Then he motioned when it was my turn to start singing.

"This is it!"

I started singing along with him, watching his lips to try and catch the words. Before too long, I was catching on, singing and laughing along with him. I was having so much fun, laughing when he rewound it for us to sing again and again. I was actually getting pretty good at it.

He grabbed me by the arm, linking mine through his. He shouted each letter, drawing out the last word with a grin, testing me to see if I could hold out Oklahoma as long as him. We both shouted, pumping our fists in the air before we fell back onto our backs on the mattresses, laughing hysterically.

"Christ, Fox got to her," I heard from the doorway, sitting up immediately. Cash stood there with Dash, both of them staring at me, almost in disappointment. Then they shut the door and walked out. I turned to Fox, wondering what to do now.

"Again?"

25

CASH

"I'm telling you, she's not guilty," Fox said as he followed me into my office.

"Why? Because she sang show tunes with you?" I snorted, sitting down at my desk.

"Well, yeah, for one thing."

I rubbed at the bridge of my nose. My head was pounding, and I was going to lose my shit soon if I didn't figure out what the connection was between that building and Grady. So far, I was getting nothing from Rafe. I even tried calling Rae, but she also came up with nothing.

"Give me a better reason than she sang 'Oklahoma' with you."

He rolled his eyes at me. "Like you need a better reason? Serial killers don't sing show tunes while they plot to kill someone."

"You do," I pointed out.

He frowned, "Right, well, I'm not a serial killer, so I don't count. I mean really baddies."

"Right, like terrorists. They aren't allowed to sing show tunes."

"Exactly!" he said, pointing at me like I finally solved the DaVinci code. "I'm telling you, no woman is going to work with a terrorist and then sit around singing musicals with me."

"Yes, she would if she wanted to appear innocent."

"Alright, then tell me about her background," he challenged me.

"I can't. I don't know who the fuck she is. She's a ghost."

"Yes, but while you were playing the mean boss that wants to tear her to shreds, I actually talked to her like a person."

"Since when?" I asked accusingly.

"Since I know she's innocent. Hey, I can be just as mean as the next guy, but I can smell the innocence on her."

I pinched the bridge of my nose, shaking my head. "Don't…don't say shit like that. It just sounds wrong."

"I'm telling you, this woman is running and scared, but it's not because of some terrorist plot. She's wrapped up in something else. She practically let it slip last night that she was abused as a kid. I'm telling you, she's not the person you're looking for."

I looked up at him sharply. "She told you that?"

"Not in so many words. Let's just say I've seen it enough to know the signs. You've seen it too, which is why I'm wondering why the fuck you're holding her like a damn prisoner."

"Because she is a prisoner. There's something you need to get through your head, Fox. She was at a suspected crime scene at the same time as a terrorist attack. Until she's cleared, I'm not letting her go. This isn't about a stolen purse or some Xboxes going missing."

"Then let me talk to her—or have one of the other guys."

"This is my job."

"This is all of our jobs. We're all qualified. Hell, I would go so far as to say Red has more experience in interrogation than you. It is sort of what he did."

I hated it when he was right. I really should have had Red in there from the start, not only because he's a damn good interrogator, but because I was too close to this from the start.

"Fine, get him down there. I'll be on the other side of the mirror."

He grinned at me when he stood. "See? I knew you'd do the right thing."

"Where is she anyway?"

"She passed out after the second time I made her watch *Oklahoma*."

"Fox," I stopped him as he turned to go. "Just remember that she's not your buddy. She's a suspect, and you need to treat her that way."

"I have my priorities in order. Maybe you need to check yours."

As he walked out the door, I stared at Betty for a moment, then picked her up and put her in my pocket to remind myself not to go crazy on the witness in the interrogation room. I called Rae again, hoping she had some intel for me.

"Your ears must have been burning," she answered immediately.

"That must mean you have something."

"On your company? Yes, but not on the girl. Sorry, there's nothing there."

Putting that aside, I'd deal with the first problem since it was the most important. "Alright, what did you find out about the company?"

"Well, it was originally started by Adam Hayes and Evan Whitlock. Adam is currently the sole owner of the company."

"Did he buy out Whitlock?"

"No, he was killed in a car accident five years ago. According to police reports, he fell asleep driving home after a late night of work. Hayes gave a bunch of money to the family, essentially buying out Whitlock's half of the business."

"That was generous of him."

"Well, without doing that, Hayes would have always been under the thumb of someone else in the family."

"What about the rest of Whitlock's family? What are they doing now?"

"They moved to Texas to live near her parents. She's remarried now with two more kids. Her husband is an investor."

"How long after Whitlock died did she remarry?"

"Um…a year," she said, almost surprised.

"She didn't need the money. Why remarry so soon after losing her husband?"

"I would guess that she's one of those women that doesn't like to be alone. Based on her social media profiles, it doesn't look like she's ever been alone for long."

I wasn't sure why that was bothering me, but right now, it didn't matter. I'd dig into it later. "What about the company? How is it doing?"

"It's in good financial standing. Most of their research is pretty well undocumented."

"What does that mean?"

"It means that they list a bunch of bullshit about what they do to keep their business sounding legit, but there's no actual information on what specific projects they're doing."

"So, we could be dealing with anything."

"Basically."

"Thanks, Rae. Let me know if you come up with anything else."

I hung up and headed into the hallway, meeting up with Red along the way.

"So, you're having me interrogate a woman."

"Yep."

"How far do you want me to go?"

I hesitated for a minute, not sure what to tell him. That part of me that remembered how scared she was at the gym told me not to push too hard, but the investigator in me said that I needed to have him push because we needed every last detail.

"Do whatever your gut tells you."

He nodded and opened the door to the interrogation room as I walked past, into the room beside it. Fox was already in there waiting for me with a bucket of popcorn, his chair tilted back as his foot rested on the ledge in front of him.

"Seriously?"

"What? I think this is going to be very interesting."

Sighing, I sat down beside him and dug my hand into the bucket. "I think you're going to be disappointed." I tossed the popcorn in my mouth as I watched Red take a seat across from Beth.

"Beth, my name is Red. I need to ask you a few questions."

"He's going for the sympathetic route," I commented.

"See? He doesn't think she's guilty either," Fox said proudly.

"Or he's trying to gain her trust."

"I know Cash has already been in here to ask you a few questions, but there are some things we need to clarify before we let you go."

"See? Sympathetic," I grinned.

"Nah, he's just signaling to you that he's not holding her."

I rolled my eyes and continued to watch.

"This man," Red pointed to the picture. "Can you tell me anything about him?"

She pulled at her shirt, clearly uncomfortable. "Like I told Cash, I don't know anything. We were stuck in the same building at the same time."

"In the elevator," Red nodded.

"Right."

"And you said you climbed out through the top of the elevator."

"That's right. That man helped me out because my shoulder was hurt."

Red nodded again. "Do you remember what floor you got out on?"

"Three. We were stopped just below it. His…friends pried the doors open."

"Not friends," I muttered. "She was scared of them."

"Which should tell you she's innocent," Fox retorted.

"Unless she was working with them because she had to."

"I know that night was scary for you, so I won't drag you through too much of it. I've been stuck in an elevator before, so I know what it's like."

"Again," I said to Fox, "he's sympathizing with her."

"No, that's a true story, man. I was there. Of course, he was hanging from the cables and I was laughing my ass off at him, but same shit."

"That's not at all like being stuck in the elevator," I snapped.

"For this purpose, it is."

"Which is why I said he was sympathizing with her," I practically yelled, getting frustrated with the man. Then I heard something and leaned forward. It sounded like music was playing somewhere. "What is that?"

"Oh, I had the soundtrack from *Oklahoma* play on repeat in the room since before she walked in."

"For what purpose?"

He sat up, his chair settling flat on the ground. "To put her at ease, of course. I laid the groundwork for you. I got her comfortable and found something that would make her feel relaxed. She's more likely to tell us what's going on if she's not ready to shit her pants."

I tuned in again to Red. "So, just so I have an approximate on how hard the power outage hit, about what time was it when you got in the elevator?"

"Um…maybe ten o'clock?"

"Ten o'clock," he muttered, going over his notes. "And how many floors did you go up?"

She frowned, not understanding the leading question. "Almost three."

"So, you were in the basement when you got on the elevator."

"Yes, I had just filled up my cart."

He slowly looked up at her. Fox and I both leaned forward, finally getting somewhere with this woman.

"So, the man got on the elevator with you from the basement."

Her mouth opened, but she didn't say anything.

"Beth, there's no entrance down there besides a fire exit. So, why were five men down there with you?"

"I didn't say—"

"The man got on the elevator with you. You went up three floors. If he had joined you on a different level, you would have said the elevator stopped and he got on. Why were you hiding that from us?"

"I wasn't," she said quickly. "I just didn't remember. I was scared and—"

"Because of the power outage, or because a large man got on the elevator with you, purposely leaving the rest of his group behind?"

"Now we're getting somewhere," I said quietly. "Still think she's innocent?"

"Beth, you let those men into the building, didn't you?"

"No!"

"How else would they have gotten in? Why would five men be hanging out in the basement? There are no offices down there. We've seen the layout of the building."

"I don't know," she rushed out. "I swear, I…they were just there."

"And you didn't let them in? Come on, Beth. How else would they have gotten in?"

"They had badges," she said quickly. "Employee badges."

"All of them?"

"Yes! I swear."

He nodded again. "And you trusted this man," he pointed to the man in the picture with her. "He made you feel safe with the other men around."

She bit her lip, nodding slightly.

"Why?"

"Because he was being nice?" she responded.

"Men like him don't make people feel nice. Men like him don't give a shit about a woman in an elevator. So, you'd better tell me why he was so nice to you. Was he on your team? Was he supposed to be there?"

"Oh, man," Fox scoffed. "That's just mean. He's tricking her."

"He's getting answers out of her."

"He was nice to me on the elevator," she finally answered. "I don't...I don't like tight spaces or being that close to men. And I couldn't see him."

Her voice was pitching, like she was reliving the experience. Her eyes were wide and her breathing was uneven. She was close to having a panic attack. Fuck, I had this all wrong. She had nothing to do with it. She was a woman trapped in an elevator.

"They sent the man with her to take her out," Fox muttered. "They needed to make sure there were no witnesses."

I agreed. "But why did they leave her alive?"

Red tapped at the picture again. "What happened in that elevator, Beth?"

"Nothing," she shook her head. "He talked to me, helped me through the panic attack."

"And when the friends showed up?"

She hung her head, almost like she was ashamed. "He was going to leave me. I called out for him."

"What was his name?"

I didn't think she was going to tell us, but then she whispered, "Seth. That's all I know. No one else said any names."

"And when you got out, they didn't try to hurt you or threaten you?"

She shook her head. "No, but it was clear that I wasn't going anywhere without them."

"And did you see anything?"

She shook her head again. "We walked out of the building and I turned away from them. I kept thinking they were going to come after me, but…"

"Seth saved you," Red finished. "Why didn't you tell us this before?"

A tear slipped down her cheek and she quickly swiped it away. "Doesn't that make me complicit or something?"

"No," Red sighed. "Give me a minute."

He shoved his chair back and walked out of the room. A moment later, he was swinging the door open and strolling in.

"Yeah, I got it," I answered before he could beat me to it.

"And to think, you almost went full-on Betty on the woman."

I pinched the bridge of my nose, blowing out a harsh breath. "Fuck. She's still involved."

"Let it go, boss," Red shook his head. "She was there, an innocent bystander. She was unlucky enough to be caught in the elevator with the dude, but lucky enough to get out with her life. She lied because she's terrified. You don't know what they said to her. They could have threatened her life."

"I know!" I snapped, pissed at myself for ignoring my initial instincts about her, all because I was hell-bent on catching a terrorist. That's how lives were ruined. "Fox, take her home."

"What about the job? Not gonna offer for her to keep it?" he grinned.

"Yeah, I can see her coming back here now. Just make sure she gets inside and she's safe."

He stood and clapped me on the shoulder. "Will do, boss. Do you want to talk to her before I take her home?"

"What for?"

"Oh, I don't know. To apologize. To tell her what a gigantic asshole you are." He shrugged. "Something along those lines, but don't rely on me to tell you what to say. Just speak from the heart."

I rolled my eyes at him and stood, shoving my way past Red and Fox. Walking into the interrogation room, I knew they were watching, using this against me in all future meetings I would have with any woman. Beth was leaning back in her chair, her arms crossed over her chest.

"I want to apologize for taking up so much of your time. After much consideration, we've determined that you're not a threat."

Her eyes slowly raised to meet mine. I expected relief or something similar, but all I saw was anger. She stood, not bothering to speak even a single word to me. Her eyes flicked to the door, and then she moved, walking right past me without so much as a mutter of disapproval. Red walked in afterward, his hands shoved in his pockets as he watched me.

"It could have happened to anyone, boss."

"I was so sure she was involved."

"Yeah, I think you saw what you wanted to."

"What's that supposed to mean?" I asked, my gaze snapping to meet his.

"It means you like that chick, and when you saw her on the footage, you let your mind put her in a box so you didn't have to deal with her."

"That doesn't even make any sense."

"Of course it does. You put all your women in a box."

"I do not."

He quirked an eyebrow at me. "Betty is in your pocket, and Sally is in your rifle case. Tell me I'm wrong."

I held in my frustrations until he walked out of the room, and then I slammed my fist into the wall. Some protector I was. I just scared the shit out of a woman who was already terrified for unknown reasons. And worse, I didn't have the time to dig into her any further because I had other shit to deal with. Fucking Rafe and his stupid ideas.

26

FOX

"You knew!" she spat as she walked away from me in the parking lot.

"Hold on," I shouted, gripping her arm and spinning her, careful not to touch her injured side. "I knew you were innocent, which is why I put you in that room. Nothing good ever comes from hiding the truth."

"Oh yeah?" she asked, her eyes gleaming. "Why don't you tell me what you're hiding?"

"Like what? I'm an open book."

"Bullshit! We all have something we're hiding. You're just better at it than most. Am I really supposed to believe that you like watching musicals?"

"I do," I countered. "I happen to love them."

She scoffed, tossing her head back in laughter. It was the most unhinged I had seen her since she arrived at our building. "Tell yourself whatever you need to so you can sleep at night."

"And what about you? I know you're running from something. Fake name, no ID, scared to be in the room with any men, and that injury would have been set properly if you'd been to the doctor. I'm guessing it happened sometime in the last year, probably less since it hasn't made your arm go completely fucking numb yet."

"That's my business," she said as she turned away from me.

"The question is," I continued as if she was still standing in front of me. "Are you hiding anything else about the research facility? Or are you just running scared from whoever you got involved with? Or maybe it's your daddy you're running from."

She whirled on me, nearly punching me as she swung. "You know nothing about my life!" Tears brimmed her eyes as she stared at me, her lower lip quivering because she was on the verge of tears. But those tears were a good sign. She held it together well the entire time she was on the OPS property. The fact that she was falling apart hinted that just maybe she was beginning to trust me. If only I could prove to her that we could help her. Or better yet…that Cash could help her.

I knew he was beating himself up right now, dying to help her in any way he could. But his pride wouldn't allow him to go after her right now. He'd find some insane way to apologize later, but by then, it would be too late.

"Beth, I've been there," I said honestly. "You may not believe me, but I understand. I can help you."

She shook her head slightly. "After what you just put me through? I don't want your help. I don't want a damn thing from you."

She started walking down the street, but I wasn't having that. I got in my truck and pulled up alongside her. "Are you going to walk the whole way?"

"Yes," she said sharply.

"Alright. I'll just be right here."

She shot me an incredulous look. "Just leave me alone. Haven't you ruined enough of my life?"

I laughed at that. "Not even close. Trust me, when you're looking at me like I just ate monkey brains, then you'll know I've ruined your life. This is just a sampling."

I drove along beside her, turning on my favorite CD and cranking it up. "The Music Of The Night" from *The Phantom Of The Opera* started playing and I sang along, letting my voice carry through the night. Beth walked faster, trying to put some distance between us, but she was no match for my truck.

"Would you stop that?" she hissed.

"Sure, just get in the truck."

"I'm not getting in the truck."

"Then I'm not going to stop singing."

I turned the music up even louder and continued singing until she finally slapped her hand against my truck and glared at me. "Fine! I'll get in the truck, but you have to turn that off!"

I grinned and turned the music off, motioning for her to get in. In a huff, she opened the door, climbed inside, and slammed it behind her. "You're a jackass."

"I've been told, but I always get my way."

"Why are you even doing this?"

"Because we had a thing back there."

She glanced back at the building. "You think we had something?"

"Yeah, didn't you feel it? You and I…we were on the verge of something great. I'm telling you, just a few more songs and we could try out for a show."

"Wait, so you weren't talking about…"

"Sleeping with you?" I chuckled. "Sorry, honey, but you're already spoken for."

"By who?"

"By whom," I corrected. "Cash, of course."

"He hates me," she responded, crossing her arms over her chest. "Besides, he has a really shitty way of showing he cares if that's how he treats all his…women."

"Oh, that's par for the course. I mean, obviously, the situation is heightened, considering what's going on. His protective instincts are going haywire."

"Can we talk about something else? I really don't want to talk about your boss."

"Come on," I teased her. "You can tell me. I won't say a word. I was once held in a POW camp for four months. They wanted intel, and I wanted a glass of fucking water. Is that really too much to ask?"

"Did you tell them anything?"

I turned and grinned at her. "Why do you think I was there for four months? It wasn't because of my winning personality."

Her face pinched slightly as she watched me. "That must have been horrible."

I brushed it off. "Horrible is going to the barber, only to find out he's closed."

"That's worse?" she asked in disbelief.

"Hey, when you find a good barber, you don't let him go. Yeah, it turns out he died or something. Kind of rude, if you ask me. There was no warning that he was sick or anything."

"Did he have cancer or something?"

I looked at her funny. "No, died from a heart attack. Why?"

She shook her head. "Never mind."

I could tell I was getting to her, which was perfect for me. A few more minutes of my charms and I'd convince her to come back to OPS and give the boss another chance.

"Right over here." She pointed to the curb and was already unbuckling her seatbelt.

"Don't you want to grab some dinner or something?"

"I think I've had enough of you for a lifetime."

"That's just because I haven't grown on you yet. I'm like mold."

She pursed her lips, nodding slightly. "That's...I'm going home now."

She shoved the door open and got out. I would have followed her, but I was double parked, and there were no free spots anywhere in sight. And I fucking hated dealing with the police. Cash already warned me to stay away at all costs.

"When you get to your apartment, I want you to flick your lights twice if you're good. Three times if you're in distress."

"Why would I be in distress?"

I sighed heavily. "Are you ever going to do as I ask, or are you always going to argue with me?"

She slammed the door and shot me the finger. I chuckled as she walked to her building and went inside. I waited for her signal, tapping my fingers on the steering wheel as I waited for her. Flashing lights shone behind me.

"Shit," I muttered, watching as a cop got out and made his way over to me.

I glanced back at the apartment window, still waiting for the signal, but it never came.

"Fuck. I guess I'm going to have to deal with the cops after all."

A harsh rap on my window drew my attention away from the apartment. "Sir, you're double parked."

"Actually, I was just dropping off a friend and—"

"Sir, there are parking spots for you to use."

I narrowed my eyes at him. "You interrupted me. Do you know how rude that is?"

"I don't give a fuck if it's rude. You're double parked. Now move it, or I'll give you a ticket."

I waved at the crowded street in front of me. "Do you see any place for me to park?"

"I don't give a fuck what you do as long as you move from your current location."

"Fine, but I need to check on my friend first. She was supposed to let me know she was okay by flickering the lights, and she hasn't done that."

"Flickering the lights, huh? You could have just walked her to the door."

"Yes," I huffed. "I could have, but I was double parked, as you already pointed out. And if I had left my vehicle, I would have gotten a ticket."

"You're still getting one," he said snidely.

"Alright," I said, shoving my door open. The time to play nice was over. I had to get to Beth, wherever the hell she was.

"Sir, get back in your vehicle."

"No, you know what? I already told you my friend is in danger, and you're fucking ignoring me. That really pisses me off."

"Sir, I will tase you if you don't get back in your vehicle!"

"Oh, yeah, sure," I snorted. "I'd love to see you try." He pulled his taser and I held up my hands. "You're gonna want to think long and hard before you deploy that thing."

"Sir! Turn around and place your hands on the car!"

That's when I heard the scream that sent chills down my spine. The cop heard it, too. "Shit! That's her. I have to go."

"Put your hands on the car!"

"She's screaming for me," I argued.

I took a step forward just as he shot the taser. The electrical wires hit me right in the chest and stunned me, but I didn't go down. I yanked them out and grabbed his gun, shooting him with his own taser. "How do you like it, asshole?"

Tossing the taser on the ground, I took off for the building, racing around it just as I saw a trunk slammed shut and two men jumping into the car. I pulled my gun and fired multiple times, but I was too far away to stop them. I got a partial plate, but that was it. Pulling my cell, I dialed Cash.

"If you're calling to lecture me—"

"Black sedan. Partial plate XGV. Two men in dark clothes. Beth is in the trunk," I said as I headed back to my car.

"Fuck! How could you let this happen?"

"I was dealing with the cops."

"The…Fox, we talked about this," I heard him say right before he rattled off my information to someone else, probably Dash. "Where is the officer now?"

I ran up to my car, looking at the officer down. "Um…he's sort of on the ground."

"Why is he on the ground?" he asked slowly.

"Because I shot him with his taser." I booted his body as gently as possible away from my truck and got in.

"Fox…"

"Hey, he shot me first. It's not my fault he went down easier than me."

Slamming the door, I slammed my foot down on the gas, burning rubber as I took off after the car. Taking a hard right, I searched for the car, but it was nearly impossible when every fucking car in the area was black.

"Tell me you have something for me," I snapped. Fuck, I was angry with myself for not going in with her.

"Dash is trying to pull up the feed now, but there aren't a lot of cameras in the area. Head back here so we can put a plan together."

"Fuck that. I'll find them on my own."

"Fox, you're not going in alone. We don't even know who has her."

"Then I'll just keep driving around until I find them," I argued, knowing it was a stupid point. Still, she was my responsibility and I let her get taken.

"Fox, get your ass back here. That's an order."

"Yeah, I've never been too good at following those," I grinned right before I hung up.

27

CASH

"It's been two fucking hours," I growled at Dash. "Tell me you have something."

I was pacing the IT room, trying to keep my cool, but Betty was burning a hole in my pocket. I wasn't sure who was responsible for snatching her, but it could be literally anyone. That asshole she worked for was practically going out of his mind when I met him. Then there were the five men she walked out of the building with. God only knows who they worked for and what they wanted. And then there was the fact that she was on the run from someone. I should have dug into that further, but I put it off because I was too focused on the disaster I was currently working. Now Beth was in the wind, and I only had myself to blame.

"The last known location of the vehicle is fifty miles south of here. But that's taking us into the country, and there are literally a million different ways they could have taken her. Without knowing who took her and cross-referencing properties they own, I don't know how the fuck to find her."

"What about lo-jack?"

"Boss," he turned to me like I was stupid. "Trust me, I've thought of everything I possibly could. She's in the wind, and unless we find out who's behind it, we're fucked."

I started pacing the room again, trying to figure out a way around this. "Let's eliminate those we know about then. Have you had any luck identifying the men she walked out of the facility with?"

"A few possible hits, but not a positive identification yet."

"Any of them matching the name Seth?"

"Nope."

Sighing, there was only one choice. "Alright, what about the boss… Hayes?"

"Why would he take her?"

"I have no fucking clue, but he's the only other person connected to her that we know of. Either we eliminate him or connect him to her in some way. I want you staying here digging into all property he's connected to in any way. I'll grab a team and head out," I said as I rushed to the door.

"To where?"

I turned back to him as I pulled the door open. "To pay Hayes a visit."

I walked out and shouted at Eli, who was at the end of the hall. "Round everyone up. We're going hunting."

A sadistic grin twisted his lips as he nodded. "On it, boss."

I walked to my office and thought of putting Betty on the pedestal, but I always carried her with me on a mission. Instead, I walked to my personal gun safe and pulled out my rifle bag, grabbing extra ammo as I slung my case over my back. Checking the magazine on my pistol, I slammed it back into place and holstered it.

Walking back out, Eli's team followed by Thumper's, headed out the front doors to the parking lot. I watched the shadows as we moved to our vehicles, but I didn't notice anything out of place. Eli slid into the front seat beside me, handing me a comm as he slammed the door.

"Who are we hunting, boss?"

"Hayes."

"What did he do?"

"Other than be an asshole? I have no idea, but I'm about to find out. I need Red on this one."

He looked over at me and nodded, knowing what I was saying. Since Fox wasn't with me, there was no one I trusted more than Red to get to the bottom of what was happening. The drive over to the office didn't take long. I parked across the street and waited for everyone else to pull in. Eli pulled out his binoculars and scanned the building. It was running on backup power now, and I could see movement inside.

"What do we have?" I asked Eli.

"Third floor, two by the windows, and three on the top floor."

"Top floor," I said with a slight grin.

"Oh, man," he laughed. "Red's going to be pissed. You know he doesn't like that shit."

"But he'll do it." I finished wiring up my comms system as Eli did beside me. "Bullseye, comm check."

"Copy that, Bullseye. Comms are live and clear," Red answered.

"Thumper's good," Tate replied.

I shook my head at Eli. "I hate when he refers to himself in the third person."

I shoved my door open and stepped out, leaving Sally in the truck. I didn't think I'd need her for this. That was for after we found out where these assholes were holding Beth. *If* they were holding Beth.

"Eli, your team is with me. Thumper, go around back and clear the field."

"On it, boss."

We walked across the street casually, trying to blend in, which was comical considering how we were all dressed.

"Movement in the lobby," Eli said as we approached. "I count five guards."

"Pretty hefty for the middle of the night," I answered.

"Are we doing this the easy way or the hard way?"

"Too many cameras. Let's get inside, then we'll make our move."

I knocked on the front door, waiting as one of the guards approached. He warily opened the door, his hand on his gun. "The office is closed."

I pulled out my official badge Rafe sent me, stating I was working with the alphabets to get this mess cleared up. After reading the inscription and frowning, he nodded and let us in.

"I'll just announce that you're here."

"Tell Mr. Hayes that we have information for him."

He nodded and radioed upstairs. Eli, Red, and Kavanaugh started spreading out around the lobby, making the other guards nervous. I glanced around as if I didn't have a care in the world, but I was checking for cameras. We'd have to clean them on the way out. The sign on the wall indicated maintenance was down the hall, and that's most likely where we'd find the control room.

I scratched my jaw, pointedly looking in that direction. Eli whistled something jaunty, making me smile. Meanwhile, Red and Kavanaugh leaned against the wall as the guards appeared even more agitated. We were definitely in the right place.

"You can go up. Sorry, you'll have to use the stairs. The elevator is stuck in the basement."

"Good to know," I grinned. "Wouldn't want to fall down an elevator shaft."

I nodded to Eli as Red and Kavanaugh followed me upstairs. Just as the door was closing, I heard Thumper's team come in from the back, taking out the guards. Eli would be in the control room in no time. I rushed up the stairs, knowing I didn't have much time. I burst into Hayes' office, glad that I caught him by surprise. He stood suddenly, stepping back when he saw us all enter.

"What's going on?"

"That's a good question, Adam. Do you want to tell me why your employee went missing just a few hours ago?"

His eyes went wide as I rounded the desk and grabbed him by the shirt, picking him up and slamming him down on the desk. I pulled my gun and pressed it into his face.

"Tell me where the fuck she is!"

"I don't know what you're talking about!" he said, trembling beneath me.

"Don't fucking lie to me! You were having her followed, weren't you?"

"Only for her safety," he said quickly.

"Why? Why would she need to be protected?"

"I…I don't know!"

Obviously, the gun wasn't scary enough. I stepped back and nodded to Red. "I think the elevator is in the basement."

He nodded and grabbed Hayes from the other side of the desk, dragging him across until his body fell to the floor. He hauled him out of the office by his arm, his legs dragging on the floor as Hayes tried to find purchase. Red walked him right over to the elevator as Kavanaugh and I pried the doors open. We were on the fourth floor, which should be enough to scare the piss out of him at the very least.

Red jerked him to the edge, leaving him hovering over the gaping hole. "Where did your men take her?" Red asked.

"I don't have any men!"

"Then why all the guards in the lobby and outside? What do you need so much protection for?"

"I swear," he sputtered. "I didn't do anything."

"Let's see about that," he said, grabbing the phone from Hayes's pocket. He tossed it to me and I redialed the last call he made.

"Boss, we've got the girl. When are you getting here?"

I narrowed my eyes at Hayes, watching as the color drained from his face. "Hayes can't come to the phone right now. He's staring down an elevator shaft, and if you touch a hair on the girl's head, I'm not only going to drop your boss down it, I'm going to come after you. Only your death will be much more painful."

The guy on the other end hung up.

"I guess he didn't want to talk, but you're going to. Otherwise, Red is going to throw you down that shaft. If you're lucky, you'll die on impact. If you're not lucky, you'll break a lot of bones and be down there for hours, possibly even days, suffering as you wait for someone to find you."

"She's a fucking nobody, man," Hayes bit out.

"Wrong answer," Red said, dragging the man's body over the edge as he planted his boot against the elevator door. I grabbed the back of his vest, ensuring he didn't follow Hayes over as well.

"Alright! Alright! I'll tell you. Just don't fucking drop me!"

Red cocked his head at him. "Are you sure? Because I don't mind doing this again."

"I swear! I'll tell you!"

Red looked back at me and I nodded. He pulled Hayes back and flung him across the floor, slamming him into the wall. I walked over and knelt beside him. "Why do you want her so bad?"

"Because she saw the men that broke in here. She wouldn't tell me what they looked like."

"Why do you need that information?"

He dropped his eyes, taking a deep breath.

"You know what? That doesn't matter right now. You think really hard about your answer. For now, I want the location of where your men took her. We'll discuss the rest when I get back."

He nodded and gave us the directions.

"Now, call your boys and make sure they keep her safe until we arrive."

I stood and pulled my own phone, dialing Lock. "Did you get him, boss?"

"Yeah, he's going to be hanging out by the elevator. I suggest you come get him really quickly. Keep him on ice until we get back."

"Got it."

I turned to Thumper. "Got any rope on you?"

"As a matter of fact, I do."

He took a length of rope off a clip on his hip and handed it over. Nodding, I took it and rigged it up enough to keep him dangling just over the edge of the elevator shaft. If he kept his toes on the edge of the elevator shaft, he'd be fine until Lock arrived.

"Now, you just hang tight," I grinned. "Help is on the way."

"You can't leave me here," he cried, looking over his shoulder at the steep drop below.

IRIS walked forward. "You know, he's right, boss. This isn't fair."

"IRIS," I warned, but I was too late. He kicked Hayes right in the chest, swinging him into the shaft as he screamed, his wrists tightening in the rope. When he swung back, he tried to get his toes to the edge, but didn't have much luck. I stepped forward and grabbed him, pulling him just close enough that his feet found purchase on the ground again.

"I knew there was a reason I should have left you at the office."

28

BETH

My face jolted to the side as something hard smacked me. Everything around me spun as my head lolled to the side. I could taste the blood in my mouth and feel the split in my lip. The last thing I remembered was walking into my apartment. Everything after that was blank.

I was tied to a chair with my arms straining from the ropes holding them behind me. The position was uncomfortable, but worse than that was the fear racing through me as I opened my eyes and saw the multiple men standing around me with guns.

"Who…who are you?" I asked, afraid I already knew the answer.

"We're asking the questions here," one of the men said, stepping forward. "Who do you work for?"

My stomach dropped out as I realized who took me. Three years ago, my life changed for the worse. I was driving home and just happened to take a wrong turn. It destroyed my life and left me running from anyone who might know me. All this time, I thought I was being safe, but now I knew that the feeling of being watched wasn't by Hayes.

Swallowing hard, I shook my head. "No one."

"Do you really expect us to believe that you just stumbled upon us?

You came looking for information, and we want to know who's looking."

When I didn't answer, his fist shot out, slamming hard into the side of my face. For the second time, it felt like a sledgehammer hit me. Blood dripped to the ground as I let my mouth hang open. Nausea swirled in my stomach as I realized what they were going to do to me. I didn't think I could take it. I wasn't trained to handle pain. I wasn't trained for anything.

And then I remembered being taken, how my fingernails scratched on the walls as I fought to not be taken. I ran one fingertip over another nail just to confirm my memories. Dried blood coated my fingers. It was all real, which meant I had really shouted for Fox. But he wasn't here. I had to hope that he heard me and he was looking for me. Otherwise, I was looking at a very painful death.

"Tell us what you know," the man snapped again.

I looked at him curiously, shaking my head. "It's been years. If I haven't said anything by now, why would you assume I know anything?"

"Years? What the fuck are you talking about? You just started working at the lab."

"The—" The puzzle pieces started to fall into place. I wasn't sure if I was relieved that I hadn't been found, or terrified that I now had another enemy. "Listen, I don't know what's going on here, but I don't know anything. Like you said, I just started working there," I struggled to explain to them. My whole body was shaking, and I was on the verge of another panic attack.

The man stormed forward, and I knew it was coming. His fist slammed into my face again and again. Then he kicked me in the chest. The chair went flying backward and my skull cracked against the pavement. I coughed harshly, turning my head to the side, hoping I didn't puke or choke on my own blood.

My vision swam as they moved around me. I prayed this didn't last too much longer. I couldn't save myself. I didn't have anything to tell them, anything that would keep me alive. "Please," I whispered, but I knew it fell on deaf ears.

I wasn't sure how much time passed. I drifted in and out of

consciousness, barely aware of anything around me. At some point, they had cut the ropes around my wrists. Now I just lay in a puddle of my own blood. My body ached and my face felt like a punching bag Muhammed Ali used on a daily basis.

But then something strange started playing. At first, I thought I was hearing things, that my mind was trying to take me someplace else, away from the pain and torment. It was a sad sort of melody, something that reminded me of a funeral.

Then I heard his voice, Fox was singing "Poor Jud Is Dead". Despite feeling like absolute shit, I started to laugh. It hurt my chest and my cheeks burned as my lips cracked further, but it was worth it when I saw him walk through the door. All the men around me stepped back, glancing over at me as I laughed too hysterically, considering the position I was in.

And then chaos kicked in. I watched through slit eyes as Fox danced around the room, throwing several knives in a row, taking out three different men with accurate precision. I shoved up on my elbow, feeling a burst of…well, it wasn't energy, but it was something. I winced as I sat up, holding my ribs.

He strolled up to another man, who glanced over at me. He was clearly out of his depth with Fox. "—And his nails had never been so clean," Fox sang. The man actually looked down at his nails just before Fox shoved a knife into his stomach. The man grunted, looking up at Fox in confusion. Then he collapsed to the ground, not dead, but not long for this life.

"Hey, sweetie pie. I bet you're wishing now I had walked you inside."

I would have rolled my eyes, but that used too much energy. "You…took them all out."

"Of course I did. What kind of man do you take me for? Now, you sit there comfortably. I have to go collect my knives. Can't leave any evidence behind," he winked.

I nodded as he walked away, watching as he went to each body and yanked his knives out of them. They didn't look like regular knives, but I didn't really know anything about knives. He wiped the blood on their clothes, then pocketed them. Just as he was heading back over to me, the windows in the warehouse busted in and men swarmed the building. Fox was too far away to protect me, and there had to be at least twenty men storming the building…and they were all headed for me.

"Fox?"

"Yep?"

"Got any brilliant plans?"

"Give me a minute. I'm thinking."

"Think faster," I hissed. "I'm pretty much useless here. You brought backup, right?"

He glanced at me and frowned. "Backup? Is that a thing?"

I stared at him incredulously as one of the men stormed over and yanked me up by my bad arm. I cried out as he hauled me up. I barely caught sight of his face, and then I knew exactly who was after me.

29

CASH

"Fox is already in there," Eli informed me as I set up Sally. "But we got a problem."

"Of course we do. It's Fox."

"Well, the good news is, he killed all Hayes's men."

"And the bad news?"

"It looks like someone else is after her."

I laid down on my belly and looked through my scope just as a man dragged her to her feet by her bad arm. I could see the pain etched on her face as she cried out.

"Fox is a sitting duck in there," Eli said urgently.

"I got it," I said tersely. This wasn't like in the Marines. This was going to be down and dirty. I found my first target, the asshole holding Beth against his body. His head was nearly hidden behind her from this angle, but I had Betty on my side and she never let me down.

I took a deep breath.

"Boss!"

The man pulled a knife, raising it to her throat.

I adjusted one click based solely on instinct. My finger slipped over the trigger.

"Boss!" Eli shouted. "Fucking do it!"

I pulled the trigger and watched through the scope as the bullet made contact with his head. Blood poured over Beth's shoulder and down her face. The knife fell from her throat. Without even taking a moment to make sure she was okay, I switched targets.

I was vaguely aware of Eli and Thumper's teams moving in. There had to be at least twenty men on the inside, not to mention the men on the outside watching the perimeter. As they made their way toward the entrance, I continued to take out men with Sally. I'd never been so happy that Fox ignored orders and went after her alone. Without him, she might already be dead. Now he stood over her, throwing his knives at anyone that came near him.

The sound of helicopters overhead had me looking up sharply. More men were on their way. What the fuck did they want her for? "Incoming!" I shouted, shoving Sally in my case and slinging it over my shoulder. I ran down the steep slope to the building, pulling my gun from my holster and firing.

"Boss, we've got the perimeter!" Eli shouted. "Get in there and get her the fuck out!"

"On it," I shouted, running flat out for the facility.

"I got this, boss!" I heard IRIS laugh over comms. I didn't want to know what he was doing, but a moment later, a high-pitched sound whizzed past me and then the door exploded in front of me. I covered my face as flames exploded out toward me. Ignoring the building flames around me, I ran through the burning doorway and straight for Beth, who was being dragged by her arm further into the building.

The first thing I saw was the massive amount of fertilizer in the building, and the flames quickly spreading toward them. When they reached the first pallet, a massive explosion rocked the building. Men were scattering, trying to find cover and finish the job. The flames were so fucking high it was nearly impossible to see.

In the distance, I saw three men converging on one target. Fox was pinned down under fire near a post. I turned and fired, taking out three of them.

Fox stepped out from behind the post, holding out his arms. "I fucking had them!"

I shook my head and ran to the back of the building where Beth was running from one man. She stumbled, falling to her knees as the man grabbed her by the hair and yanked her up in front of him. I moved into a better position, needing the best angle possible so I didn't accidentally shoot her.

"Hey, asshole!" I shouted.

As expected, he spun, pulling her in front of him for cover. He grinned at me. "You've got this wrong. I don't want her. She just needs to die."

I looked into her eyes momentarily, saw the fear and resignation, but that's not how this was going to end. Even with the building ready to burn down around us, I was calm. He started to raise his gun, but I was faster. I fired without a second of hesitation. She stiffened as the man fell behind her, crumpling to the ground. Racing over to her, I grabbed her by the arm and ran for the back exit. She was barely standing, her feet stumbling over one another. Without a second thought, I swung her up in my arms and ran for the exit, just barely making it out as the building began to crumble around us.

But as soon as we got outside, we came under more fire.

"Eli! I thought you covered the outside!"

"They just keep coming, boss! What the fuck do they want her for?"

"Fuck if I know."

Ahead of us was our only chance at escape. Dense trees covered the landscape, which would make it easier to hide, but there was only so long we could run with me carrying her like this. I ran for the tree line, not stopping until we were heavily shaded by low-hanging brush. I gently set Beth down on the ground, noticing the strain on her face as I laid her flat. Digging around in my pockets, I pulled out a kit Lock always insisted I carry on me. I hadn't thought I'd need it since my military days. Now, it was going to save our asses.

I pulled out the large needle, ignoring the way her eyes went wide. "I'm going to inject this in you."

"You're what?" she shrieked.

I didn't waste another moment, pulling up her sleeve and taking the insanely large needle and shoving it into her arm. I knew it burned like hell. In fact, it felt like fire was burning through you, but it would give her the strength she needed to get moving.

I gripped her hand in mine, staring into her terrified eyes as she panted through the heat. After a minute, the worst of it passed and she sagged back in my arms for a moment. I pulled her to me, pressing a kiss to her forehead, though I wasn't sure why. I mostly wanted to comfort her.

"Better?"

She nodded against my chest. "What was that?"

"You don't want to know. We've got to get moving now."

I stuffed my kit back in my cargo pocket and grabbed my pistol as I held out my hand to her. She got to her feet, surprised at how easily she stood. "Whoa," she muttered. "Whatever that is, I think I want more."

"One dose is good. Any more than that, it'll kill you."

Grabbing her hand, I started jogging through the trees, putting as much space between the flaming building and us. After fifteen minutes, I stopped, hunching down in the brush to check for anyone following us. We weren't exactly being silent, but I didn't notice anyone following us.

"Eli, this is Bullseye."

I waited for him to respond, but the line was dead.

"Eli, do you copy?" Still nothing. "Fuck."

"What's wrong?"

"We're cut off from everyone."

"Then we should go back," she said urgently. "Fox was back there."

Jealousy rose up inside me that she was so worried about Fox. But then again, he had been good to her when I thought she was a fucking terrorist. "Fox can take care of himself, and so can everyone else."

"Then we should go back to them," she repeated.

"No, we have no idea how bad it is. They've been in a firefight before."

"But it's my fault they're in it."

"They're in it because they choose to be," I snapped. "We came after you because it's what we do. You're the asset!"

She flinched back, hurt filling her face. "I'm an asset?"

It didn't take a genius to figure out that I'd hurt her feelings, but we didn't have time for that now. We had to find a secure location and lay low until we could get back to safety.

"Fuck, that's not what I meant. It's just...look, I need you to pay attention right now. My job was to get you out of there safely. Everything else needs to be shoved aside until I achieve that. We're separated from everyone else. We don't have a vehicle. Until I can make contact with the rest of my team, we're on our own. So, I need you to hold it together and do as I say for just a little while longer, okay?"

She gave a tight nod, but I could tell she was on the verge of breaking down. I pulled out a map, flicking on my flashlight to check our location. Fuck, we were running the wrong fucking way. Glancing around the forest, I did my best to find a way out. It wasn't going to be an easy hike, and the shot I gave her would most likely wear off long before we reached safety. I had to get the most out of her now while she was still functioning.

Folding the map, I nodded to her feet. "How are you holding up?"

"I'm...okay. I think they yanked my shoulder out of place again."

I pressed my lips together. "I can reset it. It'll hurt less now than if I do it later."

Staring at me, she gave a tight nod. "Do it."

I found a thick stick on the ground and handed it to her. "Bite down."

She took it from me and shoved it between her teeth. I got into position and jerked her shoulder back into the socket. I could have slowly worked it back into place. It would have been less painful, but we didn't have time for that. She cried out around the stick, breathing hard, her nostrils flaring with every breath.

I took the stick from her mouth, watching her curiously. "Better?" She nodded quickly. I grabbed her good arm and helped her to her feet. "We're going to have to run. I need you to tell me the minute you're starting to crash."

"To crash?"

"Trust me, you'll know what I'm talking about."

"Alright, let's do this. Do I get a gun or something?"

I laughed. "No, kitten. Not without training."

"Kitten?" she said in disgust. "Is that supposed to be a cute nickname? Because it's not."

"Kitten, because one day you'll be a full-grown cat with sharp claws. You just have to give yourself time to get there."

A small smile split her lips, though she tried to hide it. Reaching out, I took her hand in mine, trying not to think about the fact that I liked it. There were bigger things to worry about right now.

"Let's do this," she said, blowing out a breath.

We took off running through the forest for several miles. I ran at a slower pace, knowing that even with the shot I gave her, she wouldn't last long at a faster pace. It was better to get more out of her and go further than to spend all that energy running hard, but not getting as far.

I stopped near a river, splashing some water on my face. "Don't drink it," I warned her. After cooling down, I pulled out the map again, trying to judge where exactly we were. If I was correct, we were only a few miles from a small town. They might have a motel we could stay at for the night. It wouldn't be too much longer before the shot I gave her would wear off.

She sat down beside me, laying back as she stared up through the trees. "This wasn't how I saw my night going."

"It wasn't exactly in my plans either," I muttered.

"Sorry to be an inconvenience," she snapped.

I folded up the map and tucked it away. "That's not what I meant. There was a second team in there. Any idea who they were?"

"The first worked for Adam."

"Yeah, I figured as much. We paid him a little visit. He seemed to think that you knew more than you were letting on about the men who broke into his facility. Any idea why that would be?"

She continued to stare up into the sky.

"Listen, you and I need to get a few things straight right now." Her eyes slid to meet mine. "First, I'm not the enemy. I'm not here to hurt you or beat the truth out of you."

She huffed out a laugh. "That's not exactly the way you made me feel when you manipulated me into going back to your office with you, and then stuck me in an interrogation room."

"I thought you were working with terrorists," I retorted. "Someone is causing a massive failure in our system, and I need to find out who before more damage is done."

She sat up, pulling her knees in closer to her body. I knew I fucked up the first time, but now I really needed her to trust me. With two different teams attacking her, she had to know more than she was letting on.

"Beth—"

I paused at the snap of a twig. Holding my hand out, I ducked down, pulling her with me. Scanning the trees, I looked for any sign that this was more than just an animal in the forest, and what I saw had my heart rate kicking into high gear.

"Beth," I whispered. "They tracked us. We need to get out of here, and we need to do it fast. How are you at swimming?"

She winced. "Not very good."

"Can you hold your breath underwater?"

She took a shaky breath and nodded. "I can try."

"Good. We're going to slip down into the river. Try not to make any sound. I want you to hold onto my back as I swim across the river."

Her eyes shot in the direction of the vast water. "We can't make it," she said, nearing hysterics.

"We can," I said, gripping her hand tightly. "We have to. Otherwise, we're fucked. Do you understand?"

She nodded jerkily and together we slid into the water as quietly as possible. With Sally still on my back, I had to help Beth slide into place. "Ready?" I whispered over my shoulder. She gave me a thumbs-up. "Deep breath."

Together, we took in a gulp of air and then I plunged us underwater, swimming as deep as I could while swimming across the river. Beth's hands gripped me tightly, nearly strangling me. I knew she was terrified, but this was our only option. When we passed the point where the moon was reflecting off the water, I pointed to the surface, letting her know I was taking her up. I rose slowly, turning to face her and pressing my finger to my lips, letting her know to keep quiet.

As we broke the surface, I sucked in a breath of air, hearing her do the same. I quickly scanned the opposite shoreline, searching for our enemies. They were making their way toward the river, which meant they were tracking us pretty easily. "Ready?" I whispered again.

At her nod, we both sucked in air before I dove back under. I swam longer this time. We needed to get to the other side of the river and hide out until they moved on. I couldn't risk them spotting us, and the more times we surfaced the more likely it was they'd find us. Finally, just as I was running out of air, I found a boulder and latched onto it, using it to fling us to the other side.

When we came up this time, the boulder was blocking us from their view. Beth was breathing hard, though she was trying to be silent. "Stay here."

She gripped onto my sleeve, her teeth chattering as she begged me to stay with her eyes. I slowly pried her fingers from my shirt and pressed her hand to the boulder.

"I'm just moving a little ways so I can see where they are. I'll be right back."

She nodded, practically hugging the boulder as I swam around it, keeping my head low in the water. They'd definitely found where we went into the water. They were scanning the trees on this side of the shore, trying to find us. I heard the squawk of a radio, but they were too far away for me to hear what was being said.

It was clear they were coming for us when they started making their way into the water. I spun around, pressing myself to the boulder as I checked out my surroundings. There were smaller boulders along the shore, not nearly big enough to cover us both, but I could draw their fire and get her into the trees and under cover.

"They're coming for us," I said quickly. I pulled Sally off my back and opened the case, shoving it in her arms. "I'm going to draw their fire, and I want you to move when I shoot."

"Move where?" she asked incredulously. "Aren't I safer with you?"

"Not if I'm drawing fire. Whenever I fire, you move over to the next boulder," I nodded to the rocks beside us. "If anyone starts firing at you, you stop moving and take cover. When you get close enough to the trees, you run for it and duck down in the brush. Keep yourself hidden until I come for you."

"Cash—"

"We don't have time to argue about this. Do as I say," I commanded.

She nodded, biting her lip as I finished preparing my rifle. Taking a deep breath, I slowly turned around the curve of the rock, sighting my first target. Most would go for the man making his way to us, but I had plenty of time to take him out. I needed to take out the targets that were still in the tree line first. They would immediately take cover and make our escape more difficult.

With the first kill shot, I alerted them that I was close and armed. With the second kill shot, I gave away my position. I aimed again, this time for the man rushing for the shore, back to the trees. I glanced over at Beth and nodded. As I fired, she slipped under the water toward the next boulder. Bullets pinged off the rocks as they started returning fire. I needed to draw them in the opposite direction.

Taking a deep breath, I dove underwater and swam for the next boulder in the opposite direction I sent Beth. When I came up, everyone had shifted positions again. There were two men standing within ten feet of each other. I took aim, firing rapidly as I took down one and then the other. I ducked back behind the boulder just as a bullet whizzed past my head.

When I searched for Beth, I couldn't find her, but she came up moments later, even further away. The man in the water was getting closer to me, but he still wasn't my main target. I spun and took aim, but I wasn't fast enough. A bullet sliced through the water, piercing my side. I gritted my teeth and took aim, firing two shots in rapid succession.

Between the darkness and the constant barrage of bullets flying my way, it was impossible to tell how many of them were left. Beth was moving further away, and luckily, no one had noticed her yet, but the hardest part was still to come. She had to make it into the trees without anyone noticing her.

I was going to make the same move as before, ducking under the water to get to my next position, but the river was shallow here. There was no place for me to take cover as I crossed. Sucking in a few quick breaths, I ran through the water, praying I didn't take a bullet to the ass as I made my way to the next boulder.

Somehow, I came out unscathed. I pressed my hand to my pocket, thanking my lucky stars I hadn't lost Betty. I pulled out my empty magazine and grabbed a second, shoving the used magazine in my pocket, then slammed the new one into place. I had time and patience on my side, while these men were using up all their ammo, hoping to hit something. I moved around the edge of the boulder, taking a headcount of everyone I could see. Ten men still stood on the opposite embankment, and I was on my last magazine. I would need to make this count.

Firing off two shots, I was about to take my third when I heard splashing. Quickly looking to Beth, I saw her running from her spot up the embankment as the man I had left for last trudged in the water toward her. Tossing my rifle over my shoulder, I ran through the water toward him, tackling him around the waist as I took him to the ground. I flinched as a bullet landed a little too close to my head, hitting a low-hanging branch instead. The man kicked me off him, shoving me face-first into the water and pressing his weight on top of mine. His hand was wrapped around my neck, forcing me to stay down as I struggled not to suck in water. My hand grappled at my side until I finally found the leather handle of my KA-BAR and yanked it from my sheath. Swinging back forcefully, I slammed the hard steel into the man's side.

30

BETH

I ran for the shoreline like he told me to. When I saw the man racing toward me through the water, I knew it was now or never. Even though my limbs were exhausted and I wanted to lay down and take a nap, I knew this was my last chance for escape. Water dripped from my clothes as I ran to the trees, ducking behind the first one I came across.

I watched in horror as Cash raced through the water, tackling the man to the ground as the men on the opposite shore started firing at him. I covered my mouth with my hand, terrified that I would start screaming at any moment. The man kicked at Cash, flinging him off his body and rolled over him, sitting astride him as he held him under the water.

I waited for him to come up, but the longer I waited, the clearer it became that he couldn't maneuver his way out of this one. Quickly looking around, I found a rock, heavy in my hand as I picked it up. I raced back to the man just as he grunted and was flung to the side. I slammed the rock into his head just as Cash came crashing out of the river, water dripping from him as he raised his arm and slammed his knife down into the man's chest.

I stood back in shock, dropping my rock to the ground as I watched him climb to his feet and stomp out of the water, grabbing my hand as he raced to the trees. I was still in shock, barely able to think about what I'd just done or what Cash had. I could still feel the weight of my rock smashing against the man's head, the sound of his skull cracking, though I doubt I did as much damage as Cash. We stopped suddenly, Cash shoving me to the ground under a bush. He held his finger to his lips, and then he was gone. I watched as he ran a few feet away and climbed a tree. He did it so effortlessly—as if climbing trees to kill people was a regular occurrence for him.

I stifled a laugh as I imagined him and his team doing training exercises with just this scenario. I really had to pull my shit together. I looked up in the tree again, watching as he laid himself across a thick branch and held his rifle in his arms. I didn't understand how he managed to balance himself on a branch, let alone hold a rifle and aim straight at the same time. That's why he was the professional and I was the scared shitless woman on the run.

The first shot had me nearly jumping out of my skin. I laid low and covered my ears. The second shot wasn't nearly as scary as the first, but this time, I squeezed my eyes closed. With every report of the gun, I found myself cringing further in on myself. I kept waiting for someone to come running up behind me and grab me. It was clear Cash was good at his job, but there were so many of them, and I was a liability.

A hand on my shoulder had me shrieking in fear, until I looked up and saw Cash standing above me. His shirt was soaked in blood, but he didn't look any worse for wear. I stood quickly, flinging myself into his arms and holding him tight. After all I had been through in my life, this had to be one of the most terrifying moments. And when he wrapped his arms around me, warmth and comfort seeped into my skin despite both of us being drenched.

"It's okay."

"You got them all?"

"Pretty damn sure."

I nodded against his neck, but I couldn't peel myself away. I started shaking uncontrollably, hating the fact that I was about to start crying. I didn't want to be that girl. I wished I could handle this stuff, that I could brush it off as if nothing happened and walk away, but that wasn't me. And as the first tear fell, the pain and horror of the last few years washed over me like a waterfall until I was nearly crumbling in his arms.

"I've got you, kitten," he murmured. "No one's going to hurt you."

That only made me cry harder. Tears blurred my vision so much that I didn't even see the man walk up behind Cash. But he did. Spinning quickly, he shoved me behind him just as he pulled his gun, kicked the man in the chest, and then shot him in the head as he fell backward to the ground. I stared at the man, horrified by not what I saw, but how grateful I was that Cash had such great reflexes.

While I stood there like an idiot, Cash searched the rest of the area for any signs of more…what were they even called? Bad guys? Evildoers?

"We need to go," he said, taking my hand in his again. I glanced down at our locked hands, feeling a rush of warmth wrap around me. I never thought I would want his hands on me, but now, I associated his touch with the feeling of protection. He had me, and nothing would harm me.

I followed along beside him as he pulled me deeper into the trees and away from the men who attacked me. But the further we walked away, the more the pain from my shoulder injury started to flare up. At first, I thought it was just exhaustion creeping in, but then my feet started moving more sluggishly, and the aches in my face and stomach from being punched and kicked started to really take hold. This was what he was talking about. The crash.

"Cash," I mumbled, my eyes opening slowly as I thought I looked up at him. I couldn't be certain at this point. He looked back at me and swore, catching me just as I fell over. He hoisted me up in his arms, cradling my body gently as he continued on. I stared up at the hard planes of his face, how the stubble along his jaw covered him in a perfect pattern except for one long scar that ran just along his jawline. I would have reached up and touched it, but my arms were too weak, and then everything started to go dark.

When I woke, the pain was ten times worse than before I passed out. I was no longer staring up at the sky, but instead, looking at the dirty t-shirt Cash wore. Lifting my head slightly, I realized I was somehow latched onto Cash's back piggyback style. My left arm was in some kind of sling, wrapped tightly to my chest. I wasn't even holding onto him.

"Where are we?" I asked, my voice coming out strange and warbled.

"About a half mile from town."

"Town? Home?"

"No," he chuckled. "I wish, but no."

"Where are we going?"

"We're about three miles to a safe house. We'll stop in town for supplies and then head out there until I can contact my team."

"Three miles," I muttered against his back. "That feels like a lifetime."

"I know. Just hang in there. You're doing great."

I snorted at that. "I'm literally hanging off your back. I'm not doing great at anything."

I winced as he shifted me on his back, but didn't make a sound. He was doing all the work, after all. "How about another injection? That felt nice."

"That's not a good idea."

"Why not? You like toting me around?"

I thought I saw his lips pull up in a smile as he glanced over his shoulder. "Let's say I like you a lot more alive than braindead."

"Braindead," I repeated. At this point, I wasn't sure that was a bad idea. The peace of knowing all this running was over was quite appealing. On the other hand, I wanted to see Fox again and tell him thanks for saving my ass. "What about just a small shot? Like a mini one."

He sighed, stopping and getting down on his knees. He untied something, and then I was loose from his back, though still leaning heavily against him. He turned to me, his eyes looking over me. I must have looked bad based on the grimace on his face.

"You need some ice. Your cheek is swelling up."

"This is what I always look like," I teased. He winced as he sat down, and that was when I noticed the large red stain on his shirt. Forgetting my own pain, I leaned forward and yanked his shirt up, gasping when I saw the blood drying on him. There was a lot, way more than should be there.

"Did you get shot?"

He shrugged one shoulder. "Hazard of the job."

"Yeah, but aren't you trained to dodge those things or something?"

"Dodge them? No. Besides, this is just a scratch."

"That," I pointed at his stomach, "is not a scratch. It's a hole with a bullet inside."

"It was a through and through."

"And that means what? It went through your body and then through another part?"

He gave me a tired smile, leaning his head back against a tree. "It means it went in one side and out the other."

"You have two of those?" I shrieked.

He grabbed my hand, instantly soothing me. "I'm fine. I'm mostly tired from carrying your heavy ass around."

"I am *not* heavy," I snapped.

"Well, it wasn't like I was carrying a can of tomatoes."

I smiled tiredly at his joking, but the truth was, we were both exhausted. He just hid it better. "We can't go into town for supplies looking like this."

"You're not going anywhere. If I brought you anywhere near town, someone would accuse me of beating you, and then we'd be in a shit ton of trouble."

"But why couldn't we go to the police? Wouldn't they be able to help?"

"There are a handful of people I trust. I don't trust police when I don't know them. I can't judge how they'll react or who they'll contact. And since we don't know who else was after us, I can't risk anyone else finding out where we are right now."

"So, how are we going to do this?"

"We'll make it as close to town as possible and then you'll hide out while I go get supplies."

"Your shirt is full of blood," I pointed out. "You don't think anyone will be suspicious of that?"

"I'll figure something out. Are you ready to move?"

Truth be told, I wasn't sure I could even stand, but there was no way I was allowing him to keep carting me around. "You said a half mile? I think I can handle that."

He nodded in approval. "You can rest while I go into town."

"No time to waste, then."

I tried to stand up, but my body was hurting badly. Cash slipped his arms around me, helping me up. He didn't release me like I thought he would. Instead, he kept his arm wrapped around me, helping me walk across the last half mile into town. When we were just on the edge of town, he glanced over at me, taking in how hard I was breathing, and lowered me to the ground.

"That's far enough." He glanced around, checking out our surroundings. "I can't carry Sally into town with me, so I need you to keep an eye on her for me."

"Sally?"

I pulled my rifle off my back and out of the gun case. Her eyes went wide as she looked it over. "You want me to use that?"

"Only if you need to." I pulled out the magazine and sighed. "Only one round left. Use it wisely, and preferably not on me."

"I've never even held one of these before."

"If you need to use it, wait until your target is close. You don't want to waste a bullet shooting at something you know you can't hit."

He quickly took me through how to use it, but most of it was over my head. I just hoped I didn't have to actually use it. I gingerly took the gun from him, laying it across my lap as I leaned back against the tree. My eyes closed involuntarily. I wasn't sure it would matter if I had the rifle. I felt like passing out, and then this would have all been for nothing when they found me and shot me because I was sleeping.

After being taken, beaten, and running for our lives, exhaustion was pounding down on me. But the morning sun shining through the trees warmed me slightly, giving me hope that this wasn't the end. I could have sworn I felt Cash's warm hand brush against my cheek, but when my eyes fluttered open, he was gone.

31

CASH

I couldn't tear my eyes off the peaceful look on her face. Despite being beaten to hell, she looked peaceful leaning against the tree. I couldn't believe that I thought this woman could ever be involved in a terrorist plot. If I had just believed her, maybe I could have kept her safe, but instead, she was struggling to stay awake, let alone walk.

I brushed the back of my hand against her bruised cheek, vowing this would not happen again to her. I would protect her with everything in me and find out who was behind wanting her dead.

Standing, I turned and headed into town, pulling my gun from the holster at my back to check how much ammunition I had left. There wasn't much, but it would get me through as long as we weren't attacked. Right now, I needed more ammunition for Sally, and for my Beretta. After using it in the military for so long, it was like a second skin to me. I found it difficult to use any other weapon besides Sally.

The safe house would have canned food in stock, but we could really use some essentials for a few days, not to mention a change of clothes. If I was lucky, I could find a used vehicle to get us out there so we didn't have to hike it.

Luckily, I had my ID for my alter ego, Atticus Finch. It was an alias I created not long after getting out of the military when I was first starting up OPS. I knew there might be occasions when I would need a credit card and ID that wasn't directly linked to me or OPS.

As I entered town, I was well aware of how I looked. But we had chosen a safe house out here for a reason. This was a hunting community, so it was easy to get supplies where no one would look twice at you. The thrift store at the edge of town tended to put out items on clothing racks for people to browse. I quickly pulled a flannel shirt off the rack and buttoned it up, then headed inside and browsed through the women's section. After grabbing a few things for her, and then finding a few more things for myself, I paid the cashier and walked out.

My next stop was the used car dealer on the corner. I didn't need anything fancy. In fact, if I could find something about fifteen years old, that would be best. It wouldn't draw attention. Lucky for me, there was an old truck sitting on the edge of the lot with a price tag in the window of a thousand dollars. I checked under the hood and haggled the price down to eight hundred dollars.

With the keys in my hand, I now had the ability to grab a few more items before I picked Beth up. I kept worrying about her under the tree, all alone and scared. But I could only deal with one thing at a time. Pulling up to the gun shop, I got out and headed inside, grabbing what I needed. As I suspected, the cashier didn't think twice about ringing me up.

After grabbing a few groceries and some supplies to bandage Beth up, I drove out of town and parked just off the road where I left her. Except, she wasn't there. Pulling my gun, I searched the surrounding woods, my heart racing out of control. A twig snapped to my left and I spun, nearly firing at Beth as she stepped out from behind a tree.

She froze, the rifle bag slung over her shoulder as she stared at me with her hands raised. Lowering the weapon, I shoved it back in my holster and stalked over to her.

"I told you to fucking stay there."

"I had to pee."

"I thought someone had taken you," I snapped. "When I tell you to do something, you fucking do it!"

I expected her to argue back, but she was too damn tired. I immediately felt bad for yelling at her. Slipping the bag off her shoulder, I slung it over my own.

"I'm sorry. I…"

"I scared you. Got it," she said stiffly.

Sighing, I knew I was fucking this up again. "I got us a truck. No more walking."

"How did you manage that?" she asked excitedly.

It didn't matter if I trusted her. I told very few people about my alter ego. It was safer that way.

"Let's go. I'm sure you want to lay down on an actual bed."

She didn't ask any further about the truck, and when we got back to the road and she slid inside, she sighed in relief. "This feels good."

"Only a few miles to the safe house," I answered, slamming the door and walking around the truck. After being hunted nearly all night, I was wary about taking the main road back to the safe house. So, I took the long way, watching my tail the whole way. After a half hour of driving, it was clear no one was following us, so I headed to the safe house.

When I pulled down the tree-lined driveway, Beth sat up, checking out the house. It was nothing big. In fact, it was more like a hunting cabin. But appearances were deceiving. There were sensors all around the property. Dash would have been alerted as soon as we crossed the property line.

Beth got out on her side, studying the cabin. I thought for sure she was going to make some comment about how it was rundown, but instead, she smiled. "I think this is the nicest place I've stayed in years."

That surprised me, but maybe it shouldn't have, considering what I knew about her. "Here," I said, handing her the keys. "Why don't you go inside and I'll grab this stuff."

She took them from me and unlocked the door as I grabbed the stuff out of the back of the truck. By the time I got inside, she was already passed out on the couch. I walked around the property, checking all sensors and the gate, making sure we were as secure as possible. The generator had kicked in, so at least we had power. When I went back inside, I headed to the steel door that led down to the basement. It was our operational control room for the safe house, which also doubled as a safe room.

I turned on the monitor, grinning when I saw Dash staring back at me. Putting on my headphones, I waved at him. "Hey, boss. It took you long enough to check in."

"We ran into a few problems along the way."

"Yeah? Some flying squirrels? I hear they can be pretty deadly."

"Nothing I couldn't handle."

He nodded at my clothes. "Looks like one of them got you."

I glanced down, noticing the blood soaking through my shirt. I really needed to get that bullet hole patched up. "It's just a scratch."

"And our lady friend? Did she come out unscathed?"

"Not so much," I answered, sitting down in the chair. The ache in my body made itself known the moment my ass touched the seat. I was fucking exhausted. "She'll be okay. How are we looking on that end?"

"You'll be happy to know that Lock's team retrieved Hayes. Unfortunately, all his fingers and toes were still intact."

"Did you get anything out of him?"

"Just that he wanted Beth because she saw who broke into his facility. Apparently, he thinks she knows them."

I remembered Red pointing to the man who stood beside her and put his arm on her back as he led her out of the building. It was intimate in some ways, but I wasn't convinced anymore that she actually knew who he was.

"She said his name was Seth. Do we have any intel on that yet?"

"Not a peep. But, boss, the boys and I were doing some thinking…"

"That's dangerous," I grinned. "What did you come up with?"

"Well, Hayes clearly wasn't behind the second attack on Beth, so who would want her dead just as much as Hayes wanted that information?"

I leaned back in my seat and sighed. "The men that were in the building with her that night."

"That's what we're thinking."

"But they let her go," I said in confusion. "Why go back for her after the fact?"

"I went over the feed several more times. From what I can tell, Seth is the only one that wanted to let her go. You'll need her to confirm."

"I'll see what I can do," I nodded.

"You want us to send a team out to you?"

I almost said yes, but I might get more information out of her if we were alone. "Not yet. We're going to lay low for the time being. Besides, we're both wiped out."

"Just ring when you need us."

"What about Rafe? Has he called yet?"

"Silent as the lamb."

"Figures," I grumbled. "That asshole was never very good at sharing information."

"Much like you and the secret of you and your alphabet bestie."

I smirked at him, leaning forward to hit the button. "Catch ya later, Dash. Don't let me get shot."

"We've got you covered."

I flicked off the button and leaned back in the seat, closing my eyes. I was fucking exhausted, but I needed to check on Beth, put the food away, and clean myself up. The last thing either of us needed was infection to set in.

I hauled my tired ass out of the chair and climbed the stairs, pressing my hand to the wall when I felt a wave of dizziness wash over me. Damn, I must have lost more blood than I thought.

"Are you okay?"

I glanced up quickly, berating myself for not having heard her walk up. "Yeah, just checking in with the company."

"No, I meant you look like shit."

"So do you," I shot back. I finished climbing the stairs, pulling on my final reserves of strength to put the rest of the stuff away. I shoved a plastic bag her way. "I picked up new clothes for you."

"I need a shower first," she sighed, wincing when she moved the wrong way.

"Go ahead. I'll get some food started."

"Shouldn't we clean you up first?" she pointed to the wound in my side.

I really did need to take care of that, but food and water were a priority for both of us. "I'll take care of it later." I grabbed a bottle of water and handed it to her. "Make sure you drink that."

She nodded gratefully, taking it from me and instantly drinking all of it.

"Bathroom's off the bedroom," I said, pointing down the hallway.

"Thanks." She turned to go, but stopped, glancing back over her shoulder. "I mean it…for everything. You saved my life."

She continued down the hall and as soon as she was out of sight, I sat down in the seat, wincing at the pain in my side. Pulling my shirt up, I checked out the damage. It was still bleeding, but had luckily turned to a sluggish drip instead of pouring blood. I closed my eyes, just needing a few minutes to relax. I must have fallen asleep, but I jolted awake at the sound of something in the house. Grabbing my gun, I quickly headed in the direction of the bathroom.

32

BETH

With shaky hands, I pulled my shirt over my head, careful not to lift my shoulder too much. Unwrapping it from the sling Cash had made was difficult, but I wasn't going to ask him for more help. He had already done enough for me.

I stared at myself in the mirror. My hair was a mess, filled with leaves and twigs, barely still pulled back. My face looked like it was used as a punching bag, and as I stared at my ribs, the mottled bruising said it all. I was in no shape to go anywhere.

I had to slip away, though. Cash and his company didn't deserve all the crap I was bringing down on them. Between Adam and now the men from the elevator, I was a shit load of trouble. And that didn't even include the other men that were after me. What I couldn't figure out was how they found me. I was pretty sure Seth didn't give me up. He had gone with those men the night of the blackout, but someone had to have followed me, or been watching me after that night.

The only thing I could come up with was that they saw me with OPS and assumed I was talking. They probably meant to snatch me when Fox dropped me off, but Hayes's men beat them to it. Leaning against the counter, I tried not to give in to the tears, but I was so tired of running, of constantly feeling scared.

I could feel the tears slipping down my cheeks, so I quickly turned on the water and stepped inside. At least in here, the water would block out the sound of me crying. I sank down to the floor, pulling my knees up against my chest as I rested my forehead against them.

How was this my life? I was a good kid. I did what I was told, but that wasn't good enough. Trouble followed me, and men even worse. I wished I could say that my childhood was the most horrible thing that had ever happened to me, but the years after I escaped one hell hole, I found myself in an even worse situation. How I escaped that night, I still didn't know. It was sheer luck or God watching over me. But nothing had been right since. Constantly dodging danger and looking over my shoulder was my newest form of torture. Even when I tried to play things cool, I still ended up in trouble.

I needed to leave before someone else got hurt. I tilted my head back, nearly in tears as my shoulder throbbed. I was so tired of constantly moving. I just wanted to move on with my life, meet someone normal, and have the kind of life I'd always dreamed of.

I hung my head, the tears falling faster as I fell apart. Last night had really fucked with me. I'd come too close to dying so many times, and I just wasn't sure how much longer I could take it. A sob wrenched from deep within and I slapped a hand over my mouth, but it did nothing to stop the pain inside. Nothing could ever make this better.

The shower curtain was wrenched open and I quickly looked up, backing further into the shower as Cash stood before me, gun in hand. I slowly looked away from his eyes, down to his gun. Was he here to kill me? Why would he do that after risking so much to save me?

Then he shocked me by stepping into the shower, boots and all. The blood from his shirt quickly started rinsing down the drain, though not all of it would come out. When he knelt down beside me, I could see the strain in his eyes, the pain he went through just to get to his knees.

Without thinking too much about it, my hand went to the hem of his shirt, dragging it up over his head. His eyes watched me intently as I pulled it off and tossed it out of the shower. I grabbed the soap, lathering it in my hands as I gently washed him, trying to pay him back in some way for all he did for me. He sat stock still as my hands slid over the wound on his side, and then slid around to the back. I nearly started crying when I felt the hole on the other side. So much pain, all because of me. Would it ever stop?

I bit back a sob, but when he wrapped his arm around the back of my neck and pulled me toward him, I lost control. My hands slid around his back and I held him close, crying once again on his chest. I gripped him tight, holding on for dear life. I had no idea what would happen next, and that terrified me. What more could life throw at me? It seemed every time I caught a break, something else happened to mess everything up.

When I felt cried out, I pulled back, mortified that I had used him to comfort me. But when I looked up into his eyes, all I saw was sympathy and questions.

"We should get out," he murmured, his eyes dropping to my lips.

Licking them in response, I nodded and stood, just now realizing that I was naked in front of him. I ducked my head as he shut off the water and handed me a towel. I did the best I could to wrap it around me while he went to grab our clothes from the kitchen.

"Get dressed, and then we're going to talk."

I took the bag from him, knowing there was no way out of this. No matter how much I wanted to hide my past from him, or the events that recently occurred, he had a right to know. After all, he'd risked his life for mine.

I pulled out a pair of jeans and a tank top. There was no bra, but there was a pair of underwear, and luckily, he also bought me a flannel shirt that matched his. Getting dressed was an issue all its own. I couldn't do anything with only one hand, and when he saw my struggle, he came over and helped me with my jeans, sliding them up my legs as he tried to protect my modesty by looking away.

It was no use hiding anything. He'd already seen all of me in the shower. As he pulled the tank top over my head and helped maneuver my arm through the hole, his eyes lingered just a tad too long on my breasts. Then he stepped back, clearing his throat as he grabbed the flannel off the bed.

"We should make another sling for your arm. It'll help you heal faster."

"Okay," I croaked out.

He helped me finish getting dressed and then rummaged through his supplies, not finding what he wanted. "I need to check downstairs. We might have something we can use."

"What's downstairs?"

"It's a safe room and where we stay in contact with the main office."

"You have all that here?"

He gave a curt nod. "Would you like to see it?"

"Sure."

He took my hand, leading me down the stairs to what I could only imagine was some kind of next-gen technology. I'd never seen anything like this before. With computers running and what looked like code scrolling across the screen, I couldn't make heads or tails of what was what.

He picked up a remote and flicked on a screen. "These are our cameras from the outside."

"How do you monitor all this?"

"We have sensors that go off if someone crosses the property line. OPS is also monitoring it, so they'll notify us if they see anything suspicious."

He walked past the screens to the back of the room. Rummaging through the shelves, he pulled out something with a triumphant grin. "Looks like we don't need to make a sling."

He unfolded it, showing a black sling that he quickly put into place around my arm. The relief was instant. "How does that feel?"

"Amazing. I mean, not as good as if my arm wasn't hurt, but so much better."

"How did you hurt it, anyway?"

I instantly clammed up. Years of keeping secrets made it impossible for me to blurt out all the things that had happened to me in the past.

"Beth, I'm fucking tired and hungry. We both need sleep, but we also need to talk about what's going on. If we're going to get out of this alive, I need to know I can trust you, and that starts with you telling me everything you know."

I wanted to argue with him, but he was right. The time for keeping secrets was over. He'd already proven that he would go above and beyond to protect me. The longer I held onto these secrets, the more dangerous it became for everyone, and that was a bad game to play.

"Alright."

33

CASH

After a quick dinner, I patched myself up with some glue, then taped a bandage over the wound on my front and back. I did a final check of the perimeter and checked in with Dash one more time. All was quiet. There were no signs of anyone approaching the safe house, but that wasn't the only thing on my mind.

"Put Eli on the phone."

"Right here, boss," Eli said, moving into the picture.

"Everyone get out okay?"

"Well, you know IRIS. He had to blow up some shit. He singed off an eyebrow, but that's nothing unusual."

I shook my head with a laugh. "Of course he did. And our new friends?"

"Well, most of them took off after you. I'm assuming since you're still alive and kicking that you took them out."

"Piece of cake," I smirked.

"Yeah, that's what Dash said. He also said something about a nice red stain you added to your collection."

"You know how it is," I answered.

He nodded, but I could feel him searching my face for answers. "We've got Hayes on ice. What do you want to do about him?"

"Nothing for the moment. I need to talk to Beth."

He looked at me funny. "Boss, you've been with her all day, and you still haven't talked to her? What the fuck are you doing?"

"You know, the usual. Shopping."

"Getting new shoes, huh?"

"Along with a few other things."

"You should get some sleep. You look like shit."

"Well, that happens when you go traipsing through the woods without the proper gear."

"How's Sally?"

"Best friend I could ever have."

"And Betty?"

"Where she always is."

He huffed out a laugh. "Then it sounds like you're all set."

"I'll let you know what I get out of her."

Dash shoved his face back in the picture. "Remember, she's not Sally."

"Yeah, I think I've got that."

"I'm just saying, I told you last time, and you didn't seem to really take my advice."

"Duly noted. Can I get the fuck off now?"

"I don't know, can you?" Dash smirked.

"I meant off the phone, and you know it."

"Sure, you did, boss. I've seen the way you look at her."

I didn't have the energy to keep going at it with him. I was exhausted and in desperate need of some sleep. "Watch the perimeter. I'm getting some shut-eye. I'll have the sat phone on me."

"Go get some, boss," Dash cheered me on. I shot him an evil look. "Sleep. I meant *sleep*, boss. Geez, not everything is a dirty joke."

I shut off the feed and climbed back upstairs, shutting the door behind me. I thought I would find Beth on the couch, but it was empty. Shutting off the lights, I found her in the bedroom, passed out on the bed. Shucking off my pants, I climbed in beside her, scooting closer than I should have. I was cold, or that's what I told myself as I nuzzled in beside her. She was a job, and that was it. There was absolutely nothing else going on between us.

I fell asleep quickly, but my dreams tormented me. Beth was standing in front of me, a knife to her throat as she pleaded with me to save her. But I didn't have Sally with me, and before I could make a move, the man standing behind her slit her throat. I watched helplessly as she fell to the ground and stared up at me like I'd failed her.

I woke up in a cold sweat, breathing hard as I stared down at Beth peacefully sleeping. Rubbing my eyes, I sighed and tried to calm my racing heart. I never had dreams of failure. I was always confident in my abilities, so why was I suddenly worried that I would fail her? My sat phone rang on the bedside table and I quickly answered it.

"Cash."

"Boss, get the fuck out of there. You've got four trucks headed your way."

I shot up out of bed and shook Beth awake, quickly pulling on my jeans. She must have seen the urgency in my moves because she got up quickly and followed my lead.

"How the fuck did they find us?"

"I have no idea, but they're not out for a midnight drive," Dash answered.

"What direction are they coming from?"

"What direction aren't they coming from? Fuck, I've got no clear way out for you. Get the fuck down in the safe room."

"That'll only hold up for so long," I answered, slipping my shoes on, sans socks. I rushed into the kitchen and grabbed Sally, slinging her over my shoulder as I holstered my pistol. I quickly grabbed anything I could and ran for the front door with Beth on my heels, also carrying a few bags in her one good arm.

"Boss, you can't go up against them alone."

"We can't stay here. We're sitting ducks."

"We're at least an hour out. You'll be dead by the time we reach you."

"You have so little faith in me," I said as I tossed my things in the back seat of the truck and got in. Beth buckled up, looking out all around us, same as me. I shifted into reverse and backed down the drive, narrowly missing the truck that was about to crash into me. I put the truck in drive and peeled out of there, driving like a madman to avoid hitting the second one headed toward us.

"Find me a road, Dash!"

I tossed the phone over to Beth since I needed both hands to keep us on the road and alive.

"You could take them to the state park, but…"

"But what? Spit it out?"

"Well, you could end up dead."

"How does he know where we are?" Beth asked.

"He's tracking the sat phone," I answered quickly. We lurched forward as we were slammed from behind by one of the trucks.

I saw the sign that would lead us to the state park, but jerked the wheel to take another turnoff, deciding against that route. The truck directly behind us flew right past the turnoff, screeching to a halt as he waited for the other trucks to turn and follow.

"Cash, what are we doing?" Beth said nervously from beside me.

"Leading them up the mountain."

"You're doing what?" Dash screeched. "Cash, you're fucking crazy!"

I glanced in the rearview mirror, gauging how close they were. I needed to draw them in closer if this was going to work. The roads out here were insane, most of them without guardrails. And when it was construction season, which thankfully it was, the roads were even more treacherous.

I pressed down on the gas, picking up speed as we wound up the mountain road. A few cars passed us going the other direction, but luckily, the roads were pretty empty since it was still the dead of night.

"Cash…" Beth's voice shook from beside me. "This is crazy. You're going to get us killed."

"Trust me," I said, watching the road closely. I glanced over, seeing Beth squeeze her eyes closed as I wound up the mountain. I couldn't blame her, she was by the edge. But if anything happened, we were both going down. The tires caught on the gravel as I got a little too close to the edge of the mountain. She screamed as the truck momentarily swerved as I got us back on the road.

As we climbed the mountain, I continued to drive faster. After years of driving this road, I knew most of the turns by heart. I was hoping the same wasn't true for our friends. In the dark, it was nearly impossible to tell where the road curved until you were right up on it. Up ahead was a section of the road that curved more sharply, and that's where I was hoping to take out the first truck.

I pressed down on the gas as I jerked the wheel, taking the turn sharper than expected. I swerved all over the road as I tried to gain control of the vehicle. The truck behind us missed the turn, then overcorrected and swerved toward the edge of the mountain. We were just taking the next curve when I saw him heading straight over the cliff.

"One down," I grinned.

"You're fucking crazy!" Beth shouted, her voice shaking as she gripped anything she could. "You're going to kill us!"

"Not if you stop fucking screaming at me," I retorted, keeping my attention on the problem at hand.

"We need to get off this road!" She turned in her seat, then promptly freaked the fuck out. "They're still coming after us. This is insane!"

"Where would you like us to go? We're on this road, and there's no hopping off and taking the scenic route. This is the only fucking road we've got!" I snapped at her, needing her to stop fucking yelling at me.

I rounded another corner, my eyes widening when I saw a logging truck taking up more of the road than it should. I moved over, two of my wheels skidding in the gravel as I fought for control. We narrowly avoided hitting the truck, and as soon as we passed him, I maneuvered the truck back to safety.

"Any chance you feel comfortable driving?" I asked, half-joking.

"Yeah, now's the time to pull over," she retorted.

"I was actually thinking I would slide over as you shift in front of me."

I could feel the weight of her incredulous stare and glanced over at her. "Are you fucking crazy?"

"I take that as a no," I nodded. "How do you feel about firing a gun?"

"Are you just coming up with the most insane shit you can think of? I have one good arm and you want me to bend outside a window, on the edge of a fucking mountain, and fire a gun I don't know how to use at moving vehicles?"

"Relax," I snapped. "It was just a suggestion, which leads me to the third option."

She went still, knowing this was the worst and most terrifying. "Please don't say it."

"I need to take them out, and I need the truck facing the other direction."

"I'm not hearing this," she muttered, covering her ears like a toddler. "This is not happening. I'm not in this truck. Nobody is chasing me. I'm back in my shitty apartment with my air mattress, and no one is after me," she said, rocking herself as if that would make this whole situation better.

"Look, the road widens ahead to four lanes. That's our best option. I'm going to—"

She cut a nasty glare in my direction and I stopped explaining.

"Right, you don't want the details."

"Just tell me I'm going to live through this."

I really hated to lie to people. I wanted to reassure her that everything would be fine, but hell, shit went wrong all the time. And we were on a mountain road being chased by maniacs who wanted us dead.

"Most likely," I answered.

"Most likely?" she shrieked. "What does that even mean? We might live, but you're not sure? What are the odds?"

"What? Like you want percentages?" I asked, glancing over at her.

"Eyes on the road!"

"You fucking asked!"

"Not for you to look at me while you're driving like a madman on a winding road," she snapped.

I took a turn just a little too fast and nearly sent us off the edge of the cliff. I wasn't used to driving with someone who freaked out so easily over something as simple as driving fast on a curvy road with the potential of falling to our deaths.

"Then maybe you shouldn't have gotten in the truck with me," I snapped. "You know, none of this would have happened if you had just been honest with us from the start!"

"Oh, so this is my fault?"

"When there's a woman involved, it usually is her fault," I muttered.

"This is not happening to me," Beth mumbled. "I am not here. I did not escape my step-father, drug dealers, a fucking blackout, men kidnapping me, only to be taken out by a lunatic in a fast truck!"

"Yeah, we're gonna come back to all that shit as soon as I get us out of this," I retorted.

"*If* you get us out of this. You still haven't given me any odds," she said, still shaking in her seat as she grabbed the handle in the truck, hanging on as if we were going over the edge any second.

"Odds, fine...Let's say—" I swerved around another corner, narrowly missing the edge of the mountain. "Sixty percent."

"That's not odds!" she shouted.

"Woman, if you keep yelling at me, you won't have to worry about us going over the cliff. I'll throw you over!" I said, lowering my window.

"You're supposed to be protecting me."

"Then let me do my fucking job!" I shouted as we finally reached the four-lane road and I hit the brake, spinning the wheel as I pulled my gun and pointed out the window at the truck headed right for us. He hit the brakes and swerved to avoid crashing into us. His truck went right off the side of the cliff as I hit the gas again and swerved over to the side of the road, throwing the truck into park as I jumped out and fired at the next truck coming around the corner, taking out the driver's side window. His head slammed forward into the steering wheel as he swerved right into the mountainside.

I ran around the back of the vehicle, staying low as I approached the passenger side. As I lifted my head, the passenger fired out his window, shattering the glass. I quickly ducked, then threw my elbow inside, hitting him in the head and knocking him out slightly. Grabbing him by the jacket, I hauled him through the window, tossing him to the ground before I put a bullet in his head.

A scream tore through the night and I raced around the SUV, aiming at the man who had Beth by the neck, pulling her out of the truck. "Let her go!" I shouted.

"Put your gun down," he shouted, his gun aimed right at her head. He was dragging her toward the edge of the cliff. He had no intention of letting her go, but my alternative was for him to shoot her in the head right in front of me. I raised my hands, slowly lowering my gun to the ground. He was close to the edge now.

"Don't do it," I warned him. "You can walk away right now. You have no backup."

"I have a job to do."

I didn't look at Beth as I tried to calm him the fuck down. Still bent over, I slowly stood. "Aren't you wondering why they're after her? She's a nobody. She knows nothing."

"Doesn't fucking matter," he growled, still dragging her closer to the edge.

I could hear Beth whimpering. I knew she was terrified, but I couldn't think about that right now. As soon as he took his eyes off me to look over the edge, I grabbed my backup from the small of my back and fired two shots, one in his shoulder and one in his head. He dropped the gun and fell backward, but as he did, his feet tangled with Beth's and she started to fall.

I raced forward as she held out her hand. It all happened in slow motion as she slipped off the edge of the mountain and disappeared right in front of me.

"Beth!" I called off, laying on my belly to search for her.

"I'm here!" she called out, dangling ten feet below me, barely hanging onto the rock ledge. Luckily, the mountain was sloped, not a straight drop-off, so she was almost laying across the mountainside.

"Hang on! Don't move!"

I studied the terrain of the side of the mountain. There were some good places for footholds, but I needed to get down there fast. With her arm still in the sling, she was barely holding on. There was no time to run back to my truck for supplies.

"I'm coming down. Don't move unless I tell you to."

I half-expected a witty retort out of her, but instead, she kept her mouth shut and squeezed her eyes closed.

"Beth, keep watching me," I commanded, waiting for her to open her eyes. "You keep your eyes on me. Focus on what you're doing."

She gave a curt nod and tightened her grip on the rock. I started climbing down, aware that if I made even one wrong move, we were both dead. When I was right beside her, I slowly turned and faced the vast hole in front of us. Sweat dripped from me as I released my handhold and undid my belt ever so slowly.

Leaning over, I very carefully wrapped the belt around her good wrist, tying it in a knot that I knew wouldn't hold up, but might buy me a few seconds if she slipped. Then I wrapped the belt in my hand and nodded to her.

"Okay, we're going to do this together, one step at a time. You put your hand where I tell you. I'm going to shift behind you so I can help you climb up."

She nodded shakily, tears shimmering in her eyes.

"You can do this, Beth."

She swallowed hard. "I'm ready."

I turned back to face the mountainside and slowly worked my way down and behind her. "Okay, I'm right behind you. I won't let you fall. When you're ready to release your grip, press your body into the rocks."

"Okay," she said breathlessly.

Step by step, we climbed back up the mountain. "You're doing great. Now your right foot."

She moved her foot, but missed the foothold, slipping slightly. Gripping the wall tightly with my left hand, I pressed my hand to her ass, trying to hold her up.

"Get your foot in place," I grunted, feeling my hand slipping. She quickly found a foothold again and pressed her body to the rock wall, breathing hard. I took the opportunity to reposition myself.

"We need to keep going. One step at a time, okay?"

"Yeah," she answered, then started moving again. When she finally reached the top, I pushed her from behind as she dragged herself up to safety. Moments later, I pulled myself up and laid down on my back beside her. Both of us laid there, breathing hard as we stared up at the night sky.

"See? I told you we'd probably live."

She smacked me in the chest with her fist.

34

BETH

I didn't want to move. The thought of getting up from where I lay on the ground was terrifying. If I got up, that meant we had to get back in the truck and drive on the mountain road again. I closed my eyes and breathed through the panic. I thought getting kidnapped and racing through the woods was bad, but this…I was pretty sure I nearly shit my pants.

"We need to leave," Cash said, getting to his feet as if nothing happened. He held out his hand for me, watching me closely to see what I would do. I could lay here and pretend the world didn't exist, or I could haul my ass up and move on.

I gripped his hand with my one good one and struggled to my feet. We were still too close to the edge for comfort, and Cash seemed to understand that because he wrapped his arm around me and walked with me back to the truck, being extra gentle with me.

"Where are we going now?" I asked after he got back in the truck.

"Yeah, where are you going now, boss?" Dash said over the phone.

Cash snatched it off the seat with a laugh. "Are you still on?"

"Well, yeah. There was a lot of tense arguing, and then some shots were fired. I figured I'd hang on until you were both safely on the road and not hanging off the side of a mountain. Nice save, by the way."

"How the fuck do you know what just happened?"

"Oh, I hacked into a satellite. Yeah, I just got lucky that one was flying up in space over you. I saw the whole thing, man. It was pretty intense to watch. Way better than any movie. However, I would request next time that you fill me in on what you're planning. I could have made some popcorn."

Cash rolled his eyes. "How the hell did they find us? Did you manage to figure that out while you were watching the movie?"

"I still don't know. There aren't any breaches in the system, but I would assume someone has to know where our safe houses are. After all, this is a tech research company. Who knows what gadgets they're testing. Oh, and I recorded everything that happened so you can watch it when you get back."

"I don't want to see it," I chimed in. "Living it was enough for me."

"So, what you're saying is we shouldn't go anywhere related to the business."

"I wouldn't," he said nonchalantly, as if he was kicked back in his office, just chillin'.

"We just keep running?" I asked Cash.

He frowned. "Let me think for a minute."

"While you're thinking, you might want to start driving. The wreckage in the area is bound to alert the authorities, and you don't want to be there when they show up."

"Good plan," Cash said, shifting into drive. After checking his mirrors, he turned back around and continued through the mountains.

"We're not going back?"

"It's best not to return the way we came. Dash," he spoke into the phone. "We need someplace to lay low for a while. Until we know that the other safe houses haven't been compromised or how these fuckers found us, we have to go off the grid."

"Righty-o, boss. Do you want me to find someplace for you?"

I chewed my lip as I considered what I was thinking. It was a risk, but very possibly the last place anyone would look for me at this point. "I might have someplace we can go."

Cash glanced over at me with a frown. "Where?"

"They don't know who I am, right?"

"Well, yeah, they do."

"But not…not the real me."

Cash shook his head slightly. "Let me guess, Beth isn't your real name."

I shook my head. I knew he probably figured it out a long time ago, but he was letting me have my privacy for whatever reason. "If they don't know who they're looking for, they won't find us."

"Not a bad idea, boss. Care to share with the rest of us who you really are?" Dash asked.

"Not right now," I answered, still watching Cash. "I'll tell you everything, but I can't risk anyone other than you knowing."

His hands tightened on the steering wheel. I knew he didn't like excluding his team, but these were my stipulations. "Fine. Dash, I'll call you when we have a plan. And see if you can get ahold of Rafe. He and I are about to have a come to Jesus moment."

He laughed hysterically over the phone. "Oh, man! Shit, I can't believe I'm going to miss that. I'll call you when I have something."

Cash hung up the phone and continued driving. "So, where are we headed?"

"Kansas," I said quietly, turning to look out the window.

"And what's in Kansas?"

"My aunt. She's the only family I have left."

He nodded, his eyes watching the road, which I was grateful for. After the joyride we just took, I wasn't interested in repeating any of that. But mostly, I didn't want him watching me. It was hard enough to talk about without his watchful gaze on me.

"You mentioned something about escaping your stepfather. What's the story there?"

I couldn't believe I had blurted all that out, but I was terrified and out of my mind. Of course, he would remember that and bring it up again. I could tell him it was none of his business, but at this point, I wasn't sure there was any reason to keep secrets from him. He'd proven time and again that not only would he protect me, but he was perfectly capable of deciding what he wanted to do.

"My dad died when I was three. My mom couldn't take care of me on her own, or maybe she didn't want to. I don't think she liked the idea of having a kid around that depended on her. She started hanging around with all these bad guys, and when she brought them around, I would hide out in my room for hours just so I didn't have to be around all the drugs and alcohol. One day, she brought home this man, and I knew instantly that he was a creep. But if I misbehaved in my mom's eyes, she took it out on me later."

"Did he touch you?" he asked tersely.

"He certainly tried," I snorted. "When I was sixteen, he came into my room one night. I woke up to him trying to get into bed with me. I kicked him in the balls and ran. When he explained that he was just checking on me, my mom started hitting me. According to her, I was trying to tempt my stepdad into…Anyway, I ran and ended up getting caught by the police sleeping under a bridge. They wanted to take me home, but when I explained that I could never go back there, they helped me get to safety."

"And your mom and stepdad? Did the police do anything about them?"

"He was killed in a car accident—drunk driving. I never saw him again. And I knew my mom wouldn't want to see me, so I never tried to contact her again."

It was quiet for a while as he digested that. I didn't really want to talk about it anymore. I was tired and sore from our escape, and all I wanted to do was sleep. I rested my head against the window until well after the sun came up. Luckily, by the time I woke up, we were out of the mountains and driving across the desert.

"Where are we?" I asked, stretching as best I could.

"Nevada," he grumbled, rubbing at his eyes. "We need to stop and get some sleep, and I need to get rid of the truck."

"Why?"

"Because if the men that were chasing us called anyone, they have the make and model of the truck, along with the plates." He pulled into a used car dealership and put the truck in park. "Why don't you go to that motel," he nodded across the street. "Get us a room while I take care of the truck."

He pulled out some bills and handed them to me. "What should I give for a name?"

"Make one up. They don't care. That's not the type of motel that worries about things like that."

I was all too familiar with those motels. "Do you want me to carry anything over?"

"Just your bag. After you get the room, get cleaned up."

I grabbed the bag of spare clothes and walked over to the motel, worried that they'd take one look at me and call the cops. Thankfully, the man behind the counter didn't even spare me a glance. Taking the key, I went to the room and stepped inside with a sigh. It had those old bedspreads that were from the nineties, the kind that made me think bedbugs were burrowing in deep. But it was a bed and I was exhausted.

It was pointless to bring the clothes along. They were filthy, as were the ones I was wearing. There was no way I could wear these again after taking a shower, not after nearly falling off a mountain last night. I stripped out of my clothes and headed for the bathroom, turning on the shower to the hottest setting. The generic shampoo and conditioner weren't much, but at least I didn't feel like I had bugs crawling along my scalp by the time I was done.

I wrapped a towel around myself and peeked into the bedroom, glad that it was still empty. Since I had no clothes, I slipped under the covers, still wrapped in a towel, and promptly fell asleep.

The ache in my shoulder returned full force as I woke up and found myself laying in an uncomfortable position. With a groan, I rolled over and stared at the wall, wondering what time it was. The clearing of a throat had me sitting up in bed. The sheet was no longer covering me, and as I sat there staring at Cash staring at me, I realized my towel was no longer on me either.

Across the room, Cash lounged with his legs spread wide as he rested one elbow on the arm of the chair and his head resting against his fingertips. His eyes darkened as they roamed over my naked body. I could feel my nipples pebbling under the weight of his stare, but still, I couldn't move. I couldn't remember the last time I had been excited to be around a man, wondering what it would be like to touch him and have his hands on me.

He shifted in the chair, his hand moving to his crotch to adjust his growing hard-on. Embarrassment washed over me and I tugged at my towel, trying desperately to pull it up and cover myself, but the way I was laying on it left little fabric to actually cover up with. I tugged harder, only to twerk my shoulder. I gasped in pain, using my right hand to shift my arm into a better position.

"You should be wearing the sling," Cash grumbled, his voice low and gravelly.

He stood and walked over to where I had dropped the sling on the floor. After grabbing it, he stood and stalked toward me, every step more predatory than the last. I couldn't stop staring at his cock, and with every step he took, the more I realized he was lined up directly with my face. A deep blush rose in my cheeks as I imagined him unzipping his pants and pulling his cock out for me to taste.

Instead, he sat on the bed behind me, pulling my arm gently into position as he wrapped the sling around my arm. I could feel his hot breath on my neck as he leaned in closer, looking over my shoulder at the strap. His fingers brushed against my already hard nipple as he adjusted my arm.

I closed my eyes as his fingers trailed up my bicep, then gently brushed my hair aside as he finished getting the strap in place. His lips skimmed my shoulder, heating my body. For a moment, I allowed myself to imagine turning into his arms and giving myself to him. My head dropped back against his shoulder as his lips continued to explore my heated skin.

They suddenly stilled and his whole body went rigid. My eyes flew open as he stood and pressed a swift kiss to my forehead, then patted me like a dog.

"All better," he said, then walked away, as if he hadn't just kissed me...well, my shoulder. But it still counted, and it was rude to walk away from something like that. And since when did men pat women on the head?

But then it hit me. I had just told him about my stepfather last night. He probably thought he was taking advantage, or maybe he just didn't want me to know what happened. Anger surged inside me that he didn't even bother to talk to me. I stood in all my naked glory and grabbed the towel, walking into the bathroom without another word. I slammed the door behind me, making it clear just how pissed I was. When I came out, he would know he fucked up, and he would be sorry.

35

CASH

Yeah, she was pissed. She stood, not even bothering to try and hide her nudity as she glared at me and stormed into the other room, slamming the bathroom door behind her. I ran my hand over my face, cursing myself for being such a goddamn idiot. What was I thinking? I fucking kissed her, and I knew better than to involve myself with a client. They got a sort of hero-worship thing after you rescued them, which was what I had just done.

That's all this was. I kissed her because we both nearly died multiple times. Well, I was pretty good. I never really thought we wouldn't make it out of that, but she was different, fragile. She'd been through so much already, and here I was acting like a fucking fool, kissing her shoulder, ready to throw her down on the bed and shove my cock in her. All because…because of what?

Because she was fucking gorgeous. Because every time I saw that strawberry blonde hair fall over her shoulders, it felt like she was hiding secrets from me. *Dirty secrets*. Hell, I doubted her hair was even that color. I knew her name wasn't Beth. For some reason, that hadn't been the first thing I wanted to ask her. There were so many mysteries around this woman, and I found myself wanting to unlock them all.

But touching her was just fucking stupid. And then, to make

matters worse, I patted her on the head like a fucking dog. I cursed myself as I paced around the room. I had to figure a way out of this, one in which I could pretend that none of this ever happened.

I stopped pacing and grinned to myself. Why couldn't I just pretend none of that happened? I was putting on her sling and...and my lips found her shoulder and then trailed along the curve of her beautiful neck? Fuck, I was screwed.

The door to the bathroom swung open and she stepped out, still fucking naked. I was at a loss for words. She was fucking gorgeous. The curves of her body, the weight of her breasts...and her pussy on full display. I did the only sensible thing a man in my position could do. I pretended nothing had happened.

"You ready to go?" She stood in front of me, her hand on her hip as she waited on me. For what, I wasn't sure. "Do you need me to get you some more clothes?"

"Clothes? You think that's what I need?"

I stared at her in pretend confusion. "Well...you are naked."

"You kissed me," she accused.

My mouth opened and then closed. "Right, but that was an accident," I came up with. "I was helping you with your sling, but I was never—"

"Is this because of what I told you?"

Okay, now I really was confused. "What are you talking about?"

"I told you that my stepfather nearly assaulted me, and then you got all weird."

"*After* I kissed you," I pointed out.

"Exactly!" she snapped, catching me in my own lie. "Tell me what's going on."

"Can you put on some clothes first?" I asked, already feeling myself getting worked up.

"Why? You can't talk to me like this?"

"Naked? No, I'm pretty sure no man could talk to you like this."

"Well, that's just too bad. You're going to tell me what's going on, or I'll just stand here naked."

"That's going to be pretty embarrassing when I carry you out of here." I glanced at my watch. "We need to be on the road in an hour."

"I can wait."

"So can I," I said, taking a seat in the chair by the window. I crossed my arms over my chest, once again pretending that this was totally normal. That I could stare at her naked body and not react to it. It was damn fucking hard, and so was I, but I wasn't giving in on this point. I would not get involved with a client.

"Why are you being so stubborn?"

"I'm not stubborn. I'm logical."

"You're a pain in the ass," she retorted. Biting her lip, she walked over to the chair and snatched her dirty clothes, tugging them on. I shifted in my chair, growing more uncomfortable by the minute as I watched her ass sway as she pulled on her pants, struggling with only one arm. "You could help, you know," she shot over her shoulder.

"I'm pretty sure I can't," I said, clearing my throat. I was painfully hard now. If I stood and walked over to her, I would do things I really shouldn't do.

"Fine. Be a jerk."

"Trust me, you want me to be a jerk."

But that all went out the window the moment she pulled the sling off and cringed in pain. Getting to my feet, I stalked over to her and grabbed the top to help her into it. She slowly looked over her shoulder at me, her eyes asking me for something I couldn't give. We had issues to deal with, and none of those would be solved with a quick roll in the sack.

"Let's get this on you."

"I thought you didn't want to help."

I gripped the shirt even tighter, fighting the urge to do what I really wanted. "We have to leave," I said, sliding the shirt over her head and helping her arms through. After getting her flannel shirt on, I stepped back, rubbing my hand across the back of my neck.

"I'll be in the truck."

I turned and stormed out of the room, berating myself for being so weak. As I sat in the truck and waited for her, I wondered if it would really be that terrible to give in and take what I wanted. But as she walked out of the room, looking a little more than dejected, I realized too many people had already used her. I wouldn't be one of them.

"Ready?" I asked as she got in the truck.

"Sure."

I put the truck in reverse and pulled out of the lot. It was going to be a long drive to Kansas.

We drove for most of the morning in silence. The air was broken in our new-old truck, so the windows were down and the hot breeze was the only thing keeping us moderately cool. We would stop in Colorado for the night before continuing in the morning. I had a lot on my mind, worrying about how Hayes was involved in this, what Beth knew that might get us into trouble, and my own company.

I tightened my grip on the steering wheel as I glanced over at her, trying to find a way to move past what happened this morning. The only thing I could think of was to tell her exactly how it was, and that might cause a greater fallout in the end. But it had to be done.

"I don't sleep with clients," I said bluntly, not bothering to look over at her.

"Excuse me?"

I pressed my lips together, irritated I had to talk about this. "You're a client, and I get it. I saved your life and now you think there's something between us. It happens a lot. But Beth, no matter how many times I save your life, nothing's going to happen between us."

I sat there, waiting for a response when she finally gave a one-word answer. "Wow."

I waited for more, but it didn't come. Finally, I tore my eyes from the road and looked over at her. "Wow, what?"

"You really think a lot of yourself."

"That's not at all what I meant."

She spun toward me, her face pinched in anger. "You really think I'm so desperate for affection that I would fall to your feet and beg you to sleep with me?"

"Again, that's not what I meant."

"I'm not some damsel in distress!"

I snorted at that. "Then why do I keep having to rescue you?"

"You know, it's like you open your mouth and the stupid just falls out."

"I think I liked it a lot more when you were timid and shy," I muttered.

"I've never been timid and shy, just cautious."

"Bullshit," I spat, glancing over at her. "When I met you, I could feel the fear coming off you."

"Because you're twice the size of me!"

I jerked the wheel to the side of the road and put the truck in park. "You know what I think?"

"Why don't you tell me," she said snidely.

I put my hand on the back of the seat and leaned in closer. "I think your stepdad did a lot more than you're letting on. Maybe he didn't go as far as I thought, but he fucked with your head, and now you look at every man like he's going to do the same thing."

"That's not true," she said weakly. "If it was, would I have walked around in front of you naked?"

I couldn't explain that one other than she was attracted to me. "It doesn't matter what you did this morning. I remember when we met, how terrified you were of me. You didn't want anyone touching you. You back away from men when they walk by. You flinch at sudden noises. Every action you take tells me everything I need to know."

I watched as her throat bobbed. "And what is that?"

I stared at her intently, reading the fear in her eyes—not from me, but that I knew the truth. "He cornered you, probably a lot. He said things, maybe even did things, that suggested he was going to take something you weren't willing to give. He probably jacked off in front of you." Her nostrils flared and her pulsed thrummed hard in her neck. "He may not have raped you, but in your head, he did. And that's just as fucking bad because you can't ever escape that."

Tears pricked her eyes and she quickly brushed them away, refusing to look at me any longer.

"I've seen it before, and the only reason I can think of that you aren't terrified of me anymore is that you trust me," I said quietly.

"It doesn't matter if I do. We're stuck together for now."

"It matters to me. I know it's hard to put your faith in anyone after your trust has been broken, especially when you were so young. I would never do anything to make you think I was like him, and that's part of the reason I won't sleep with you."

She scoffed at me, wiping the last of the tears from her face. "You wish I would sleep with you. The truth is, you're just too damn cocky for your own good. I'd rather sleep with Fox."

I smirked at her, putting the truck in drive. "Yeah, and then you could have sing-alongs every night before bed. But the truth is, Fox is crazier than I am. You haven't even begun to see what he's capable of."

"Trust me, I've seen worse than him."

"Worse than your stepdad?"

"Definitely," she muttered.

"So, who are you running from?"

She huffed in irritation. "Bad guys."

"I figured as much," I said, rolling my eyes. "Who?"

"I'm not sure exactly," she mumbled. "I was taking a friend home. She lived in Southern California. I took a wrong turn and ended up on some long road to a farm or something. Except it wasn't a farm."

"What was it?"

"A heroin distribution center."

"No shit?"

She nodded sagely. "And stupid me, I had no idea something was wrong until I wandered into a barn looking for someone and found myself surrounded by a shitload of drugs and at least thirty armed men."

"So, what you're saying is you just sort of stumble into trouble."

She laughed slightly, shaking her head at me. "I guess you could say that after what happened at the research facility." She went quiet for a moment. "I thought it was just Adam after me."

"Do you know what those men wanted?"

"No, and I wish I had never been there. I only took the job because it paid more. I was trying to save up to get further away and maybe live a normal life."

I frowned at that. "How did you get away from them?"

I glanced over at her when she didn't respond, but she was lost in thought, staring out the window. "Beth?"

36

BETH

I had been driving down this road for nearly a half hour with no signs of life anywhere in sight. A few times I saw signs that it was private property, but I kept driving because there wasn't really a place to turn around on this narrow, gravel road. Finally, up ahead, I spotted an old farmhouse. I just needed some directions to get out of here and back home.

I pulled to a stop in front of the house and stretched as I got out. Maybe if they were really nice, they'd invite me inside for a drink of water. I was so damn thirsty. I walked up to the house and banged on the door, but no one answered. The sun was already setting, and from what I could tell, there were no lights on in the house. I walked around the porch, looking in windows, but there was nobody.

I heard a noise off in the distance and walked down the steps toward the barn. Something was going on in there, so they must have been working late. So glad that I was finally going to talk to another human being, I didn't notice the odd smell, or the fact that when I flung open the door, a heavy white powder hung in the air.

Stumbling back a step, I hid behind a crate, looking at the massive production in front of me. I'd been around drugs growing up. My mom was one of the biggest buyers on our block. But I'd never actually seen the whole opera-

tion in motion. I glanced back at the door, wondering how the hell I was going to get out of here without being seen. I quickly pulled out my phone, making sure it was on silent as I opened my camera. If I got caught, I needed to have evidence on my side.

Peeking around the corner, I started snapping photos, zooming in on what I thought were important things around the warehouse.

"Tucker's on his way here," one of the men said loudly. "Let's get this place cleaned up. He'll be here any minute. And he's bringing a friend."

"Who?"

"Who do you think?"

"Christ, not that fucker. I hate Walton."

I frowned, wondering who Walton was. The name sounded familiar, but I couldn't place it. I slipped around some more crates, sticking to the shadows as best I could, then snapped a few more pictures when I came across a crate that wasn't sealed. Peeking inside, my eyes widened. It was filled with stacks of hundred-dollar bills. After a few more pictures, I uploaded the pictures to my secure cloud account.

Slipping my phone in my back pocket, I made my way back to the door, ready to get the hell out of there. But when I pulled open the door, I knew I wasn't leaving. Someone was standing by my car with a radio in his hand. I was so fucked.

"Mr. Walton," another voice said.

I gasped, pressing myself against a crate just as a man walked past me. Narrowing my eyes, I finally realized who they were talking about when I saw his face. It was the governor, and he was here at a drug distribution center, or whatever the hell this was.

"Tucker," Walton said as he approached. I quickly pulled out my phone and snapped a few pictures just as the men shook hands. "I'm assuming everything is running smoothly and on time."

I quickly switched to video and stayed as far back as possible.

"We just got another shipment from Mexico."

"That was supposed to be here a week ago. What's the holdup?"

"Our drug runners had a little trouble getting through the border inspection."

"I thought you bought off a guard," Walton said angrily. "That's why I've been feeding so much money into this organization. Hell, I need to put the funds back before anyone notices."

"Hey, I didn't tell you to allocate money from the state to this project. It was supposed to be a personal loan."

"You needed more money," Walton snapped. "I couldn't pull that much money without someone noticing."

"Yeah, just the whole goddamn state government now," Tucker snapped.

"Relax, I have it covered. No one will find out, not as long as you keep your fucking mouth shut and get these drugs onto the streets."

The door opened where I came in and the man by my car walked through. "Boss, we've got a problem. There's a car out front. From what I can tell, it's a woman," he said, holding up my purse.

I ended the video and quickly sent it off to the cloud. Then I sent a text, telling my aunt to check our cloud account. I held my breath as I listened intently.

"Where is she?"

"No idea. She's parked right by the house."

"Then fucking find her!" Tucker yelled. "Christ, what the hell did you do with the dogs?"

"Boss—"

"I don't want your fucking excuses!"

I stepped back, trying to blend further into the shadows, but I accidentally kicked a bucket and everything went silent. I stood still, but I knew I just gave myself away. I glanced around for a place to hide, but they would eventually find me. I had the evidence, but anyone could hack into my phone and see what I'd done. A few feet away was a large barrel that had bleach written across the side. I had no idea if throwing my phone in there would erode it or not, but I had to try. I quickly pried the lid, grimacing at the smell, and tossed my phone inside. All the images and video were on the cloud, and I had to hope they couldn't access that.

I ducked down behind the barrels, closing my eyes and praying they didn't find me. Moments later, I was hauled up by my arm and dragged out in front of thirty men who all stood around armed to the teeth and glaring at me. The man gripping my arm tossed me to the ground. I barely caught myself before my head slammed into the concrete. Shaking from fear, I looked up at the men in front of me, but didn't dare stand.

"Who are you?"

"No one," I shook my head. "I just got lost."

"This is private property," he spat.

My eyes flicked to the governor. Part of me hoped that he would take pity on me, that he would stand up for me. Instead, he glanced at the man who spoke to me and shook his head. My heart sank as he motioned for the man behind me to pick me up. I was grabbed roughly and dragged to my feet. They started pulling me away and I knew that was the moment I would die.

"Wait!" I shouted. "If you kill me, everything I took pictures of will go to the news outlets!"

"Stop!" the governor shouted. He stalked toward me, his face mottled with anger. "What the fuck are you talking about?"

I shook as I stared the man in the face. If he was going to have me killed, I would only have this one chance to save myself. "I saw what you were doing and I took pictures. And that conversation about you supplying the state funds to a drug operation? It's all on video."

"Where is it?" he asked angrily.

"You'll never know," I answered, thinking I was being pretty clever.

He turned away from me and then spun around, slamming his fist into my face. I fell hard to the ground, blood gushing from my nose and mouth. Then his foot landed hard in my stomach multiple times until I felt like I would pass out. He grabbed me by the hair and lifted me bodily off the ground.

"You tell me where the fuck it is."

I gasped for air, staring at him through bruised eyes. "In the bleach," I murmured.

He dropped me to the ground and walked away. I wanted to watch the reaction on his face, but I couldn't move to save my life. Everything on me hurt. But I heard his reaction after someone fished my phone out of the bleach. His anger surged through the building, and I momentarily wondered if I had made a mistake in telling him what I knew. Maybe my death would have been swift.

"Tie her up in the other room. I want to know what the fuck is on that phone!"

I was carted off to a room with no windows at the back of the barn and locked inside. They didn't even bother to tie me up, probably because I was too banged up to move. I wasn't sure how long I lay there for. I was pretty sure at least a day had passed, but I had lost consciousness at some point and the time flew by.

When someone finally came back for me, I wished I were dead. I was dragged off the floor and propped in a chair. The governor walked in and slammed the door behind him.

"I'm going to make this very clear to you. If you don't tell me where you uploaded those photos, I'm going to make sure every single person you love dies a very slow, painful death."

I laughed at him. "I don't have anyone I love."

"What about your mother?"

"Go ahead and kill her," I mumbled.

"And your aunt?"

That gave me pause. I loved my aunt more than anything in this world. I just stupidly thought they wouldn't know about her. She was the only person that was ever there for me. She helped me after what my stepdad did. I was able to function because of her.

"If you don't want her to die a slow, painful death, I suggest you tell us where that information is."

My eyes slipped closed and tears leaked down my face. I wanted to tell them to save her, but deep down, I knew they would kill both her and me just to ensure there were no loose ends. So, I could tell them and hope they gave her a quick death, or I could let the chips fall where they may. At least then there was still a chance this would get out. If she uploaded it immediately, their crimes would be out there for everyone to see.

"Not going to say anything to save the last person you care about?"

We pulled into the motel well past the time I was ready to go to sleep. Reliving those days at the farm and telling Cash what I could reminded me of everything I had to lose and what I could still lose if they found me. Whenever I thought of those times, I fell into a depression for days, but I couldn't afford that right now. Tomorrow, we would be at my aunt's house, and she needed to see that I was okay.

"I'm going to run out for some clothes. Why don't you go lay down?"

I glanced over at Cash, realizing that I hadn't spoken a word to him since he asked me about the farm. Still, I didn't know what to say. I nodded and took the money from him, then rented a room. I handed him the spare key and walked into the room, not even bothering with a shower as I plopped down in bed. I was asleep before I had a chance to pull the covers over me.

37

CASH

After making sure Beth was safely inside the motel room, I went in search of supplies for us. Honestly, I was running, not from her, but from what she told me. It was like hearing a recording of the events that happened, and it scared the shit out of me to hear her relive it. When she stopped talking, I drove in silence, knowing she gave me all she could for one day.

All the life was sucked out of her just from telling me that one story, more than when she told me about her stepdad. I knew there was more to the story that I didn't know yet, but I couldn't push. I had so many questions, mostly about how she escaped and if she still had that evidence. We'd need it to keep her safe.

But I had other things to take care of too. I had a business I left behind, a pain in the ass alphabet agent who was doing everything he could to piss me off, and half the country was falling apart. I needed to check in with my team and find out what was going on.

"Dash, give me some good news," I said tiredly.

"Well, I got a haircut today. It's not exactly what I wanted. They tried to pull this hippie bullshit on me and ended up shaving one half of my head. When I saw it, I nearly pulled my gun on the guy."

"Dash—" I tried interrupting, but he kept going.

"So, I said to the guy, you'd better fix this before I send Fox or IRIS after you. And the guy had the nerve to look at me like I was fucking crazy. I mean, how hard is it to cut hair?"

"I thought you said this was good news."

"Right, well, after I threatened him, he sent over this really hot chick. She cut my hair and fixed it as best she could. Then I took her out for ice cream."

"Ice cream?" I asked, pinching the bridge of my nose.

"Well, it was too late for coffee, and I thought it was a really good meet-cute. I'm trying out some new moves on the ladies."

"Dash, has anyone ever told you that Scottie's rubbing off on you just a tad too much?"

"Not at all. In fact, I think—"

"You know what?" I interrupted. "Can we just get to the point of this call?"

"Sure thing, boss. What's up?"

"How's everything going at the company?"

"Well, Fox is beating everything to shit because he feels terrible about Beth. By the way, are we all still going to go with the lie that her name is Beth?"

"It's not her name."

"Yeah, that's what I just said," he retorted. "Any luck finding it out?"

I glanced at the door to the thrift store I was standing in like she might walk through the door at any moment. "I'm finding out more than I thought I would, but I haven't gotten her name yet."

"Seriously? After all this time together, you haven't just asked her?"

"There were more important things to deal with."

"Like what?"

"Like outrunning trucks that were racing us through the mountains."

"Well, yeah, but that was a long time ago. Besides, that would have been the perfect time to ask her. High-pressure situations make people blurt all kinds of shit out."

"I know, which is how I found out a lot about her," I gritted out.

"And you just happened to forget to ask her about her name?"

"Dash! Can we please focus?"

"Right, sorry, boss. What can I do for you?"

"Did you get ahold of Rafe?"

He laughed outright. "Yeah, he's fun. I've been tracking your sat phone and giving him regular updates."

"You did what?" I hissed.

"He wants to know where you are, and frankly, he's more intimidating than you."

"Dash, if I wanted him to know where I was, I would have told him."

"Yeah, but he's got Hayes, and he says he really needs to talk with you. Something about the end of the world and crazy shit like that. But hey, if it makes you feel better, I've given you a good fifty-mile head start."

"Look, don't tell him anything else. I need to hide Beth, and then I'll meet up with him."

"I'm not a total moron, boss. I have plans in place that even he can't touch."

"Like what?"

"Rae. Yeah, she's actually pretty close to you. Apparently, she has some old boyfriend that she's been shacking up with."

"A boyfriend?"

"Okay, he's a hacker, but don't tell her I told you. He's some super secret hacker and we're not allowed to know anything about him."

I nodded at that. "You already have a file on him, don't you?"

"Yep, it's all here waiting for you when this shit is over."

"Thanks, I guess."

"Just doing my job, boss. And when you actually find out this chick's name, let me know and I'll do the same for her."

"How about we respect her privacy just a little?" I asked.

"Oh, I see how it is. You're feeling protective of her."

I was, and that was a huge problem for me. If only he knew what almost happened. I would be so screwed. "I'm thinking that until we know what we're up against, we need to keep her identity hidden."

He was silent for a minute. "Boss...tell me you didn't fuck her."

I rolled my eyes. "No, I didn't fuck her."

"But you want to." I heard the laughter in his voice. "Man, I called it. I so called it. Fox is going to be so pumped up."

"As much as I would love to sit here and talk with you about my love life and how it affects Fox, I want to get some shut-eye."

"Love life? Boss, you're in deeper than I thought."

"I'm hanging up now."

"Because you know I'm right!" he shouted as I hung up.

Stuffing my phone in my pocket, I quickly walked around the store and grabbed new clothes for us, this time grabbing Beth a few extra pairs of underwear and some sports bras. I didn't know her size, but I could guess based on what I saw this morning.

I was so proud of myself for remembering the little things, even grabbing her a few toiletries, that I wanted to show it all to her when I walked into the motel room. However, she was already passed out on the bed. Sighing, I set the stuff down and got cleaned up, needing a shower to relieve the tension in my shoulders. I wasn't used to not being around to care for my company. My only saving grace was that I knew my guys always had my back, and they always would.

I was just getting out of the shower when I heard her crying in bed. Wrapping a towel around myself, I walked over to the bed and sat down, placing my hand on her back. "Beth?"

She didn't answer, just rolled over with her eyes still closed. She was crying in her sleep. Against my better judgment, I laid down beside her and pulled her into my arms. She came willingly, snuggling into my chest and burying her nose in my neck.

I stared up at the ceiling and tried not to let this affect me—not physically, but mentally. This woman was worming her way into my head more and more every day, no matter how hard I fought it. I was a sucker for a sob story, but I had never let it affect me in this way. But she was different.

I told myself it was just a physical attraction, but that wasn't true. She had a strength to her that she didn't know about yet. That's why I called her kitten. Deep down, those claws were waiting to come out and fight back. She was a fighter, just like me. Yeah, she was a little damaged, but with time and training, she would be strong again, and I would be there to witness it. I knew it deep in my soul.

Both of us lay there wide awake, but not moving. I didn't know how to explain that she was practically laying across my chest with her legs entwined with mine or the fact that I was holding her to me like I needed her to breathe. I tried to come up with something logical to say, like...we got cold in the middle of the night. Except it was sweltering in the room, and despite that, I was still more comfortable now than I had ever been in my life.

"We should probably get up," she finally whispered.

"Yeah," I agreed, but still, neither of us moved.

"I'm guessing this was something that happened in our sleep," she continued.

I could lie and agree with her, but I didn't really want to, which surprised me. "You were crying in your sleep. I...I pulled you into my arms."

Her head jerked up in surprise as she looked at me. "You did?"

I shifted to face her, but didn't let her go. "I don't like to see you cry."

Her bright eyes shone with a light I hadn't seen before, and then they dropped to my lips. "You won't get involved with me, though," she stated. "You can't."

"No," I admitted, but I wasn't sure how true that was anymore.

"And I'll be moving on. I have to find someplace safe to stay."

That would be happening over my dead body. "I can help you with that." I knew a great place she could stay, where she would never have to worry about anyone coming after her again.

"Thank you."

"You're welcome," I said, my voice low as I leaned forward and pressed my lips to hers. She opened for me immediately, gasping as I slipped my tongue in her mouth and rolled to the side, maneuvering her under me. Now my leg was intertwined with hers. I kissed her harder as my hand slid up to cup her cheek. I was careful of her arm, not to hurt her further. When this was over, I was taking her to the fucking doctor. I hated seeing her in constant pain.

Despite my growing erection, I pulled back. I wasn't going to fuck her quick and hard in a cheap motel room. She'd already dealt with enough shit. She needed something real to hold onto. I kissed her one last time and pulled back, staring into her eyes.

"Eva," she murmured.

I studied her face, smiling slightly. She looked like an Eva. "It suits you. What's your last name?"

She smiled at me. "Are you going to call Dash and tell him?"

"You know I am," I grinned.

"James."

"Why did you tell me?"

Her fingers slid up into my hair as she stared into my eyes. "Because I trust you. You'll keep me safe."

"With my life," I vowed.

I wanted to stay in bed with her all day, even if we were hiding out in this motel. I wanted to know all about her, and not just because of how it affected what was going on with Hayes, but because things were different between us. I'd never felt this need to protect a woman like I did with Eva. I'd never wanted something more. Marriage and kids were something for the distant future. It wasn't like I was planning our future or anything, but the more time I spent with her, I at least wanted the chance with her. Maybe things wouldn't last. Maybe we'd realize we were totally wrong for each other. But kissing her now was like a wakeup call—that these things come when you least expect it.

"We should get on the road. We're only a few hours from your aunt's house."

"Cash," she stopped me before I could get up. "When she got that message from me, she ran. She saw the pictures and the video, and she knew she was in trouble. Just…take it easy on her."

"Of course," I answered immediately. "Eva, I'm not going to go storming in there demanding answers."

"But I know you want to. I still have a lot to tell you."

"Eva, we have so much shit on our plate right now. I'm going to be honest with you, it'll be easier to take care of you and your aunt if I have all the facts. I can't keep you safe if I don't know everything."

"I understand."

"Let's go eat. I have a feeling there'll be a lot more to deal with once we reach Kansas."

"Like what?" she asked in confusion.

"Like Dash spilling the beans on more than he should." I sat up, tossing away the sheet.

"Can I borrow your phone?"

"For what?"

"I want to let my aunt know we'll be arriving soon."

"Sure, just don't stay on too long. I'll clean up while you get ahold of her."

She gave me a shy smile, taking the phone from me. "Thank you."

I kneeled on the bed, leaning forward as I pressed my lips to hers. "Anytime."

38

BETH

"What do you think Hayes is hiding?" I asked as we crossed the state line into Kansas.

"I'm not sure. He owns a research facility. It could be damn near anything."

"But why is everyone so concerned about the power outage? They happen all the time."

"Not on this scale. Nobody's really come out and admitted anything yet, but the entire power grid for the West Coast is down."

"Why don't people know that?" I asked in shock.

"There's not really an easy way to spread the word when there's no power. Cell phones aren't working right, there's no TV. Hell, there aren't even any newspapers right now."

"And this power outage is special, why?"

He glanced over at me, his face pinched. "It was a domestic terror attack. Someone set off a graphite bomb over an electrical substation."

I was baffled by that. I didn't really know anything about politics or security, so I didn't understand how they could automatically call it a terrorist attack. "But if you don't know who's behind it, how can you be sure it's a terrorist attack?"

"A bomb being deployed over an electrical substation brought down the entire West Coast, causing massive power failure, chaos, and the domino effect will just keep going if we can't plug the holes. It caused terror and hysteria, therefore, a terror attack."

"And you think Hayes was somehow involved in this."

"I can't be positive about anything, but this is the kind of shit I do. When the power went out, all these backup generators kicked in. The entire block his building is on didn't."

"What does that prove?"

"Nothing, but it was a clue. Add in that he increased his security and was acting strangely when I approached him...not to mention the strange men that were in his facility..."

"I'm sorry, I'm not trying to say you're wrong, but it seems like you're grasping at straws. So what if the backup power didn't come on? And he could have increased security because of a project he was working on."

"And he sent men to grab you because of what?" he asked, glancing over at me.

I sighed in frustration. "I honestly don't know. Because men broke in and they were planning to steal something. He thinks I could know something."

"Exactly."

"Exactly, what? I still don't get how you piece together that he's part of the threat from those few details."

"It's what I do. I know that sounds like bullshit, but when you've been around this shit for as long as I have, you see the puzzle before the pieces are all put together. You learn to spot the clues and read into what they could be instead of what it looks like."

"So, you're like a code breaker?"

He laughed at that. "I wouldn't exactly say that. Let's say I'm paranoid and I tend to see the bad before the good, which is why I assumed you were part of the threat when I saw you walk out with those men."

"But you don't think Hayes is behind the threat, right?"

"I can't be sure, but I think he plays a major role in it, whether he knows it or not. When I met with him, he was pissed and jumpy as hell. I think those men stole something, and I think he knows exactly what could happen if it falls into the wrong hands."

"Don't they keep records of projects?"

"Of course, but if they're doing something they shouldn't or creating something they don't want anyone to know about, they're not going to exactly detail what they're doing. If you created a nuclear weapon, would you label the project *Nuclear Weapon*?"

"*I* would," I retorted. "But then again, I may not be the best person to ask about this stuff."

"That's not a bad thing. Sometimes, it's best to be the person who doesn't understand how evil everyone can be."

"I've already had my fair share of that," I muttered. Sighing heavily, I stared out the window. "I'm so nervous to see my aunt."

"When was the last time you saw her?"

"Years ago," I admitted. "She took me in after everything with my stepdad. And after I graduated high school, I was taking classes at a community college for a while."

"Did you finish?"

"No, I was stupid. Some of my friends wanted to move out to California, and I thought it was a great idea. I followed them out there and went home for the holidays. I just wanted to feel alive. Going to school almost felt too normal. I guess I was in a rebellious phase or something." I huffed out a laugh. "My life would have been so different if I had stayed home with her and finished school."

"I think we could all say that about ourselves. Hell, I would be a lot different if I never joined the military."

I shot him a berating look. "You made something of yourself. Like you said, trouble finds me."

"Yeah," he nodded, "but once this is all over, we'll get that evidence and blow up the governor's life. Then you'll be known as the woman who took down one of the most crooked politicians of our time."

"I don't want to be known at all. I just want to live a normal life where no one knows me."

"This is it, right?" he asked, turning down the long driveway.

"I think so. It looks abandoned."

"Maybe she doesn't live here anymore."

"I wouldn't be surprised if this was it. Aunt Amelia was living with some conspiracy theorist at the time. His name is Noah. He's one of those preppers that thinks the world is about to end, zombies are real, and the government is bugging everyone's homes and listening in."

"You'd be surprised how much of that is true," he muttered. "Are they still together?"

"As far as I know. When I sent Aunt Amelia that text, I think Noah did something with it. It's off the cloud."

We started slowing as we approached the house. "Wait, so you don't know if they have it?"

"When I checked the cloud a few months after it all happened, the evidence was gone, but I can't imagine they would get rid of something like that."

"Eva, you talked to your aunt, right?"

I huffed out a laugh. "Well, no, not on the phone. When I escaped and she ran, the only way we could communicate with each other was through the cloud."

He slammed on the brakes and faced me, his face urgent. "You said you talked to her this morning."

"I sent her a picture to let her know I was okay. And I included a message."

"What kind of message?" he snapped.

I shook my head, confused as to why he was getting so upset. He glanced at the house and then at our surroundings. "What do you—"

"Eva, this is fucking serious. Did you ever actually talk to her?"

"No, but I—"

"Then how do you know you were even talking to her?"

"Because we always shared pictures. It's our form of communication."

"And anyone could figure that out," he snapped, pulling his gun from his holster. He shifted into reverse and started backing out just as the front door on the porch opened.

"Wait, that must be Noah."

Cash hit the gas, spinning the wheel as he turned us in the other direction.

"Cash, what are you doing? My aunt is in there!"

He put the truck in drive and hit the gas. "It's a fucking setup."

"What are you talking about?" I shouted, about to call him crazy, when bullets started pinging off the truck. I screamed as Cash grabbed me and yanked me down.

"Stay down!" he shouted, driving faster down the driveway.

"What's going on?"

"You weren't talking with your aunt. They must have figured out how you were talking to her. You said they knew about her."

"Yes, but how would they get into our account?"

"Eva, I could have any of my techs in your cloud account in minutes," he said, swerving onto the road.

I heard the sound of a helicopter overhead and looked out through the windshield.

"Fuck!" Cash slammed his hand on the steering wheel. He grabbed his sat phone and quickly dialed, swerving as he tried to drive and dial at the same time. "Dash, it's a fucking setup. Get me to Rafe right now! I need backup."

I stared out through the passenger side window as the house slowly faded in the distance. If this was a setup, where was my aunt?

"Cash, we have to go back," I said in a panic.

"We can't. They were waiting for us."

"That's my aunt, the last of my family. I can't leave her with them!"

I grabbed at his arm, trying to get him to turn around, but he fought me off.

"We're not turning around!"

"I can't leave her!"

I grabbed the handle on the door, yanking it open. Cash shouted at me, trying to hold onto me as I fought to get away. It wasn't logical or rational in any way, but I had to get to her. If there was even a chance to save her, I had to try. I flung him off me as he hit the brakes, then threw the door open and jumped out of the truck that was still moving. I hit the ground hard, rolling and hurting my shoulder once again. But none of that mattered as I stood and took off running for the house.

I didn't make it far, though. Cash tackled me to the ground, grabbing my hands as I struggled to get away from him.

"Stop, just fucking stop!" he shouted. "We can't go back there. We don't have the manpower or the weapons!"

"I can't leave her," I shouted, tears pouring down my cheeks. "I can't lose her!"

"She's not there," he snapped. "They've most likely been there since a few weeks after you contacted her."

I squeezed my eyes shut, not wanting to admit the truth. "Is she dead?" I asked.

"I don't know, but we can't stick around here." His gaze jerked back to the road, at the end of the driveway where a truck was peeling out onto the road. He hauled me up quickly, pushing me to the truck. "Get inside now!"

I raced back to the truck, jumping inside just as someone started shooting at us again. I ducked down, covering my head as Cash threw the truck in drive and slammed his foot down on the gas. I screamed as more bullets slammed into the truck. This was all my fault. We would have been further away if it weren't for me losing my shit and jumping out of the truck.

The sat phone rang and Cash handed it to me. "Put it on speakerphone," he said quickly.

I answered, keeping my head down.

"Dash, where is he?"

"Gone Elvis," he replied.

"What does that mean?" I screeched.

"Beth, that you?" he asked.

"Who else would it be?" I practically yelled at him.

Cash snatched the phone from me. "Tell me you have something for me!"

"I got you John Wayne." I could hear the laughter in his voice, but had no idea why he thought this was funny.

"What the hell is John Wayne?"

"It's a can opener," Cash said as he took a hard right down a gravel road.

"Why would a can opener be helpful?" I asked, looking up just in time to see the helicopter starting to set down in the middle of the road. "Oh shit!" I screamed as Cash jerked the wheel and drove into the field, the truck bumping over the uneven ground. A spray of bullets in our direction had Cash grabbing me and shoving me back down.

"How far out?" Cash asked.

"She should be coming up on your ass any minute now."

"Who is she?" I asked again.

"John Wayne."

"The can opener?"

"Rae," he answered. "Because she always opens a can of worms."

39

CASH

The truck bounced all over the uneven field. I had to get us the fuck out of here if we were going to have any chance of surviving. The back window cracked, then shattered as bullets pierced the truck. I was practically holding Eva down on the floorboards to keep her from getting hit.

I pushed us to seventy miles an hour, hoping I could outrun the truck that was now on our tail. I heard the sound of the chopper behind me, lifting off the ground, and prayed Rae was close by. I had everywhere to go, but nothing to keep us safe.

"Cash!" Eva cried out, terrified as she huddled low.

"Just stay down!"

She pointed out my window where the helicopter was flying past us. I swore, trying to figure out a way out of this. I swore I would protect her, but right now, that didn't seem like a possibility.

The helicopter turned, settling higher above us, ready to fire. I swerved out of its path, knowing it was a mere adjustment for them.

"John Wayne has arrived!" Dash shouted over the phone.

"Where the fuck is she?" I asked as I looked around.

"You'll hear her in about—"

The helicopter exploded in a fiery blaze, falling from the sky just to the left of us. My tires spun in the dirt as I got further away from the crash site, but I turned right into a low spot in the field, filled with mud and puddles of water. The tires spun as I tried to push us through, but we jerked to a stop in a particularly wet spot.

"Fuck!" I yelled, slamming my hand on the steering wheel as I shifted into reverse, trying to get us out. A quick look out the driver's side window only made things worse. There was an SUV barreling down on us. "Eva, get in the seat and strap in!"

She scrambled up into the seat as I shifted back and forth, rocking the truck to get us out. The SUV was nearly on us.

"Cash!" she screamed just as I looked up and stared down the front end of the SUV. I shifted one last time, finally gaining purchase as the truck lurched forward, but not fast enough. I felt the impact deep in my bones as the truck absorbed the impact and started to roll. The last thing I saw was Eva reaching out to grab onto my hand before something slammed into my head and everything went dark.

ALSO BY GIULIA LAGOMARSINO

Thank you for reading In The Trenches. Don't miss out on my next book in Owens Protective Services. Click here for Nuclear Option!

Join my newsletter to get the most up-to-date information, along with new content in the Reed Security series.

https://giulialagomarsinoauthor.com/connect/

Join my Facebook reader group to find out more about my obsession with Dwayne Johnson!

https://www.facebook.com/groups/GiuliaLagomarsinobooks

Reading Order:

https://giulialagomarsinoauthor.com/reading-order/

To find the individual series, follow the links below:

For The Love Of A Good Woman series

Reed Security series

The Cortell Brothers

A Good Run Of Bad Luck

The Shifting Sands Beneath Us- Standalone

Owens Protective Services

Printed in Dunstable, United Kingdom